ESSENTIAL
SPANISH
PHRASEBOOK & DICTIONARY

Nicole Irving & Leslie Colvin
Illustrated by Ann Johns

Designed by Lucy Parris
Edited by Michelle Bates
Series editor: Sue Meredith

Language consultants: Graciel.la Edo de Grigg, Marión
Lorente Moltó and Margarita Díaz Gutiérrez

Cover designed by Stephen Wright
and Andrea Slane
With thanks to Lucy Owen

Cover photographs: *Cathedral, La Sagrada Familia, Barcelona* ©
Pictures Colour Library; *Fireworks* © Jim McDonald/Corbis

Some of the material in this book was originally published in
Essential Spanish

Original designs by Adrienne Kern

First published in 2000 by Usborne Publishing Ltd, Usborne
House, 83-85 Saffron Hill, London EC1N 8RT, England.
www.usborne.com
Copyright © 2000, 1990 Usborne Publishing Ltd.

Printed in Italy.

Contents

About the phrasebook

This book gives simple, up-to-date Spanish to help you survive, travel and socialize in Spain. It also gives basic information about Spain and tips for low budget travellers.

Finding the right words

Use the Contents list on page 3 to find the section of the book you need. If you don't find a phrase where you expect it to be, try a related section. There are food words, for example, on several pages. If you still can't find the word, try looking it up in the dictionary.

Go for it

Remember that you can make yourself clear with very few words, or words that are not quite right. Saying "¿Madrid?" while pointing at a train will provoke *si* or *no* (yes or no). The Spanish listed on the opposite page is absolutely essential.

You will feel more confident if you have some idea of how to pronounce Spanish correctly and of how the language works. If Spanish is new to you, try looking through the sections on pages 55-60. A good pronunciation tip is to make your voice go up at the end of a question. This will help it to sound different from a statement.

Being polite

Words like *por favor* (please) or *gracias* (thank you) make anything sound more polite and will generally guarantee a friendly response.

There are other ways of being polite in Spanish. The words *Señor* (Sir) and *Señora* (Madam) are often used to address older people whose names you don't know.

Spanish has four words for "you". You say *tú* to a friend and *vosotros/vosotras* to friends. *Usted* is polite and used for an older person or someone you don't know. *Ustedes* is the plural polite form. You can find out more about these forms on page 57. Using *tú* or *vosotros/vosotras* to people who don't expect it can be very rude. In this book the most appropriate form has been used, according to the occasion. Sometimes you will have to judge whether polite or informal is best, so both are given. If you are ever in doubt, use the polite form.

The language in this book is everyday, spoken Spanish, ranging from the formal to the colloquial. An asterisk after a Spanish word shows that it is slang or fairly familiar, e.g. *los viejos** (parents).

Masculine or feminine?

Adjectives with two forms in Spanish are given twice, e.g. red – *rojo/roja*. The first is masculine (m) and the second is feminine (f). You can find out more about masculine and feminine in Spanish on page 56.

Questions

In written Spanish you put an upside down question mark at the start of a question and a standard one at the end, e.g. *¿Quieres comer?* (Do you want to eat?)

¡Perdone! Nos hemos perdido.
Excuse me, we're lost.

¿Dónde van?
Where are you going?

yes	sí
no	no
maybe	quizás
I don't know.	No sé
I don't mind	No me importa
please	por favor
thank you	gracias
excuse me	perdone[1]/perdona[2]
sorry	perdone[1]/perdona[2]
I'm very sorry.	Lo siento mucho
not at all	de nada
hello, hi	hola
goodbye, bye	adiós
see you, bye	hasta la vista
see you later	hasta luego
good morning	buenos días
good evening	buenas tardes
good night	buenas noches
see you soon	hasta pronto
How are things?	¿Qué tal?
Mr, Sir	señor
Mrs, Madam	señora
Miss	señorita
and	y
or	o
when?	¿cuándo?
where is?	¿dónde?
why?	¿por qué?
because	porque
how?	¿cómo?
how much?	¿cuánto?
How much is it?	¿Cuánto cuesta?
What is it/this?	¿Qué es esto?
it is	es
this is	esto es
is there?	¿hay?
there is	hay
I'd like	quisiera[1]/quiero[2]

Getting help with Spanish

I don't understand.
No comprendo/entiendo.

Can you write it down?
¿Puede escribirlo?

Can you say that again?
¿Puede repetir?

A bit slower, please.
Un poco más despacio, por favor.

What does this word mean?
¿Qué significa esta palabra?

What's the Spanish for this?
¿Como se dice esto en español?

Have you got a dictionary?
¿Tiene un diccionario?

Do you speak English?
¿Habla inglés?

Más despacio, por favor.
Slower, please.

Signs you may see

Salida de emergencia	**Emergency exit**
¡Cuidado!	**Beware**
¡Cuidado con el perro!	**Beware of the dog**
Prohibido el paso	**Keep out, no entry**
Prohibido fumar	**No smoking**
Propriedad privada	**Private property**
¡Peligro!	**Danger**
Agua potable	**Drinking water**
Prohibido nadar	**No swimming**

¿Está María, por favor?
Is Maria there please?

[1] Polite form. [2]Familiar form.

Asking the way

Me he perdido.
I'm lost.

¿Puede ayudarme?
Can you help me?

¿Dónde está la Oficina de Información y Turismo?
Where is the tourist office?

¿Podría dibujarme un mapa?
Can you draw me a map?

¿Hay servicios públicos por aquí?
Is there a public toilet around here?

Fact file

You will find an *Oficina de Información y Turismo* (tourist office) in most big towns and cities. In tourist areas even small towns have one. Opening times are usually 9-1 and 3.30-6 on weekdays and 9-1 on Saturday. Most tourist offices provide town plans and leaflets on local sights free of charge. They also give advice on places to stay and travel arrangements. They often employ someone who speaks English.

Go straight ahead. Siga todo recto.	**It's on the left/right.** Está a la izquierda/derecha.
Follow the signs for Cadiz. Siga las señales para Cádiz.	**Go left/right.** Vaya a la izquierda/derecha.
Take the first on the left. Tome la primera a la izquierda.	

Take the second turning on the right.
Tome la segunda bocacalle a la derecha.

It's ...	Está ...
Go ...	Vaya ...
Carry on ...	Siga ...
straight ahead	todo recto
Turn ...	Gire ... Tuerza ...
left	izquierda
right	derecha
Take ...	Tome ...
the first	la primera
the second	la segunda
the third	la tercera
the fourth	la cuarta
turning	la bocacalle
crossroads, junction	el cruce
roundabout	la glorieta
traffic lights	el semáforo
pedestrian crossing	el paso de peatones
subway	el paso subterráneo
Cross ...	Cruce ...
Follow ...	Siga ...
street	la calle
road	la carretera
main ...	... principal
path	la senda, el camino
square	la plaza
motorway	la autopista

ringroad	la carretera de circunvalación
one way	dirección única
no entry	dirección prohibida
no parking	prohibido aparcar
car park	el aparcamiento
parking meters	los parquímetros
pedestrian area	la zona peatonal
pedestrians	los peatones
pavement	la acera
town centre	el centro de la ciudad
area, part of town	el barrio
outskirts, suburbs	las afueras
town hall	el ayuntamiento
bridge	el puente
river	el río
park	el parque
post office	la oficina de correos
shops	las tiendas
church	la iglesia
school	el colegio, la escuela
museum	el museo
railway line	la vía del tren
just before the	justo antes de
just after the	justo después de
at the end	al final
on the corner	en la esquina
next to	al lado de
opposite	enfrente de
in front of	delante de
behind	detrás de
above	encima, por encima
beneath	abajo
over	sobre
under	debajo de
in	en, dentro de
on	en, encima de
here	aquí
there	allí
over there	por allí
far	lejos
close, near	cerca
nearby, near here	cerca de aquí
around here	por aquí
somewhere	en alguna parte
in this area	en esta zona
10 minutes walk	a diez minutos a pie
5 minutes drive	a cinco minutos en coche
on foot	a pie

¿Cómo se va al camping?
What's the best way to the campsite?

¿Puede indicármelo en el mapa?
Can you show me on the map?

¿Dónde está la playa más cercana?
Where's the nearest beach?

¿Queda muy lejos?
Is it far?

¿Por dónde se va al albergue juvenil?
How do I get to the youth hostel?

Travel: trains, underground, buses

Getting information

¿A qué hora sale el próximo tren a Madrid?
What time is the next train to Madrid?

¿Cuánto dura el viaje?
How long is the journey?

¿Tengo que cambiar de tren?
Do I have to change?

Fact file

For getting around Spain, *autobuses interurbanos* (long-distance buses) are a good option as they are frequent, cheap and go to remote places. There are many bus companies, and buses to the same destination may leave from different places. For information, try the tourist office, bus station or, in a small place, a bar. Get tickets at the bus station or on the bus.

RENFE (Spanish railways) runs a complicated train service.

The standard trains are *Expreso* and *Rapido*. *Talgo, Ter* and *Electotrén* are faster and more pricey. Buy tickets in advance to save confusion over which supplements you have to pay. Fares are cheaper on off-peak *dias azules* (blue days). There are a few private railway companies – details from tourist offices.

Some cities have a *metro*, but they all have *autobuses urbanos* (city buses). Ten ticket booklets, e.g. *Bono-bus*, work out cheaper – available from *estancos* (tobacconists). There's little public transport on Sundays.

¿Dónde tengo que cambiar para ir al Retiro?
Where do I change for el Retiro?

¿Qué acaban de decir por el altavoz?
What did they just say over the loudspeaker?

¿De qué andén sale el tren para Sol?
Which platform for Sol?

Tickets

¿Dónde puedo comprar un billete?
Where can I buy a ticket?

Quisiera un billete de ida a Granada.
Could I have a single to Granada?

¿Hacen algún tipo de descuento?
Can I get a reduction?

¿Cómo funciona esta máquina?
How does this machine work?

I'd like to reserve a seat.	Quisiera hacer una reservation.	**ticket machine**	la máquina
railway station	la estанción de tren	**student fare**	la tarifa de estudiante
underground station	la estанción de metro	**ticket**	un billete ...
bus station	la estанción de autobuses	**a single**	... de ida
		a return	... de ida y vuelta
bus stop	la parada de autobús	**supplement**	el suplemento
train	el tren	**left luggage locker**	la consigna automática
underground train	el metro	**map**	un mapa
tram	el tranvía	**timetable**	un horario
bus, coach	el autobús	**arrivals/departures**	llegadas/salidas
leaves at 2 o'clock	sale a las dos	**long distance**	largo recorrido
arrives at 4.30	llega a las cuatro y media	**local, suburban**	cercanías
		every day, daily	diario
first	primero/primera	**weekdays and Saturdays**	laborables
last	último/última	**Sundays and holidays**	domingos y festivos
next	próximo/próxima		
cheapest	más barato/barata	**in summer-time**	en verano
ticket office	la taquilla, la ventanilla	**out of season**	fuera de temporada
		except	excepto

Buses

¿De dónde sale el autobús para Valencia?
Where does the bus for Valencia leave from?

¿Este autobús va a Barcelona?
Is this the right bus for Barcelona?

¿Puede decirme cuándo tengo que bajar?
Can you tell me when I should get off?

Travel: air, sea, taxis

> *Quisiera confirmar mi vuelo.*
> **I'd like to confirm my flight.**

> *¿A qué hora debo presentarme?*
> **What time should I get there?**

> *¿Dónde tengo que facturar el equipaje?*
> **Where do I check in?**

Fact file

Airports and ports often have signs and announcements in English. There's usually a bus or train from the airport into town.

Taxis are cheap with metered fares, but it's wise to ask what the fare will be first. Taxis usually take up to four passengers. They charge extra at night, on Sundays and for large bags.

> *Mi equipaje no ha llegado.*
> **My luggage hasn't arrived.**

> *Tenía que encontrarme con la Señora Serra.*
> **Mrs Serra is supposed to be meeting me.**

Where is the taxi stand?
¿Dónde está la parada de taxis?

Take me to ...
A ...

What's the fare to ... ?
¿Cuánto costaría ir a ...?

Please drop me here.
Pare aquí por favor ...

airport	el aeropuerto
aeroplane	el avión
flight	vuelo
port	el puerto
ferry	el barco
(sea) crossing	travesía
I feel sea sick	Estoy mareado/ mareada
on board	a bordo
Mediterranean	Mediterráneo
suitcase	la maleta
backpack/rucksack	la mochila
bag	una bolsa
hand luggage	el equipaje de mano
trolley	el carrito
information	información
customs	la aduana
passport	el pasaporte
departure gate	la puerta de salida
boarding pass	la tarjeta de embarque
No smoking	No fumador
travel agent	una agencia de viajes
airline ticket	un billete de avión
cut price	de precio reducido
standby	aviso
charter flight	un vuelo charter
flight number	el número de vuelo
a booking	una reserva
to change	cambiar
to cancel	cancelar
a delay	un retraso

Fact file

Bikes and mopeds are often available for hire in tourist areas. You can ride mopeds from age 14, but make sure you are insured. It is illegal not to wear a crash helmet.

Remember the Spanish drive on the right. Drivers must always carry their driving licence with them. Theft from cars is a problem in some areas, so keep your documents with you and your things well out of sight.

Fill it up, please.
Lleno, por favor.

I have a puncture.
Se me ha pinchado una rueda.

The engine won't start.
El motor no arranca.

The battery's flat.
La batería está descargada.

How much will it cost?
¿Cuánto costará?

for hire
de alquiler

Can I hire ... ?
¿Alquilan ... ?

Where are you going?
¿A dónde vas?

I'm going to Cadiz.
Voy a Cádiz.

Se me ha averiado el coche.
I've broken down.

¿Dónde está el taller más cercano?
Where's the nearest garage?

town centre	centro de la ciudad
give way	ceder el paso
toll	peaje
insurance	el seguro
driving licence	el carnet de conducir
(car) documents	los papeles
petrol station	una gasolinera
petrol	la gasolina
lead-free petrol	gasolina sin plomo
oil/petrol mixture	mezcla de aceite y gasolina
garage, repair shop	un taller
oil	el aceite
litre	un litro
car	un coche
bicycle	una bicicleta
moped	una motocicleta
motorbike	una moto
crash helmet	un casco
radiator	el radiador
lights	las luces
chain	la cadena
wheel	la rueda
gears	las marchas
cable	el cable
pump	una bomba
tyre	el neumático

Los frenos no funcionan.
The brakes don't work.

No sé por qué no funciona.
I don't know what's wrong.

¿Puede repararlo usted?
Can you fix it?

Accommodation: places to stay

At the tourist office

¿Tienen una lista de campings?
Do you have a list of campsites?

Fact file

The *Oficina de Información y Turismo* (tourist office) will supply lists of places to stay. Cheap accomodation includes: *fondas* – rooms, often above a bar; *casas de huespedes* – guest houses; *pensiones* – rooms, price may include food; *hostales* – cheap hotels. You might also see signs for *camas* (beds), *habitaciones* (rooms) and *camas y comidas* (beds and meals) advertised in private houses or above bars.

Camping

Fact file

Campings (campsites) vary in price and quality and can be crowded in summer.

Is there a campsite around here?
¿Hay un camping por aquí?

Where are the showers?
¿Dónde están las duchas?

tent	una tienda
caravan	una caravana
hot water	agua caliente
cold water	agua fria
drinking water	agua potable
camping gas	camping gas
tent peg	una estaquilla
mallet	un mazo
sleeping bag	un saco de dormir
torch	una linterna
a box of matches	una caja de cerillas
loo paper	el papel higiénico
can opener	un abrelatas

¿Tienen sitio para acampar?
Do you have a space?

Somos tres personas con una tienda.
There are three of us with a tent.

¿Hay alguna tienda?
Do you have a shop?

¿Es potable el agua del grifo?
Is it OK to drink the tap water?

Hotels

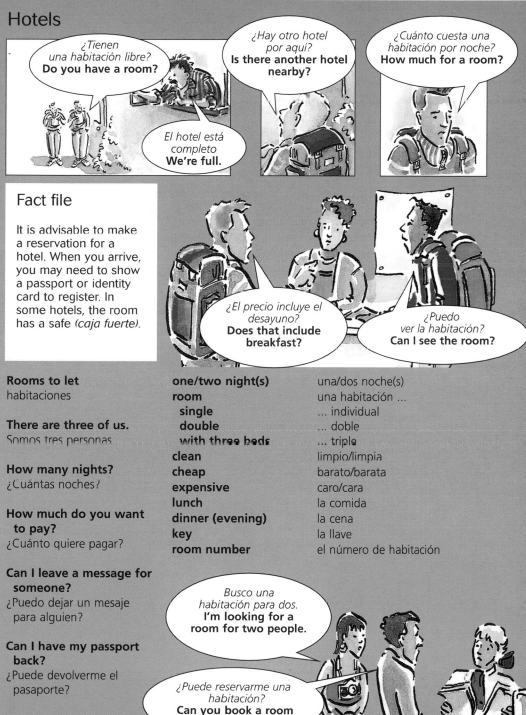

¿Tienen una habitación libre?
Do you have a room?

El hotel está completo
We're full.

¿Hay otro hotel por aquí?
Is there another hotel nearby?

¿Cuánto cuesta una habitación por noche?
How much for a room?

Fact file

It is advisable to make a reservation for a hotel. When you arrive, you may need to show a passport or identity card to register. In some hotels, the room has a safe *(caja fuerte)*.

¿El precio incluye el desayuno?
Does that include breakfast?

¿Puedo ver la habitación?
Can I see the room?

Rooms to let	**one/two night(s)**	una/dos noche(s)
habitaciones	**room**	una habitación ...
	single	... individual
There are three of us.	**double**	... doble
Somos tres personas	**with three beds**	... triple
	clean	limpio/limpia
How many nights?	**cheap**	barato/barata
¿Cuántas noches?	**expensive**	caro/cara
	lunch	la comida
How much do you want	**dinner (evening)**	la cena
to pay?	**key**	la llave
¿Cuánto quiere pagar?	**room number**	el número de habitación

Can I leave a message for someone?
¿Puedo dejar un mesaje para alguien?

Can I have my passport back?
¿Puede devolverme el pasaporte?

Busco una habitación para dos.
I'm looking for a room for two people.

¿Puede reservarme una habitación?
Can you book a room for me?

Accommodation: staying with people

Greetings

¡Hola!
Hello.

¿Como estás?
How are you?

¿Dónde puedo dejar mis cosas?
Where can I put my things?

¿Dónde voy a dormir?
Where am I sleeping?

¿A qué hora desayunáis?[1]
What time do you have breakfast?

¿Puedes despertarme a las siete?[2]
Could you wake me up at seven?

For more polite or formal greetings, use the expression most appropriate to the time of day followed by *Señor* or *Señora* (see page 4). Also use the polite form *¿Como está?* (How are you?)

Washing

¿Cómo funciona la ducha?
How does the shower work?

Is it OK to have a bath?
¿Puedo bañarme?
Do you mind if I wash a few things?
¿Puedo lavar algo de ropa?
Where can I dry these?
¿Dónde puedo secar esto?

bathroom	el cuarto de baño
bath	el baño
shower	la ducha
toilet	los servicios
loo	el lavabo
towel	una toalla
soap	jabón
shampoo	el champú
toothpaste	el dentrífico
toothbrush	el cepillo de dientes
deodorant	el desodorante
hairdryer	el secador
hairbrush	el cepillo para el pelo
washing powder	jabón en polvo

[1] To be polite, when speaking to a stranger or an older person, say *¿A qué hora desayunan?*
[2] To be polite, *Puede despertarme a las siete?*

Being polite

¿Puedo ayudar a pagar los gastos?
Can I pay my share?

No, no te preocupes.
No, it's OK.

Gracias por hospedarme.
It's nice of you to let me stay.

No hay problema.
No problem.

alarm clock	un despertador
on the floor	en el suelo
an extra ...	otro/otra...
blanket	manta
quilt, duvet	edredón
sheet	sábana
pillow	almohada
electric socket	un enchufe
T.V.	la tele
needle	una aguja
thread	el hilo
scissors	unas tijeras
iron	una plancha
upstairs	arriba
downstairs	abajo
cupboard	un armario
bedroom	el dormitorio
living room	la sala de estar
kitchen	la cocina
garden	el jardín
terrace	la terraza
balcony	el balcón

I'm tired.
Estoy cansado/cansada.

I'm knackered.
Estoy muerto/muerta de cansancio.

I'm cold.
Tengo frío.

I'm hot.
Tengo calor.

Can I have a key?
¿Puede darme una llave?

What is there to do in the evenings?
¿Qué se puede hacer por las noches aquí?

Where's the nearest phone box?
¿Dónde está la cabina más próxima?

¿Puedo llamar por teléfono?
Can I use your phone?

¿Cuánto cuesta llamar a Gran Bretaña?
How much is it to call Britain?

Pagaré la llamada.
I'll pay for the call.

Saying goodbye

Muchas gracias por todo.
Thank you for everything.

¡Adiós!
Goodbye.

15

Banks

Quisiera cambiar esto.
I want to change this.

¿Aceptan Eurocheques?
Do you accept eurocheques?

¿Puedo ver su pasaporte?
Can I see your passport?

Post office

¿Me dá un sello para esta carta?
Can I have a stamp for this?

¿Dónde está el buzón más cercano?
Where's the nearest postbox?

Fact file

The unit of currency is the *peseta (Pta)*. The 5 *pesetas* coin is called a *duro*. Banks open 8.30-2 on weekdays, 9-1 on Saturday (not always in summer). You can change money elsewhere (look for the sign *cambio*) but you may get a poorer exchange rate. There's a good system of cashpoints. Most take foreign cashpoint cards.

Money problems

He perdido mis cheques de viaje.
I've lost my traveller's cheques.

Los números de serie eran ...
The serial numbers were ...

¿Cómo puedo obtener cheques de repuesto?
How do I get replacements?

Estoy esperando un envío de dinero, ¿ha llegado?
I'm expecting some money, has it arrived?

bank	el banco	reverse charge call	una llamada a cobro revertido
cashier's desk, till	la caja	Hang on.	un momento
foreign exchange	cambio		
enquiries	información		
money	el dinero		

The cashpoint machine (ATM) has swallowed my card.
El cajero se ha tragado mi tarjeta

small change	el suelto
traveller's cheques	unos cheques de viaje
credit card	una tarjeta de crédito
commission	la comisión
money transfer	una transferencia

Where can I send an e-mail?
¿Dónde puedo enviar un e-mail?

post office	la oficina de Correos
postcard	una postal
letter	una carta

What is the exchange rate?
¿A cómo está el cambio?

parcel	un paquete
envelope	un sobre
by airmail	por avión
registered letter	una carta certificada
stamp	un sello
telephone office	central telefónica
telephone	un teléfono
telephone box	una cabina de teléfono
mobile phone	un teléfono portátil
directory	una guía telefónico
phone number	el número de teléfono
wrong number	el número equivocado

Fact file

Most of the payphones on the street take coins. For international calls look for the sign *Teléfono Internacional*. You can also phone from bars, department stores or a *Telefónica*. These phones are metered and you pay after the call.

You can buy stamps in a post office or an *estanco* (tobacconist).

Phones

Este teléfono no funciona.
This phone doesn't work.

¿Es éste el prefijo de Barcelona?
Is this the code for Barcelona?

Hola. ¿Está María?
Hello, is Maria there?

Por favor, dígale que he llamado
Please tell her/him I called.

¿Cuándo volverá?
When will she be back?

Mi número es ...
My number is ...

¿Puedo dejar un recado para ...?
Can I leave a message for ...?

¿Podría decirle que me llame?
Can she/he call me back?

17

Cafés

café	el café
bar	el bar
table	una mesa
Cheers!	¡Salud!
something to drink	algo de beber
something to eat	algo de comer
snack	un bocado
black coffee	un café solo
white coffee	un café con leche
decaffeinated	descafeinado
tea (with milk)	un té (con leche)
hot chocolate	un chocolate caliente
fruit juice	un zumo de fruta
orange juice	un zumo de naranja
coke	una coca-cola
mineral water	un agua mineral
still	sin gas
sparkling	con gas
beer (bottled)	una cerveza
beer (draught)	una caña
glass of red wine	un vino tinto
bottle of ...	botella de ...
half a bottle of white wine	media botella de vino blanco
sugar	el azúcar
with ice	con hielo
slice of lemon	una rodaja de limón
olives	unas aceitunas
omelette	una tortilla
cheese sandwich	un sandwich de queso
ham (cured)	jamón serrano
ham (cooked)	jamón de York
ice cream	un helado

Fact file

There is little difference between a Spanish bar, café and *cafetería*. Most of them open 9.30am to 11pm. Prices vary (smart means pricey). If you sit down, a waiter serves you but everything is cheaper at the bar.

Look out for *tapas* (starter-like dishes), see page 21. Other snacks include *churros* (doughnuts), omelettes (*española* has potato, *francesa* is plain) and sandwiches.

¿Vamos a tomar un café?
How about a coffee?

¿Está ocupada esta silla?
Is this chair free?

¿Puedo ver el menú?
Can I see the menu?

Un café solo, por favor.
A black coffee, please.

¿Tienen batidos?
Do you have milk-shakes?

Eating out

Choosing a place

¿Dónde vamos?
Where shall we go?

No me gustan las pizzas.
I don't like pizzas.

Vamos a comer una hamburguesa.
Let's go for a hamburger.

Spanish food	la comida española
Italian ...	... italiana
Chinese ...	... china
cheap restaurant	un restaurante barato
take-away (food)	para llevar
menu	el menú
starter	el primer plato
main course	el segundo plato
dessert	el postre
price	el precio
soup	la sopa
fish	el pescado
meat	la carne
vegetables	las verduras
cheese	el queso
fruit	la fruta
chips	patatas fritas
sausages	unas salchichas
salad	ensalada
hamburger	una hamburguesa

fried egg	huevo frito
spaghetti	unos espaguetis
rare	muy poco hecho/hecha
medium	poco hecho/hecha
well done	muy hecho/hecha
mustard	la mostaza
salt	la sal
pepper	la pimienta
dressing	la vinagreta
mayonnaise	la mayonesa

Is everything all right?
¿Todo bien?
Yes, it's very good.
Si, está muy bueno.

Deciding what to have

¿Puede hacer uno sin queso?
Can I have one without cheese?

¿Qué es eso?
What's that?

Tomaré uno de esos.
I'll have one of those.

Problems

Yo pedí una paella.
I ordered paella.

¿No tienen salsa de tomate?
Don't you have any ketchup?

La carne está poco hecha.
The meat isn't cooked enough.

¡Por favor!
Excuse me!

¿Puede traernos la cuenta, por favor?
Can we have the bill please?

Yo no había pedido eso.
I didn't order this.

Fact file

Spanish food is good value and well worth exploring, but to eat out cheaply you need to be adventurous – there aren't many fast-food places.

Look out for bars that serve *tapas* (snacks or starter-like dishes). These include olives, *chorizo* (spicy salami) seafood such as *gambas* (prawns) or *calamares* (squid), *habas* (beans), etc. The dishes are often on the counter so you can point to show what you want. Have one *ración* (portion) as a snack or several as a meal. Alternatively order *unos platos* (a large plateful).

Tapas are cheap, but remember that in most bars, prices are even lower if you eat at the counter.

There are lots of restaurants serving good, inexpensive food. Try *un retaurante* or, for local food, *una fonda*. Most of these display a *menú turistico* (set menu) with its price. This is usually three courses with a drink and is often good value. *El menú del dia* (dish of the day) or the *platos combinados* (various dishes served on one plate) can be cheap.

Most bills say *Servicio incluído* (service included) but tipping is normal practice so it's best to leave a small tip.

Fact file

Breakfast is coffee with pastries or toast. Mid-morning snacks are common. The main meal is at about 3 and it is often three courses. Soups may be cold. Water, wine and bread are always served and pudding is often fruit. The evening meal is lighter and late, at 9, 10 or even 11. On weekends, it is normal to go out before dinner for drinks and tapas. This is called: *ir de vinos* or *ir de tapas*.

Enjoy your meal.
¡Buen provecho!

I'm hungry/thirsty.
Tengo hambre/sed.

I'm not hungry/thirsty.
No tengo hambre.

¡La comida está lista!
It's ready.

¡Serviros!
Help yourselves.

¿Qué lleva este plato?
What's in this?

¿Puedes pasarme el agua?
Can you pass the water?

Ya he comido bastante, gracias.
I've had enough thanks.

¿Quieres ensalada?
Would you like some salad?

La comida estaba muy buena.
The food was delicious.

Sólo un poco.
Just a little.

¿Más pan?
Some more bread?

Helping

¿*Puedo ayudar?*
Can I help?

¿*Puedo poner la mesa?*
Can I lay the table?

¿*Puedo fregar los platos?*
Can I do the washing-up?

breakfast	el desayuno	**tuna fish**	el atún
lunch	la comida, el almuerzo	**hake**	la merluza
dinner (evening)	la cena	**monkfish**	el rape
bowl	un tazón		
glass	el vaso	**rice**	el arroz
plate	el plato	**pasta**	la pasta
knife	un cuchillo	**potatoes**	las patatas
fork	un tenedor	**onions**	las cebollas
spoon	una cuchara	**garlic**	el ajo
bread	el pan	**tomatoes**	los tomates
jam	la mermelada	**peppers**	los pimientos
butter	la mantequilla	**peas**	los guisantes
margarine	la margarina	**aubergine**	la berenjena
chicken	un pollo	**asparagus**	los espárragos
pork	la carne de cerdo	**spinach**	las espinacas
beef	la carne de vaca		
veal	la carne de ternera	**raw**	crudo/cruda
liver	el hígado	**(too) hot, spicy**	(demasiado) picante
squid	el calamar	**salty**	salado/salada
prawns	las gambas	**sweet**	dulce

Special cases

No me gusta el pescado.
I don't like fish.

Soy vegetariano[1].
I'm a vegetarian.

Soy alérgico a los huevos[2].
I'm allergic to eggs.

[1] If you're a girl, say *vegetariana*. [2] If you're a girl, say *alérgica*.

> ¿Qué desea?
> **Can I help you?**

> Quisiera uno de estos.
> **I'd like one of these.**

> ¿Cuánto cuesta esto?
> **How much is it?**

Fact file

Opening times vary but bear in mind that many shops close for lunch. Shops generally open Monday to Friday 9.30 to 1.30 and 4 or 5 to 7.30 or 8, and 9.30 to 2 on Saturday. Many bakers are also open on Sunday morning.

Department stores open 10 to 8 without a break, Monday to Saturday. Look out for the sign *cerrado los* (closed on ...).

An *estanco* sells stamps as well as cigarettes. A *ferretería* sells handy things for camping but try a *tienda de deportes* for camping equipment. A *farmacia* has medicines and plasters and a *perfumería* sells make-up, shampoo, soap etc. but things like this are cheaper in department stores, e.g. *el Corte Inglés.*

The best and cheapest place for food and everyday things is a *tienda de comestibles.* They can be small but they sell everything including wine, meat, fruit and vegetables. Some sell bread, but each village has at least one *panadería.* There are few greengrocers. People buy their fruit and vegetables from a *tienda* or a market.

Markets are held regularly. Big towns have them daily and smaller places twice a week. They're colourful and lively as well as being good for food and local produce.

For picnic things, go to a *tienda* or buy sandwiches from a *tapas* bar (see page 21). In cities you might find a *charcutería* where you can buy sausages, salamis, ham etc.

> ¿Podría escribir el precio, por favor.
> **Please could you write down the price?**

> Está bien.
> **That's fine.**

> Quinientas veintitrés pesetas.
> **It's 523 pesetas.**

> Me lo llevo.
> **I'll take it.**

shopping centre	el centro commercial
shop	una tienda
department store	unos grandes almacenes
market	el mercado
supermarket	un supermercado
general shop	una tienda (de comestibles)
grocer	un colmado[1]
baker	una panadería
cake shop	una pastelería
butcher	una carnicería
delicatessen	una charcutería
fruit/veg stall, greengrocer	una verdulería
fishmonger	una pescadería
healthfood shop	una tienda naturista, herboristería
hardware shop	una ferretería
chemist	una farmacia
camera shop	una tienda de fotografía
gift department	objectos de regalo
tobacconist	un estanco
news kiosk	un quiosco de periódicos
bookshop	una librería
stationer	una papelería
record shop	una tienda de discos
computer store	una tienda de ordenadores
video shop	vídeo club
flea market	un rastro
junk shop	un baratillo
sports shop	una tienda de deportes
shoe shop	una zapatería
shoe mender	un zapatero
hairdresser	una peluquería
barber	un barbero
laundry	una lavandería
travel agent	una agencia de viajes
open	abierto/abierta
closed	cerrado/cerrada
entrance	la entrada
exit	la salida
check-out	la caja
stairs	una escalera
price	el precio

¿Dónde está el centro comercial?
Where's the main shopping area?

¿Venden pilas?
Do you sell batteries?

¿Dónde se puede comprar pilas?
Where can I buy batteries?

¿Dónde pueden arreglarme esto?
Where can I get this repaired?

¿Dónde hay una buena tienda de gafas de sol?
Where's a good shop for sunglasses?

---

[1] The word *colmado* is used in Catalonia. See page 54 for the different regions of Spain.

¿Qué desea?
Can I help you?

¿Puedo ver ése?
Can I see that one?

¿Cuánto cuesta?
How much is it?

Estoy mirando.
I'm just looking.

Quiero pensarlo un poco.
I want to think about it.

Necesito una crema bronceadora.
I need some suntan lotion.

¿Tienen una más grande?
Do you have a bigger one?

sunscreen	una crema con protección
make-up	el maquillaje
(hair) gel	el gel fijador
mousse	el mousse
tampons	unos tampones
tissues	unos pañuelos de papel
razor	una maquinilla de afeitar
shaving foam	espuma de afeitar
contact lens solution	la solución para las lentes de contacto
plasters	unas tiritas
film	una película
English newspapers	unos periódicos ingleses
postcard	una postal
writing paper	el papel de escribir
envelope	un sobre
notepad	una libreta
ball-point pen	un bolígrafo
pencil	un lápiz
poster	un poster
stickers	unos adhesivos
badges	unas insignias
sunglasses	unas gafas de sol
jewellery	las joyas
watch	un reloj
earrings	unos pendientes
ring	un anillo
purse	un monedero
wallet	una cartera
bag	una bolsa
smaller	más pequeño/pequeña
cheaper	más barato/barata
another colour	otro color

Quisiera dos panecillos.
I'd like two rolls.

¿Puede darme setenta pesetas de uvas?
Can I have 70 pesetas worth of grapes?

¿Puede darme un poco de ese pâté?
Can I have a bit of that pâté?

carrier-bag	una bolsa	**peanuts**	unos cacahuetes
small	pequeño/pequeña	**apples**	manzanas
large	grande	**pears**	peras
a slice of (meat)	una tajada	**peaches**	melocotones
a bit more	un poco más	**nectarines**	nectarinas
a bit less	un poco menos	**plums**	ciruelas
a portion	una porción	**cherries**	cerezas
a piece of	un trozo de	**strawberries**	fresas
a kilogram	un kilo	**apricots**	albaricoques
half a kilo	medio kilo	**melon**	un melón
100 grammes	cien gramos	**bananas**	plátanos
organic	orgánico	**oranges**	manzanas
bread	el pan		
stick	una barra		
round loaf	una hogaza		
wholemeal bread	pan integral		
savoury pie	una empanada		
sweets	unos dulces		
chocolate	el chocolate		
crisps	unas patatas fritas, unas papas		

Fact file

There are many different types of bread that you can try. A standard loaf is *una barra*. If you want something smaller, ask for *una barra pequeña*.

Un poco más, por favor.
A bit more please.

¿Así?
Like that?

Vale, así está bien, gracias.
OK, that's enough, thanks.

clothes	la ropa
shirt	una camisa
T-shirt	una camiseta
sweatshirt, jumper	un jersey
fleece	un polar
dress	un vestido
skirt	una falda
trousers	unos pantalones
jeans	unos vaqueros, unos tejanos
shorts	unos pantalones cortos
tracksuit	un chandal
top	la parte de arriba
bottom	la parte de abajo
trainers	unas zapatillas de deporte
shoes	unos zapatos
sandals	unas sandalias
boots	unas botas
belt	un cinturón
(ski) jacket	un anorak
boxer shorts/pants	unos calzoncillos
knickers	unas bragas
bra	un sostén, un sujetador
tights	unas medias
socks	unos calcetines
swimsuit, trunks	un bañador
small	pequeño/pequeña
medium	mediano/mediana

Fact file

For reasonably priced clothes, try hypermarkets such as *Continente, Alcampo* and *Pryca*. Look out for sales: *las rebajas de inverno* (after Christmas) and *las rebajas de verano* (before the end of the summer). A well-known charity shop is *Cruz Roja* (Red Cross shop).

large	grande
extra large	extra grande
too big	demasiado grande
smaller	más pequeño/pequeña
long	largo/larga
short	corto/corta
tight	ceñido/ceñida
baggy	suelto/suelta
fashion	la moda
a look, style	un estilo
fashionable	de moda
trendy, cool	moderno/moderna
out-of-date, untrendy	pasado de moda
smart	elegante
dressy	bien vestido/vestida
scruffy	desaliñado/desaliñada
sale	las rebajas
changing room	el probador

¿Puedo ir en vaqueros?
Are jeans all right?

¿Puedes prestarme tu chaqueta?
Can I borrow your jacket?

¿Llevo el traje de baño?
Shall I bring my swimming stuff?

Music

¿Dónde hay una buena tienda de discos?
Where's a good place to buy CDs?

Can I put some music on?
¿Puedo poner música?
I listen to (lots of) ...
Escucho mucho ...
I've never heard any ...
Nunca he oído ...
Can you tape this for me?
¿Puedes grabarme este disco?

Turn it up.
Sube el volumen.
It's too loud.
Está demasiado alto.
Turn it down.
Baja el volumen.

¿Tienen esto en casete?
Do you have this on cassette?

¿Has visto el vídeo?
Have you seen the video?

¿Tienen una sección de jazz?
Do you have a jazz section?

¿De quién es?
Who's this by?

Playing an instrument

Do you play an instrument?
¿Tocas algún instrumento?

I play the guitar.
Toco la guitarra.

I sing in a band.
Canto en un grupo.

Which instrument do you like best?
¿Qué instrumento prefieres?

I play in a band.
Toco en un grupo.

I'm learning the drums.
Estoy aprendiendo a tocar la batería.

¿Qué típo de música te gusta?
What kind of music do you like?

¿Has oído su último disco?
Have you heard the latest album?

¡Son malísimos!
They're useless.

¿Puedes prestarme este CD?
Can I borrow this album?

¡Es fantástico!
It's brilliant.

music	la música
music shop	una tienda de música
radio	la rádio
CD	CD
CD player	un reproductor de compact disk
personal CD player, Walkman[1]	un estéreo personal, un Walkman
hi-fi	una cadena de alta fidelidad
headphones	unos auriculares
single	un single, un sencillo
mini disc	mini disc
a blank tape	una cinta
pop video	un vídeo-pop
song, track	una canción
lyrics	la letra
tune, melody	una melodía
rhythm	el ritmo
live music	música en directo
group, band	un grupo
solo artist	un solista
singer	el cantante
accompaniment	el acompañamiento
fan	un/una fan
tour	una gira
concert, gig	un concierto
the Top 40[2]	los cuarenta principales
number one	el número uno
hit	un éxito
latest	último/última
new	nuevo/nueva
piano	el piano
keyboards	el teclado
electric guitar	la guitarra eléctrica
bass guitar	la guitarra baja
saxophone	el saxofón
trumpet	la trompeta
harmonica	la armónica
violin	el violín
flute	la flauta
choir	un coro
orchestra	una orquesta

Types of music

This list includes music you're likely to hear in Spain. For other types of music, try using the English word as the names are often the same.

house music	house
heavy metal	heavy metal
rock	rock
rap	rap
hip-hop	hip-hop
techno	techno
reggae	reggae
funk	funk
flamenco	flamenco
Afro-cuban	música afro-cubana
Brazilian	musica brasileña
rock & roll	rock & roll
jazz	jazz
folk	folk
pop	pop
dance, disco	disco
classical	clásica
70's music	música de los setenta

[1] Walkman is a Sony product. [2] The most common pop chart in Spain is the Top 40.

Hola, ¿qué hacemos?
Hello, what's happening?

¿Tienes alguna idea?
Have you got any ideas?

¿Hacemos algo esta noche?
Shall we do something tonight?

Estoy ocupado[1].
I can't, I'm busy.

¿A qué hora?
What time?

¿Dónde nos quedamos?
Where shall we meet?

Nos vemos en la fuente.
See you at the fountain.

Do you know a good place to ...	¿Conoces un buen sitio para ...
go dancing?	ir a bailar?
listen to music?	eschuchar música?
eat?	comer?
go for a drink?	ir de copas?
nightclub	un club nocturno, una disco
disco	una discoteca
rave	un rave
party	una fiesta
picnic	un picnic, una excursión
barbecue	una barbacoa
theatre	un teatro
show, entertainment	un espectáculo
cinema	un cine
a film	una película
a performance, showing	una sesión
ballet	ballet
opera	opera
ticket office	la taquilla
Is there an admission charge?	¿Hay que pagar entrada?
Can I get a ticket in advance?	¿Puedo comprar una entrada con antelación?
student ticket	una entrada de estudiante
What time does it ...	¿A qué hora ...
start?	empieza?
finish?	acaba?
open	abre?
close?	cierra?
today	hoy
tomorrow	mañana
day after tomorrow	pasado mañana
(in the) morning	(por la) mañana
(in the) afternoon	(por la) tarde
(in the) evening	(por la) noche
this week	esta semana
next week	la próxima semana
entertainment guide	una guía

32

[1] Say *Estoy ocupada* if you're a girl.

Fact file

If you want to find out what to visit, go to the tourist office. Here you will get free maps, town plans and leaflets.

To find out what's on, look at the back pages of local newspapers. Most cities have listings magazines and towns have *carteleras* (billboards). Many films are dubbed but some are in *version original* (original language) or *vo*.

People go out late. The last film showing is at 10.30 or 11. Clubs may not fill up until 1 am.

What is there to see around here?	¿Qué se puede ver por aquí?	**the old town**	el centro histórico
		cathedral	la catedral
tour	una excursión	**church**	una iglesia
region	la región	**castle**	un castillo
countryside	el campo	**tower**	una torre
mountains	la montaña	**city walls**	las murallas
lake	el lago	**ruins**	unas ruinas
river	el río	**caves**	unas cuevas
coast	la costa	**theme park**	el parque de atracciones
on the beach	en la playa		
in town	en el centro	**festival**	el festival
at X's place	en casa de X	**fireworks**	los fuegos artificiales
museum	un museo	**bullfight**	una corrida de toros
art gallery	una galería de arte	**interesting**	interesante
exhibition	una exposición	**dull, boring**	aburrrido/aburrida
craft exhibition	una exposición de artesanía	**beautiful**	bonito/bonita

cinema	un cine	**actor/actress**	el actor, la actriz
film society/club	un club de cine	**fringe**	experimental/ independiente
theatre	un teatro		
library	una biblioteca	**film buff**	un experto en cine
film, movie	una película	**production**	una producción
play	una obra de teatro	**plot**	el argumento
book	un libro	**story**	la historia
magazine	una revista	**set**	el decorado
comic	un comic	**special-effects**	los efectos especiales
novel	una novela	**photography**	la fotografía
poetry	poesía	**TV, telly**	la tele
author	el autor	**TV (silly box)**	la caja tonta*
director (film)	el director	**remote control**	el mando a distancia
cast	el reparto	**cable TV**	la televisión por cable

34

satellite TV	la televisión satélite	war film	una película de guerra
digital TV	la televisión digital	a western	una película del oeste
programme	el programa	sci-fi	ciencia ficción
channel	el canal	suspense	suspense
news	las noticias	sex	sexo
weather	el tiempo	violence	violencia
documentary	el documental	political	político/política
cartoons	dibujos animados	satirical	satírico/satírica
game show	un programa concurso	serious	serio/seria
soap opera	el culebrón	offbeat	original
ads	los anuncios	commercial	comercial
dubbed	doblado/doblada	exciting	emocionante
in English	en inglés	over the top	exagerado/exagerada
with subtitles	con subtítulos	good	bueno/buena
famous	famoso/famosa	OK	bien
award-winning	ganador/a de un premio	bad	malo/mala
		lousy	malísimo/malísima
blockbuster	la película taquillera	silly	tonto/tonta
a classic	un clásico	funny, fun	divertido/divertida
comedy	una comedia	sad	triste
thriller	thriller/una película policíaca	scary.	de miedo
		Where can I hire a video?	¿Dónde se puede alquilar un vídeo?
musical	un musical		
horror film	una película de terror	Do I have to be a member?	¿Tengo que ser un miembro?
adventure story	una historia de aventuras	soap opera	el culebrón

¿Me puedes prestar algo para leer?
Can you lend me something to read?

Leí ese libro en la escuela.
I did that book at school.

¿De qué va?
What's it about?

Es fantástico.
It's brilliant.

¿Has leído esto?
Have you read this?

Es aburridísimo.
It's so boring.

¿De quién es?
Who's it by?

¿Estás sola?
Are you alone?

¿Tienes alguna hermana?
Have you got any sisters?

¿Dónde te alojas?
Where are you staying?

No, estoy viajando con amigos.
No, I'm travelling with friends.

I'm English.
Soy inglés/inglesa.

My family is from ...
Mi familia es de ...

I've been here for two weeks.
Hace dos semanas que estoy aquí.

I'm on an exchange.
He venido en un intercambio.

I'm on holiday.
He venido de vacaciones.

I'm staying with friends.
Estoy en casa de unos amigos.

I am a friend of ...
Soy amigo/amiga de ...

I'm studying Spanish.
Estoy estudiando español.

I'm travelling around.
Estoy viajando por el país.

My parents are divorced.
Mis padres están divorciados.

My birthday is on the ...
Mi cumpleaños es el día ...

I'm an only child.
Soy hijo único/hija única.

My name is ...	Me llamo ...
I live ...	Vivo ...
in the country	en el campo
in a town	en una ciudad
in the suburbs	en las afueras
in a house	en una casa
in a flat	en un piso
I live with ...	Vivo con ...
I don't live with ...	No vivo con ...
my/your	mi, mis[1]/tu, tus[1]
family	la familia
parents	los padres
father/mother	el padre/la madre
stepfather	el padrastro
stepmother	la madrastra
husband/wife	el marido/la esposa
boyfriend	el novio
girlfriend	la novia
brother	el hermano
sister	la hermana
step brother	el hermanastro
step sister	la hermanastra
alone	solo/sola
single	soltero/soltera
married	casado/casada
surname	apellido
nickname	apodo
my address	mi dirección
my e-mail address	mi e-mail
Do you have e-mail?	¿Tienes e-mail?

[1] Use *mi* and *tu* with singular words, *mis* and *tus* with plural words.

Other people

¿Conoces a Carlos?
Do you know Carlos?

Es alto.
He's tall.

Me cae fatal.
I can't stand her.

¿Quién es aquél?
Who's that?

Es muy divertido.
He's a good laugh.

Me gusta.
I like him.

¿Qué le pasó a Paola?
What's happened to Paola?

¿Cómo es?
What's she like?

Ella no está mal.
She's quite pretty.

Nos llevamos bien.
We get on OK.

friend	un amigo/una amiga	short	bajo/baja
mate, pal	un tío/una tía*	**fat**	gordo/gorda
boy/girl	un chico/una chica	**thin**	delgado/delgada
someone	alguien	**fair**	rubio/rubia
has long hair	tiene el pelo largo	**dark**	moreno/morena
short hair	el pelo corto	**pretty**	guapa
curly hair	el pelo rizado	**is good-looking**[1]	está bueno/buena*
straight hair	el pelo liso	**isn't good-looking**[1]	no es guapo/guapa
has brown eyes	tiene los ojos castaños	**is OK (looks)**[1]	está bien
		ugly	feo/fea
he/she is[1]...	el/ella es ...	**a bit, a little**	un poco
tall	alto/alta	**very**	muy

¿Conoces a alguien aquí?
Do you know anyone here?

¿Me puedes dar tu número de teléfono?
What's your phone number?

¿Qué quieres beber?
Do you want a drink?

¿Quieres bailar?
Do you want to dance?

[1] There are two words for "is": es means "is (always)" e.g. Es alto (he is tall); está means "is (at the moment)" eg Está de mal humor (he is in a bad mood).

so	tan
really	realmente
completely	completamente
nice, OK	simpático/simpática
horrible, nasty	horrible
is cool, trendy, hip[1]	está al día
is old-fashioned, square[1]	está anticuado/ anticuada
clever	listo/lista
thick	burro/burra
boring	aburrido/aburrida
shy	tímido/tímida
mad, crazy	loco/loca
weird	raro/rara
lazy	perezoso/perezosa
laid back	tranquilo/tranquila
up-tight	tenso/tensa
mixed up, untogether	desorientada
selfish	egoísta
jealous	celoso/celosa
rude	mal educado/educada
macho	machista
a bit smooth	un poco falso/falsa
stuck up	pretencioso/ pretenciosa
sloaney	pijo/pija*
cool	chulo/chula
a creep	un pelotillero/ una pelotillera

an idiot	un/una idiota
a prat	un/una gilipollas*
in a bad mood	de mal humor
in a good mood	de buen humor
hassled, annoyed	enfadado/enfadada
upset	preocupado/ preocupada
depressed	deprimido/deprimida
happy	feliz

Have you heard that ... ?
¿Sabes que ... ?

Carlos is going out with Paola.
Carlos está saliendo con Paola.

Juan fancies Maria.
A Juan le gusta María.

He/she kissed me.
Me besó.

They split up.
Han roto.

We had a row.
Tuvimos una pelea.

Leave me alone.
¡Déjame en paz!

¿Podemos vernos otra vez?
Can I see you again?

¿Puedo ir también yo?
Can I come too?

Lo siento, no puedo.
Sorry I can't.

¿Quieres venir?
Want to come?

Quizás otro día.
Maybe some other time.

¿Haces algún deporte?
Do you do any sport?

¿Haces jogging?
Do you go jogging?

No estoy nada en forma.
I'm really unfit.

Yo juego al rugby.
I play rugby.

No juego al squash.
I don't play squash.

¿Juegas al tenis?
Do you play tennis?

¿Cada cuándo?
How often?

¿Quieres jugar una partida de badminton?
Do you want a game of badminton?

No tengo una raqueta.
I haven't got a racket.

Voy a correr cada mañana.
I go jogging every morning.

Catch!
¡Cógela!

In!/Out!
¡Dentro!/¡Fuera!

Throw it to me.
Tíramela.

Who won?
¿Quién ganó?

You're cheating!
¡Haces trampas!

How do you play this?
¿Cómo se juega?

What are the rules?
Explícame las reglas del juego.

What team do you support?
¿De qué equipo eres?

Is there a match we could go to?
¿Podríamos ir a ver algún partido?

Fact file

Spanish bull fighting is famous but it's not as popular as football. People play football, go to matches and watch it on TV, particularly in bars on Sunday evening. The big teams are *Real Madrid*, *F.C. Barcelona* and *Real Sociedad*. Tennis and basketball are popular. In the Basque country people play pelota (balls are hit against a wall with wicker rackets). There's an annual *Vuelta ciclista a España* (round Spain cycle race). Winter sports are becoming popular, with most resorts in the Pyrennes and the Sierra Nevada.

sport	un deporte	**track suit**	un chandal
match	un partido	**once a week**	una vez a la semana
a game (of)	una partida (de)	**twice a week**	dos veces a la semana
doubles	dobles		
singles	individuales	**I play ...**	Juego al ...
race	una carrera	**I don't play ...**	No juego al ...
marathon	un maratón	**tennis**	tenis
championships	unos campeonatos	**squash**	squash
Olympics	los juegos Olímpicos	**badminton**	badminton
World Cup	La Copa del mundo	**football**	fútbol
club	un club	**American football**	fútbol americano
team	un equipo	**basketball**	baloncesto
referee	un árbitro	**volleyball**	balonvolea
supporter	un/una hincha	**table tennis**	tenis de mesa
training	entrenamiento	**cricket**	cricket
practice	práctica	**baseball**	béisbol
a goal	un gol	**I do/go ...**	Hago ...
to lose	perder	**I don't do/go ...**	No hago ...
to draw	empatar	**judo**	judo
sports centre	un centro de deportes	**karate**	karate
stadium	un estadio	**aerobics**	aerobics
gym	un gimnasio	**weight-training**	levantamiento de pesos
court	una pista		
indoor	cubierta	**bowling**	los bolos
outdoor	al aire libre	**dancing**	baile
ball	una pelota	**yoga**	yoga
net	una red	**I go jogging**	Voy a correr
trainers	unas zapatillas de deporte		

41

No soy muy aficionada al submarinismo.
I'm not keen on scuba diving.

Me gusta volar en ala delta.
I love hang gliding.

Prefiero el esquí acuático.
I prefer water-skiing.

No lo he intentado nunca.
I've never tried.

No sé nadar.
I can't swim.

¿Son fuertes las corrientes?
Are the currents strong?

¿No es peligroso, verdad?
It's not dangerous, is it?

I like ...	Me gusta ...
I don't like ...	No me gusta ...
I love ...	Me encanta ...
I prefer ...	Yo prefiero ...
swimming	la natación
(scuba) diving	el submarinismo
sailing	la navegación
surfing	hacer surf
water skiing	el esquí acuático
canoeing	el piragüismo
rowing	el remo
sunbathing	tomar el sol
boat	una barca
sail	la vela
surfboard	una plancha de surf
sea	el mar
beach	la playa
swimming pool	la piscina
in the sun	al sol
in the shade	a la sombra
mask	las gafas de natación
snorkel	el tubo
flippers	las aletas
wetsuit	el traje de buceo
life jacket	un salvavidas
fishing	la pesca
fishing rod	la caña

¿Has hecho alguna vez montañismo?
Have you ever been climbing?

¿Me pueden dar clases?
Can I get lessons?

¿Es caro?
Is it expensive?

¿Dónde puedo alquilar esquíes?
Where can I hire skis?

¿Te gusta patinar?
Do you like skating?

cycling	el ciclismo
racing bike	una bici de carreras
mountain bike	una bici todo terreno
touring bike	una bici de paseo
BMX	una bici BMX
horse riding	la equitación
horse	un caballo
walking, hiking	el excursionismo
skateboard	un monopatín
roller skating	el patinaje sobre ruedas
ice rink	la pista de hielo
skates	los patines
skiing	el esquí
cross-country skiing	el esquí alpino
snowboarding	snowboard/esquiar con tabla
ski run	la pista
ski pass	el pase/el ticket
chair lift	la telesilla
drag lift	el telearrastre, el telesquí
skis	los esquíes
ski boots	las botas de esquiar
ski goggles	las gafas de esquiar
snow	la nieve

Soy principiante.
I'm a beginner.

Soy bastante bueno.
I'm quite good.

¡Ya no puedo más!
I've had enough.

Venga, puedes hacerlo.
Come on, you can do it.

¿Qué haces?
What do you do?

¿Dónde estudias?
Where are you studying?

¿Qué tipo de escuela es?
What sort of college is it?

¿A qué hora acabas?
What time do you finish?

¿Tienes que trabajar mucho en casa?
Do you have a lot of work?

Sí, cantidad.
Yes, loads.

I do ...	Estudio ...
computer studies	informática
maths	matemáticas, mates
physics	física
chemistry	química
biology	biología
natural sciences	ciencias naturales
geography	geografía
history	historia
economics	económicas
business studies	estudios empresariales
languages	idiomas
French	francés
English	inglés
Spanish	español
German	alemán
Italian	italiano
literature	literatura
philosophy	filosofía
sociology	sociología
religious studies	religión
general studies	estudios generales
design and technology	diseño y tecnología
art	arte
art history	historia del arte
drama	teatro
music	música
PE	educación física
school	un colegio, una escuela
boarding school	un internado
state education	enseñanza pública
private education	enseñanza privada
term	un trimestre
holidays	las vacaciones
beginning of term	el principio del trimestre

uniform	un uniforme
school club	un club
form leader	el encargado/ la encargada
lesson, lecture	una clase
private lessons	clases particulares
conversation class	clase de conversación
homework	deberes
essay	un trabajo escrito
translation	una traducción
project	un proyecto
an option	una optativa
revision	un repaso
test	un exámen
oral test	un exámen oral
written	escrito
presentation	una exposición oral de un tema
continuous assessment	evaluación continua
mark, grade	nota
teacher	el maestro/la maestra
lecturer	el profesor/la profesora
(language) assistant	ayudante de conversación
good	bueno/buena
bad	malo/mala
strict	estricto/estricta
discipline	la disciplina
to repeat (a year)	repetir curso
to skive, to bunk off	hacer novillos, hacer campana
a grant	una beca
a loan	un préstamo
free	gratis

I'm a student.
Soy estudiante.

I'm still at school.
Aún voy a la escuela.

I want to do ...
Quiero hacer ...

He is skiving, bunking off.
Está haciendo novillos.

Fact file

Types of schools and colleges:
– *un colegio de enseñanza secundaria* (first stage of secondary school – for all pupils aged about 12 to 16)
– *un instituto de bachillerato* (second stage, 16 to 18 – similar to sixth form college)
– *una escuela de formación profesional* (as above, but with technical, vocational slant)
– *una universidad* (university)

School is compulsory until 16. State schools are mixed and there is no uniform. At each stage of secondary education the forms are called *el primero, el segundo* and *el tercero*[1]. There is continuous assessment as well as a test for each subject every year. Anyone who fails has the option of retaking the test in September. At about 18 many pupils sit the *Selectividad*, the university entrance exam. Pupils have to travel to a university to sit this. *El servicio militar* (national service) is compulsory for men. The first call-up stage is at age 19 but it can be deferred for up to 15 years. A period of community service can be served instead.

¿Qué quieres hacer cuando acabes?
What do you want to do when you finish college?

¿Qué asignaturas haces?
What subjects are you doing?

¿En qué curso estás?
What year are you in?

¿Cuándo tienes los exámenes?
When are your exams?

¿Cuál te gusta más?
What do you like best?

[1] Literally, these mean the first, second and third.

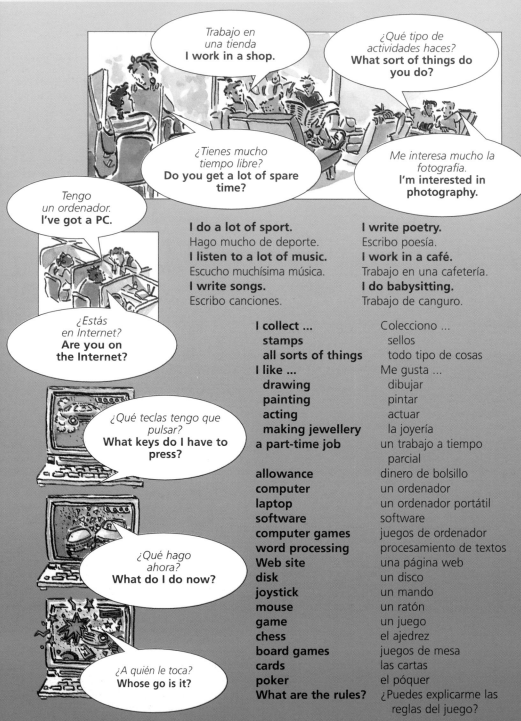

Trabajo en una tienda
I work in a shop.

¿Qué tipo de actividades haces?
What sort of things do you do?

¿Tienes mucho tiempo libre?
Do you get a lot of spare time?

Me interesa mucho la fotografía.
I'm interested in photography.

Tengo un ordenador.
I've got a PC.

¿Estás en Internet?
Are you on the Internet?

¿Qué teclas tengo que pulsar?
What keys do I have to press?

¿Qué hago ahora?
What do I do now?

¿A quién le toca?
Whose go is it?

I do a lot of sport.
Hago mucho de deporte.
I listen to a lot of music.
Escucho muchísima música.
I write songs.
Escribo canciones.

I write poetry.
Escribo poesía.
I work in a café.
Trabajo en una cafetería.
I do babysitting.
Trabajo de canguro.

I collect ...	Colecciono ...
stamps	sellos
all sorts of things	todo tipo de cosas
I like ...	Me gusta ...
drawing	dibujar
painting	pintar
acting	actuar
making jewellery	la joyería
a part-time job	un trabajo a tiempo parcial
allowance	dinero de bolsillo
computer	un ordenador
laptop	un ordenador portátil
software	software
computer games	juegos de ordenador
word processing	procesamiento de textos
Web site	una página web
disk	un disco
joystick	un mando
mouse	un ratón
game	un juego
chess	el ajedrez
board games	juegos de mesa
cards	las cartas
poker	el póquer
What are the rules?	¿Puedes explicarme las reglas del juego?

What do you want to do later?
¿Qué quieres hacer después?
When I finish ...
Cuando acabe ...
One day ...
un día..
I want to be a ...
Quiero ser ...

I want ...
to live/work abroad
to travel
to have a career
to get a good job
to get my
   qualifications
to carry on studying

Quiero ...
vivir/trabajar en el extranjero
viajar
tener una carrera
obtener un buen trabajo
obtener los títulos
   necesarios
continuar estudiando

What do you think about ...?
¿Qué piensas sobre ...?
I don't know much about ...
No sé mucho sobre ...
Can you explain ...?
¿Puedes explicar ...
I feel angry about ...
Me enfada que ...

I think ...
Creo que ...
I belong to ...
Soy de ...
I believe in ...
Creo en ...
I don't believe in ...
No creo en ...

You're right.
Tienes razón.
I don't agree.
No estoy de acuerdo.
I'm for, I support ...
Estoy a favor de ...
I'm against ...
Estoy en contra de ...

the future	el futuro	**deforestation**	la desforestación
(in) the past	el pasado	**acid rain**	la lluvia ácida
now, nowadays	ahora	**nuclear power**	la energía nuclear
religion	la religión	**recycling**	el reciclaje
God	Dios	**politics**	la política
human rights	los derechos humanos	**government**	el gobierno
gay	gay	**democratic**	democrático/
feminist	feminista		democrática
abortion	el aborto	**elections**	las elecciones
drugs	las drogas	**party**	el partido
drug addict	drogadicto/drogadicta	**revolution**	la revolución
HIV	VIH positivo/positiva	**the left**	la izquierda
Aids	el Sida	**the right**	la derecha
unemployment	el desempleo/el paro	**fascist**	fascista
Third World	el Tercer Mundo	**communist**	comunista
peace	la paz	**socialist**	socialista
war	la guerra	**greens, green**	los verdes
terrorism	el terrorismo	**movement**	
environment	el medio ambiente	**conservative**	conservador/
pollution	la polución		conservadora
conservation	la conservación	**politically active,**	políticamente,
global warming	calentamiento global	**committed**	activo/activa
greenhouse effect	efecto invernadero	**march, demo**	una marcha, una
ozone layer	la capa de ozono		manifestación

Illness, problems, emergencies

It hurts a lot.	Duele mucho.
It hurts a little.	Duele un poco.
I've cut myself.	Me he cortado.
I think I've broken my ...	Creo que me he roto ...
My ... hurts	Me duele ...
eye	el ojo
ear	el oido, la oreja
I've been stung by a wasp.	Me ha picado una avispa ...
I've got mosquito bites.	Tengo picaduras de mosquito.
He/She's had too much to drink.	Ha bedido demasiado.
I feel dizzy.	Me siento mareado/ mareada.
I'm constipated.	Tengo estreñimiento.
I'm on medication for ...	Estoy tomando medicamentos para ...
I'm allergic to ...	Soy alérgico/alérgica a ...
antibiotics	los antibióticos
to some medicines	algunos medicamentos
I have ...	Tengo ...
food poisoning	una intoxicación
diarrhoea	diarrea
cramp	una rampa
sunstroke	una insolación
a headache	dolor de cabeza
a stomach ache	dolor de estómago
my period, period pains	el periodo, la regla*
an infection	una infección
a sore throat	dolor de garganta
a cold	un resfriado
flu	una gripe
a cough	una tos
hayfever	fiebre del heno
asthma	asma
a toothache	dolor de muelas
a temperature	fiebre
a hangover	una resaca
doctor	un doctor, un médico
female doctor	una doctora
dentist	un/una dentista
optician	un/una oculista, un óptico/una óptica
chemist	una farmacia
pill	una pastilla
suppository[1]	un supositorio
injection	una inyección

No me encuentro bien.
I don't feel well.

¿Qué te pasa?
What's wrong?

Tengo ganas de vomitar.
I'm going to be sick.

Lo siento mucho.
I'm really sorry about this.

Quiero ir al médico.
I need to see a doctor.

¿Hay alguna farmacia abierta por aqui?
Is there a chemist open around here?

¿Puedes darme algo para fiebre del heno?
Can you give me something for hayfever?

[1]These are often prescribed in Spain.

He perdido una lente de contacto.
I've lost my contact lens.

Se me han roto las gafas.
I've broken my glasses.

Me han robado mis cosas.
Someone's stolen my things.

No ví lo que pasó.
I didn't see what happened.

Fact file

In Spain it's always advisable to carry proof of identity, so keep your passport with you. You may be asked to show your *papeles* (documents, ID). When carrying anything valuable or important, keep it out of sight.

For minor health problems or first aid treatment, go to a chemist. For something more serious go to a doctor. Look for an *Ambulatorio de la Seguridad Social* (local surgery). In an emergency go to a *Hospital de la Seguridad Social* (state-run hospital). In each case you should expect to pay. You should be able to claim back on insurance, but keep all the paperwork.

Emergencies

Emergency phone numbers: police 091; ambulance 3354545 and fire brigade 080.

There's been an accident.	Ha habido un accidente.
Help!	¡Ayuda!
Fire!	¡Fuego!
Stop thief!	¡Al ladrón!
Please call ...	Por favor, llame a ...
an ambulance	una ambulancia
the police	la policía
the fire brigade	los bomberos

my wallet	mi cartera
(hand)bag	mi bolso
my things	mis cosas
my papers	mis papeles
my passport	mi pasaporte
my key	mi llave
my mobile	mi móvil
all my money	todo mi dinero
lost property	objetos perdidos
I'm lost.	Me he perdido.
I'm scared.	Tengo miedo.
I'm in trouble.	Tengo problemas.

I need to talk to someone.
Necesito hablar con alguien.

I don't know what to do ...
No sé qué hacer ...

I don't want to cause trouble, but ...
No quiero molestar, pero ...

A man's following me.
Un hombre me está siguiendo.

Can you keep an eye on my things?
¿Puedes vigilar mis cosas?

Has anyone seen ... ?
¿Alguien ha visto ... ?

Please don't smoke.
Por favor, no fume.

It doesn't work.
¡No funciona!

There's no water/power.
No hay agua/corriente eléctrica.

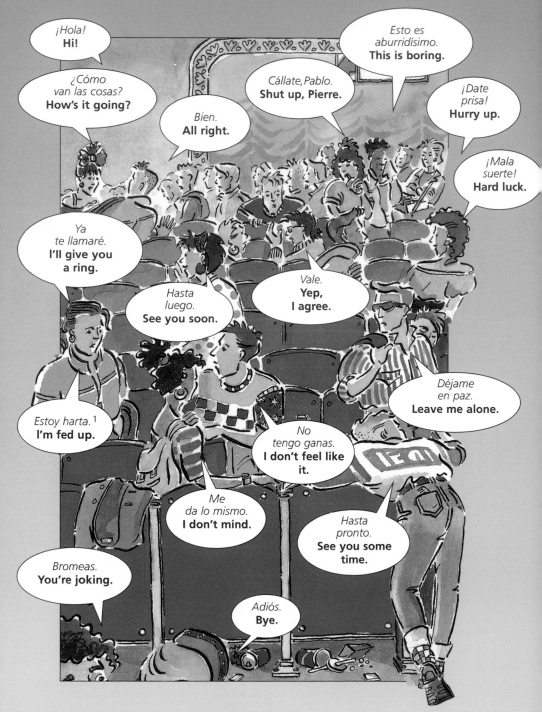

¹ If you're a boy, say *Estoy harto*.

This book has included informal Spanish and slang where appropriate, but these two pages list a few of the most common words and phrases.

When using slang it is easy to sound off-hand or rude without really meaning to. Here, as in the rest of the book, a single asterisk after a word shows that it is mild slang, so be careful how you use it. You will find more examples of slang in the dictionary.

Contractions and alternative pronunciations

How are you?	¿Qué tal? (Qué tal estás)
How are things?	¿Cómo va? (Cómo van las cosas?)
See you later.	Ta luego.* (Hasta luego.)
houses	casa* (casas)[1]
market	mercao* (mercado)

Abbreviations

TV	la tele (televisión)
teacher	el profe* (el profesor)
disco, club	la disco (la discoteca)
mate, pal	el/la compa* (el compañero/la compañera)
OK	vale

American and English imports

Un parking, un spot **(a commercial, an ad),** el look, sexy, stop, el estress **(stress),** el corner **(in football),** el club, el marketing, el heavy metal, el cassette or casete, el Walkman, el estereo, el cheque...

Fillers and exclamations

you know	sabes
well ...	bien
... er ...	bueno
then	luego, entónces
Really?	¡Ah, sí?
Hey!	¡Vaya!

Wow!	¡Caray!
by the way	por cierto
I mean, that's to say (means somthing is "so so" or OK)	o sea psss
shows you agree	ya, ya

Slang

great, fantastic	(ser)[2] guay* (ser) superguay*, (ser) bestial*
great, amazing	(ser)[2] alucinante*
very, hyper	super-, hiper-, ultra-
grotty	cutre*
good-looking	(estar)[2] cachas*
square person	(ser)[2] un/una carca (ser) un/una facha
parents	los viejos*
my boyfriend	mi chico*
my girlfriend	mi chica*, mi niña
friend, mate	un/una colega*
police	la pasma*
a bore, a pain	(ser)[2] un/una pelma un/una palizas* un/una plasta* un/una plomo* un/una peñazo* un muermo*
a flirt	(ser)[2] un ligón/una ligona*
stingy person	un/una rata*
skiver	un/una jeta*
thief	un chorizo/una choriza*
knowall	un enterado/una enterada
nutter	un chalado/una chalada*
pesetas/money	las pelas*
1000 ptas note	un talego*
job	un curro*
sandwich	un bocata*
jacket	una chupa*
a hassle	un lío
to steal, nick	mangar*, birlar
to eat	papear*
to like, dig	molar*
to be cheesed off	estar cabreado/cabreada*
to be low	estar depre*

[1] The plural "s" is often dropped in southern Spain. [2] Use with *ser* or *estar* (to be) as shown. See page 58.

Countries, nationalities, faiths

Countries

Africa	Africa
Asia	Asia
Australia	Australia
Austria	Austria
Bangladesh	Bangladesh
Belgium	Bélgica
Brazil	Brasil
Canada	Canadá
Caribbean	El Caribe
Central America	Centro-américa
China	China
Dominica	Dominica
England	Inglaterra
Europe	Europa
France	Francia
Germany	Alemania
Great Britain	Gran Bretaña
Greece	Grecia
Hungary	Hungría
India	India
Ireland	Irlanda
Israel	Israel
Italy	Italia
Jamaica	Jamaica
Japan	Japón
Kenya	Kenia
Middle East	Oriente Medio
Mexico	Méjico
Netherlands	Holanda
New Zealand	Nueva Zelanda
North Africa	Africa del Norte
Pakistan	Pakistán
Poland	Polonia
Portugal	Portugal
Russia	Rusia
Scandinavia	Escandinavia
Scotland	Escocia
South America	Sudamérica
Spain	España
Switzerland	Suiza
Tunisia	Túnez
Turkey	Turquía
United States	Estados Unidos
Vietnam	Vietnam
Wales	Gales

country	el país	**continent**	el continente
north	el norte	**south**	el sur
east	el este	**west**	el oeste

Nationalities

You can say "I come from" + country:
e.g. *Soy de España*
or:
I am + adjective for nationality:
e.g. Soy español/española

Here are some common adjectives:

American	americano/americana
Australian	australiano/australiana
Austrian	austríaco/austríaca
Belgian	belga
Canadian	Canadiense
Dutch	holandés/holandésa
English	inglés/inglesa
French	francés/francesa
German	alemán/alemána
Indian	indio/india
Irish	irlandés/irlandesa
Italian	italiano/italiana
Pakistani	paquistaní
Scottish	escocés/escocesa
Spanish	español/española
Swiss	suizo/suiza
Welsh	galés/galesa

Faiths

agnostic	un agnóstico/ una agnóstica
atheist	un ateo/una atea
Buddhist	budista
Catholic	católico/católica
Christian	cristiano/cristiana
Hindu	hindú
Jewish	judío/judía
Muslim	musulmán/musulmana
Protestant	protestante
Sikh	sikh, sig

Numbers

0 cero	**30** treinta
1 uno[1]/una	**31** treinta y uno
2 dos	**40** cuarenta
3 tres	**50** cincuenta
4 cuatro	**60** sesenta
5 cinco	**70** setenta
6 seis	**71** setenta y uno
7 siete	**72** setenta y dos
8 ocho	**80** ochenta
9 nueve	**81** ochenta y uno
10 diez	**82** ochenta y dos
11 once	**90** noventa
12 doce	**91** noventa y uno
13 trece	**92** noventa y dos
14 catorce	**100** cien, ciento[2]
15 quince	**101** ciento uno
16 dieciséis	**200** dos cientos/cientas
17 diecisiete	**300** tres cientos/cientas
18 dieciocho	**1,000** mil
19 diecinueve	**1,100** mil cien
20 veinte	**1,200** mil dos cientos
21 veintiuno	**2,000** dos mil
22 veintidós	**2,100** dos mil cien
23 veintitrés	**10,000** diez mil
24 veinticuatro	**100,000** cien mil
25 veinticinco	**1,000,000** un millón

Colours

colour	color
light	claro
dark	oscuro
blue	azul
navy	azul marino
green	verde
yellow	amarillo/amarilla
orange	naranja
purple	morado/morada
pink	rosa
red	rojo/roja
white	blanco/blanca
grey	gris
brown	marrón
black	negro/negra

Days and dates

Monday	lunes
Tuesday	martes
Wednesday	miércoles
Thursday	jueves
Friday	viernes
Saturday	sábado
Sunday	domingo
January	enero
February	febrero
March	marzo
April	abril
May	mayo
June	junio
July	julio
August	agosto
September	septiembre
October	octubre
November	noviembre
December	diciembre
day	el día
week	la semana
month	el mes
year	el año
diary	una agenda
calendar	un calendario
yesterday	ayer
the day before yesterday	anteayer
today	hoy
the next day	el próximo día
tomorrow	mañana
the day after tomorrow	pasado mañana
last week	la semana pasada
this week	esta semana
next week	la semana próxima
What's the date?	¿Qué día es hoy?/¿A cuántos estamos?
on Mondays	los lunes
in August	en agosto
(on) 1st April	el uno de abril
in the year 2000	en el año dos mil
in 2005	en el año dos mil cinco

[1]*Uno* drops the "o" before masculine nouns, e.g. *un libro* (one book). [2]*Cien* changes into *ciento* when followed by a smaller number.

Time

hour	hora
What time is it?	¿Qué hora es?
It's 1 o'clock.	Es la una
2 o'clock	Son las dos
minute	minuto
morning	la mañana
afternoon	la tarde
evening	la noche
midday	el mediodía
midnight	la medianoche
quarter past two	los dos y cuarto
half past two	los dos y media
quarter to two	las dos menos cuarto
five past two	las dos y cinco
ten to two	las dos menos diez
in ten minutes	dentro de diez minutos
half an hour ago	hace media hora
at 09.00	a las nueve
at 13.17	a las trece y diecisiete

Seasons and weather

season	la estación	**sky**	el cielo
spring	la primavera	**sun**	el sol
summer	el verano	**clouds**	las nubes
autumn	el otoño	**rain**	la lluvia
winter	el invierno	**snow**	la nieve

It's fine.	Hace buen tiempo.
It's sunny.	Hace sol.
It's hot.	Hace calor.
It's windy.	Hace viento.
It's raining.	Está lloviendo.
It's foggy.	Hay niebla.
It's snowing.	Está nevando.
It's icy.	Hay hielo.
It's cold.	Hace muchísimo frio.
It's freezing.	Está helado.
It's horrible.	Hace un tiempo horrible.

What's the weather like?
¿Qué tiempo hace?

What's the weather forecast?
¿Cuál es el pronóstico del tiempo?

Fact file – Spain and South America

The Spanish that is used in this book is Castilian Spanish – the most widely spoken language in Spain. Outside of Spain, it is the language of most of South and Central America. This developed because of the widespread colonisation by Spain in the 16th and 17th century. Spain itself has four official national languages: Castilian, Catalan, Galician and Basque. The first three are all derived from Latin.

Castilian Spanish is spoken in the north, centre and south of Spain. Castilian itself has many dialects, which mainly involve differences in pronunciation. These occur in the Canary Islands and the south of Spain, in Andalucia, Extremadura and Murcia.

The Spanish of South and Central America (Latin American Spanish) developed originally from the Spanish of southern Spain. This is the area where the "c" is not lisped, as it is in most of Spain, and this along with some other local variations formed a basis for the language.

Catalan is spoken in the north-east of Spain – the area of Catalonia proper, coastal Valencia and the Balearic Islands (Majorca, Minorca and Ibiza). In these areas, Catalan is an official language alongside Castilian Spanish. It is taught in schools and widely spoken.

Galician is spoken in Galicia (in the north-west) along with Castilian Spanish. It is also spoken in parts of the neighbouring communities of Asturias and Castilla-Leon. Galician is very similar to Portuguese.

Basque is spoken in the Basque region (northern Spain).

Vowel sounds

In Spanish, vowel sounds are always short:

a sounds like "a" in "cat".

e sounds like "e" in "let".

i sounds like "i" in machine.

o sounds like "o" in "soft".

u sounds like "oo" in moon. It is silent after "q" and usually silent after "g" if it is followed by "e" or "i".

Groups of vowels

When in Spanish you have two or more vowels together, you usually pronounce each vowel in turn. For example, **eu** is said "e-oo" as in *Europa*, and **iu** is said "ee-oo", as in *ciudad*. The same applies to double vowels, for example **ee** is said "e-e" as in *leer*.

Consonants

c is hard as in "cat", except before "i" or "e" when it is like "th" in thumb.

ch sounds like the "ch" in "cheese".

d is like an English "d" except when it is on the end of a syllable. Then it is like "th" in "that".

g is like the "g" in "good" except before "e" or "i". Then it sounds like "ch" in the Scottish word "loch". When "g" is followed by "ue" or "ui", the "u" is not sounded but the "g" still sounds like the "g" in "good", for example in guerra and guitarra.

h is never pronounced.

j sounds like "ch" in the Scottish word "loch".

ll sounds like the "y" in "yes" but preceded by a hint of an "i".

ñ sounds like the "ni(o)" sound in "onion".

qu is the same sound as the hard "**c**" as in "cat".

r is a rolled or nearly trilled "r". Double "rr" sounds about the same. At the beginning of a word, "r" is strongly trilled, and on the end of a word it is not trilled quite so much.

v sounds like "b" in "big". There is no difference between a Spanish *b* and a Spanish *v*.

y sounds like "y" in "yes" when it is in the middle of a word. On the end of a word or on its own, e.g. *y* (and), it sounds like a Spanish *i* - like the "i" in "machine".

In Spanish you stress the last syllable of most words ending in a consonant. For words ending in a vowel, stress the second-to-last syllable. Any Spanish word that does not follow this pattern is written with a stress mark or accent. This shows you which part of the word you should stress, for example *árbol*.

The alphabet in Spanish

Applying the points made above, this is how you say the alphabet:
A, Be, Ce, CHe, De, E, eFe, Ge, Hache, I, Jota, Ka, eLe, eLLe, eMe, eNe, eÑe, O, Pe, Qu, eRe, eSe, Te, U, uVe, W=uve doble, X=equis, Y=igriega, Z=ceta.

How Spanish works

Nouns

All Spanish nouns are either masculine (m) or feminine (f). Nouns for people and animals have the obvious gender, e.g. *el padre* (father) and *el toro* (bull) are masculine and *la madre* (mother) and *la vaca* (cow) are feminine. For most nouns, though, the gender seems random, e.g. *autobús* (bus) is masculine and *casa* (house) is feminine. A few nouns can be either gender, e.g. *el/la turista* (tourist m/f).

The singular article (the word for "the" or "a") shows the noun's gender: with (m) nouns, "the" is *el,* e.g. *el autobús* (the bus) and "a" is *un*, e.g. *un autobus* (a bus); with (f) nouns, "the" is *la*, e.g. *la casa* (the house) and "a" is *una*, e.g. *una casa* (a house.)

Don't worry if you muddle up *el* and *la*, you will still be understood. It is worth knowing the gender of nouns since other words, particularly adjectives, change to match them. If you're learning a noun, learn it with *el* or *la*. In general, nouns ending in "o" are masculine and those ending in "a" are feminine.

Plurals

In the plural, the Spanish for "the" is *los* + masculine noun and *las* + feminine noun, e.g. *los autobuses* (the buses), *las casas* (the houses).

Uno and *una* become *unos* and *unas*, e.g. *unos autobuses* (some buses), *unas casas* (some houses).

To make nouns plural, add "es" to any that end in a consonant, e.g *un tren, dos trenes* (a train, two trains) and add "s" to most nouns ending in a vowel, e.g. *un billete, dos billetes* (a ticket, two tickets).

A (to) and de (of, from)

In Spanish, "to" is *a*. When *a* precedes *el,* they contract to *al*, e.g. *Voy al mercado* (I'm going to the market).

The Spanish for "of" and "from" is *de*. When *de* precedes *el,* they join up and become *del*, e.g. *Soy del norte* (I'm from the north).

Spanish uses *de* to show possession where English does not, e.g. *el libro de Ana* (Ana's book), *el suéter del niño* (the kid's jumper).

Adjectives

In Spanish, most adjectives come after the noun they refer to, e.g. *la película larga* (the long film). They also agree with the noun – they change when used with a feminine or plural noun.

With feminine nouns, adjectives ending in "o" and a few others change to "a", e.g. *corto* becomes *corta: la novela corta* (the short novel). Others don't change, e.g. *feliz* (happy).

With plural nouns, most adjectives that end in a vowel have an "s", e.g *rojo* (m) becomes *rojos: los trenes rojos* (the red trains); *roja* (f) becomes *rojas: las camisetas rojas* (the red T-shirts). Those that end in a consonant have "es", e.g. *difícil* (difficult) becomes *difíciles*: *los exámenes difíciles* (the difficult exams).

Some common adjectives come before the noun, e.g. *gran* (big), *poco/poca* (little).

Making comparisons

To make a comparison, put the following words in front of the adjective: *más* (more, ...er), e.g. *más bonita* (prettier); *menos* (less), e.g. *menos bonita* (less pretty); *tan* (as), e.g. *tan bonita* (as pretty); *el/la más* (the most, the ...est), e.g. *la más bonita* (the prettiest);

más ... que (more ... than, ... er... than), *e.g. El es más alto que ella* (he's taller than her);
menos que (less ... than), e.g. *Ella es menos alta que él* (she's less tall than him);
tan ... como (as ... as), e.g. *El es tan delgado como ella* (He's as thin as her).

There are exceptions, e.g. *bueno/buena* (good), *mejor* (better), *el/la mejor* (the best); *malo/mala* (bad), *peor* (worse), *el/la peor* (the worst).

Very + adjective

Spanish has two ways of saying that something is "very good/easy etc.". You can use *muy* (very) + the adjective, e.g. *muy fácil* (very easy), or the adjective + *-ísimo/ísima*, e.g. facilísimo/facilísima (very easy). Vowels on the end of the adjective are dropped, e.g. *caro* (expensive), *carísimo* (very expensive). This second way is used a lot in colloquial Spanish.

Este/esta (this)

The Spanish for "this" is *este* + (m) noun, e.g. *este chico* (this boy), *esta* + (f) noun, e.g. *esta chica* (this girl), *estos* + plural (m) noun, e.g. *estos chicos* (these boys), *estas* + plural (f) noun, e.g. *estas chicas* (these girls).

Ese/esa, aquel/aquella (that)

There are two words for "that": *ese* when the person or thing referred to is near the person you're speaking to, e.g. who's that bloke on your right?, and *aquel* when the person or thing is far from both of you, e.g. that bloke over there.
Ese and *aquel* change as follows: *ese* or *aquel* + (m) noun, *esa* or *aquella* + (f) noun; *esos* or *aquellos* + plural (m) noun; *esas* or *aquellas* + plural (f) noun.

I, you, he, she etc.

Spanish often leaves out "I", "you", etc. The verb changes according to who or what is doing the action (see Verbs, page 58) so they are not needed, e.g. *Estoy pensando* (I am thinking, literally "am thinking"); *Es un bar* (It's a bar, literally "Is a bar"). It helps to know these words as the verb has various forms to correspond to each of them.

I yo

you tú, usted, vosotros/-as, ustedes
There are four words for "you": *tú* is singular informal; say *tú* to a friend or someone your own age or younger. *Usted,* often writted *Vd.*, is singular polite (pol). Use it to a person you don't know or you want to show respect to (someone older); *Vosotros/-as* is plural informal, (m)/(f). Use it like *tú* but when speaking to more than one person. Use *vosotras* when talking to girls or women only; *ustedes* (written *Vds.*) is plural polite (pl.pol). Use it like *usted* but for more than one person. If in doubt, use the polite forms.

he él **she** ella **it** él/ella
There's no special word for "it". The verb is used on it's own.

we nosotros/-as
Nosotros means "we" for males or males and females, *nosotras* means "we" for females only.

they ellos/ellas
Ellos is for males, *ellas* for females.

How Spanish works

My, your, his, her etc.

These words agree with the noun they relate to, e.g. *mi hermano* (my brother), *mis padres* (my parents), *nuestra casa* (our house) etc:

In front of singular noun		plural noun
my	*mi*	*mis*
your	*tu*	*tus*
his/her/its, your (pol)	*su*	*sus*
our	*nuestro/-a*	*nuestros/-as*
your	*vuestro/-a*	*vuestros/-as*
their, your (pl.pol)	*su*	*sus*

Verbs

Spanish verbs have more tenses (present, future, simple past etc.) than English verbs, but there are simple ways of getting by which are explained here.

Present tense

Spanish verbs end in "ar", "er" or "ir" in the infinitive[1], e.g. *comprar* (to buy), *comer* (to eat), *escribir* (to write), and follow one of these three patterns. Drop "ar", "er", or "ir" and replace it with the ending you need:

to buy	compr ar
I buy	*compr o*
you buy	*compr as*
he/she/it buys, you buy (pol)	*compr a*
we buy	*compr amos*
you buy	*compr áis*
they buy, you buy (pl.pol)	*compr an*

to eat	com er
I eat	*com o*
you eat	*com es*
he/she/it eats, you eat (pol)	*com e*
we eat	*com emos*
you eat	*com éis*
they eat, you eat (pl.pol)	*com en*

to write	escribir
I write	*escrib o*
you write	*escrib es*
he/she/it writes, you write (pol)	*escribe*
we write	*escrib imos*
you write	*escrib ís*
they write, you write (pl.pol)	*escrib en*

Spanish verbs are mostly used without "I", "you" etc. (see I, you, he, she etc. on page 57). It helps to learn them as a list, e.g. como, comes etc.

Spanish doesn't distinguish as much as English between present (I write) and present continuous (I'm writing). Unless you want to stress that the action is happening now (e.g. He's sleeping), the present tense is used, e.g. *Viene hoy* (she is coming today, literally "she comes today").

Ser and estar (to be)

Spanish has two verbs "to be". Ser is used to describe people and things, e.g. *Soy ingles* (I am English), *Es un camarero* (He's a waiter), and to tell the time, e.g. *Son las tres* (It's three). *Estar* is for saying where people and things are, e.g. *Está lejos* (It's far) and describing anything changeable or short-lived, e.g. *Está de mal humor* (He's in a bad mood). Both are irregular:

to be	ser	estar
I am	*soy*	*estoy*
you are	*eres*	*estás*
he/she/it is, you are (pol)	*es*	*está*
we are	*somos*	*estamos*
you are	*sois*	*estáis*
they are, you are (pl.pol)	*son*	*están*

[1]The infinitive is the form in which verbs are given in dictionaries.

Other useful irregular verbs

to have	tener
I have	tengo
you have	tienes
he/she/it has,	tiene
you have (pol)	
we have	tenemos
you have	teneis
they have, you have (pl.pol)	tienen

to go	Ir
I go	voy
you go	vas
he/she/it goes,	va
you go (pol)	
we go	vamos
you go	vais
they go, you go (pl.pol)	van

to do	hacer
I do	hago
you do	haces
he/she/it does,	hace
you do (pol)	
we do	hacemos
you do	hacéis
they do, you do (pl.pol)	hacen

to be able to (can)	poder
I can	puedo
you can	puedes
he/she/it can,	puede
you can (pol)	
we can	podemos
you can	podéis
they can, you can (pl.pol)	pueden

Stem-changing verbs

These are verbs whose stem (the part before the "ar", "er", or "ir" ending) changes as well as the endings. These three are especially useful:

to want	querer
I want	quiero
you want	quieres
he/she/it wants,	quiere
you want (pol)	
we want	queremos
you want	queréis
they want, you want (pl.pol)	quieren

to prefer	preferir
I prefer	prefiero
you prefer	prefieres
he/she/it prefers,	prefiere
you prefer (pol)	
we prefer	preferimos
you prefer	preferís
they prefer, you prefer (pl.pol)	prefieren

to play	jugar
I play	juego
you play	juegas
he/she/it plays,	juega
you play (pol)	
we play	jugamos
you play	jugáis
they play, you play (pl.pol)	juegan

Reflexive verbs

Spanish has far more reflexive verbs than English. They all have "se" infinitive[1] endings, e.g. lavarse (to get washed/wash oneself), levantarse (to get up, literally "to get oneself up").
Here is the present of a common one:

I get up	me levanto
you get up	te levantas
he/she/it gets up,	se levanta
you get up (pol)	
we get up	nos levantamos
you get up,	os levantáis
they get up,	se levantan
you get up (pl.pol)	

Talking about the future

"Ar", "er" and "ir" verbs (see present tense) all have the same endings in the future tense:

I shall buy	comprar é
you will buy	comprar ás
he/she/it will buy, you will buy (pol)	comprar á
we will buy	comprar emos
you will buy	comprar éis
they will buy, you will buy (pl.pol)	comprar án

Another future tense is made with the present of *ir* (to go) + *a* + the verb's infinitive, e.g. *Voy a comprar* (I'm going to buy). It is used for something that is just about to happen.

Talking about the past

The most useful past tense in Spanish is the simple past tense. "Ar" verbs have one set of endings and "er" and "ir" verbs have another:

to buy	compr ar
I bought	compr é
you bought	compr aste
he/she/it bought, you bought (pol)	compr ó
we bought	compr amos
you bought	compr ásteis
they bought, you bought (pl.pol)	compr aron

to eat	com er
I ate	com í
you ate	com iste
he/she/it ate, you ate (pol)	com ió
we ate	com imos
you ate	com ísteis
they ate, you ate (pl.pol)	com ieron

The past tenses of "to be" and "to do" are also useful:

to be	ser	estar
I was	fui	estuve
you were	fuiste	estuviste
he/she/it was, you were (pol)	fue	estuvo
we were	fuimos	estuvimos
you were	fuísteis	estuvísteis
they were, you were (pl.pol)	fueron	estuvieron

The past tense of *ir* (to go) is the same as the past tense of *ser*, so *fui* can also mean "I went", *fue* (he/she/it went), *fuimos* (we went) etc.

to do	hacer
I did	hice
you did	hiciste
he/she/it did, you did (pol),	hizo
we did	hicimos
you did	hicisteis
they did, you did (pl.pol)	hicieron

Negatives

To make a sentence negative, put *no* in front of the verb, e.g. *No comprendo* (I don't understand), *No me levanto* (I don't get up).

Other useful negative words include *nunca* (never), *nadie* (noboby), *nada* (nothing), *ninguno/ninguna* (any).

Making questions

To make a question, just give a sentence the intonation of a question – raise your voice at the end. Questions can begin with words like:

who?	¿quién?	how?	¿cómo?
what?	¿qué?	where?	¿dónde?
when?	¿cuándo?	how much?	¿cuánto
which? what?	¿cuál?		/cuánta?

This dictionary lists essential words. If the word you want is missing, try to think of a different one that you could use instead. In the English to Spanish list (pages 62-103), illustrations with labels provide lots of extra words. Below are some tips on using the dictionary.

Entry

A typical entry in the English to Spanish list looks like this:

This is the word you looked up.

This is the Spanish translation.

air aire [m] *aire;*

This is the Spanish pronunciation hint. Read it as if it were an English word and you will be close to the Spanish.

"or" introduces an extra Spanish translation. Words in brackets hint at the difference in meaning:

advertisement (in paper) **anuncio (m)** *anoontheeo,* or (at cinema, on TV) **publicidad (f)** *poobleethdath*

Expansions

Some words have expansions to include words that are associated with them:

contact lens lentillas [f] *lentilyass;* soft/hard lens: **lentillas duras/blandas** *lentilyass doorass/blandass;* cleansing/rinsing solution: **líquido limpiador de lentillas** *likeedo leempeeador*

Masculine and femine

Most Spanish nouns (see page 56) are masculine or feminine ("el" or "la"). So that you know which each is, they are listed with either **[m]** or **[f]** after them.

Most Spanish adjectives (see page 56), have two forms: masculine and feminine. The feminine is usually formed by knocking off the masculine "o" at the end of the word and inserting an "a". Although they are not both spelt out, both of the pronounciations are shown.

adopted adoptivo/a *adoptibo/adoptiba*

In some instances the adjective is the same for both masculine and feminine:

snobbish esnob [m/f] *essnob*

Slang

* indicates that words are familiar or mild slang, and are best avoided in formal situations:

guy hombre [m]/ tío* [m] *ombre/ teeo*

Verbs

Verbs (see page 58) are listed in the infinitive form, e.g. "to eat", but you will find them listed under "e" for eat, etc.

to eat comer *komer*

a, an **un [m]** *oon,* **una [f]** *oona;* **unos [mpl]** *oonos* **unas [fpl]** *oonas*

about (approximately) **aproximadamente** *aproksseemadamente;* what's it about? (film, book) **¿De qué trata?** *de ke trata*

above **encima de** *entheema de*

abroad **en el extranjero** *en el el eksstranhero*

accent **acento [m]** *athento*

to accept **aceptar** *atheptar*

accident **accidente [m]** *aktheedente*

accommodation (places to stay) **alojamiento [m]** *alohamyento*

to ache **doler** *doler;* to have a headache/ backache etc **tener dolor de** *tener dolor de*

to act (theatre) **interpretar** *eenterpretar*

actor **actor [m]** *aktor*

actress **actriz [m]** *aktreeth*

to add **añadir** *anyadeer*

address **dirección [f]** *deerektheeon*

adopted **adoptivo [m]/ adoptiva [f]** *adopteebo/ adopteeba*

adult **adulto [m]/ adulta [f]** *adoolto/ adoolta*

adventurous **aventurero [m]/ aventurera [f]** *abentoorero/ abentoorera*

advertisement (in paper) **anuncio [m]** *anoontheeo,* or (on TV) **publicidad [f]** *poobleetheedath,* or (classified ads) **anuncios por palabras** *anoontheeos por palabrass*

advice **consejo [m]**

konsseho

aerobics **aerobic [m]** *aerobeek*

Africa **Africa** *Afreeka*

after **después** *desspooess*

afternoon **tarde [f]** *tarde*

again **de nuevo, otra vez** *de noqebo, otra beth*

against **contra** *kontra*

age **edad [f]** *edaḍ;* underage: **menor [m/f]** *menor*

to ache   **tener dolor de**

Tengo dolor de cabeza. *Tengo dolor de kabetha*

Tengo dolor de muelas. *Tengo dolor demooelass.*

Tengo dolor de oídos. *Tengo dolor de oeedoss*

Tengo dolor de estómago. *Tengo dolor de esstomago.*

Tengo dolor de riñones *Tengo dolor de reenyoness.*

ago **hace** *hathe;* ten days ago: **hace diez días** *hathe dyeth deeyas*

to agree **estar de acuerdo** *esstar de akooerdo*

aid **ayuda [f]** *ayooda*

AIDS **SIDA [m]** *sseeda*

air **aire [m]** *aeere;*

air-conditioned **aire acondicionado [m]** *aeere akondeetheeonado*

airline **línea aérea** *leenea aerea*

airmail **correo aéreo [m]** *correo aereo*

airport **aeropuerto [m]** *aeropooerto*

alarm clock **despertador [m]** *desspertador*

album **álbum [m]** *alboom*

alcohol **alcohol [m]** *alkohol*

alcoholic **alcohólico [m], alcohólica [f]** *alkoleeko/ alkoleeka,* non-alcoholic: **sin alcohol** *seen alkol*

all **todo/a/os/as** *todo/a/oss/ass;* all right: **de acuerdo, vale** *de acooerdo, bale*

allergy **alergia [f]** *alercheea*

almost **casi** *kassee*

alone **solo/a** *ssolo/a*

already **ya** *ya*

also **también** *tambyen*

alternative **original** *oreeheenal*

always **siempre** *syempre*

amazing **increíble, genial** *eenkreyble, heneeal*

ambulance **ambulancia** *amboolantheea [f]*

America **América** *Amereeka*

American **americano/a**
amereekano/a
and **y** ee
angry **enfadado/a**
enfadado/a
animal **animal [m/f]**
aneemal
ankle **tobillo [m]** tobeelyo
to annoy **enfadar** enfadar;
to get annoyed: **enfadarse**
enfadarsse
annoying **molesto**
molessto, or **fastidioso**
fassteedeeosso
answer **respuesta [f]**
resspooessta
to answer **responder**
ressponder
answering machine
**contestador automático
[m]** kontesstador
aootomateeko
antibiotic **antibiótico [m]**
anteebeeoteeko
antiseptic
antiséptico [m]
anteessepteeko
any **algún/a/os/as** algoon/
a/oss/ass; **cualquier/a**
kooalkeyer/a
anyone **cualquiera**
kooalkeyera
anything **cualquier cosa**
kooalkeyer kossa
anywhere **en cualquier
sitio** en kooalkeyer
sseeteeo
apple **manzana [f]**
manthana; apple pie: **tarta
de manzana [f]** tarta de
manthana; apple turnover:
empanada de manzana
empanada de manthana
appointment **cita [f]**
theeta
apricot **melocotón [m]**
melokoton
April **abril** abreel

Arab **árabe** arabe
archeology **arqueología
[f]** arkeoloheea
architecture **arquitectura
[f]** arkeetektoora
area **región [f]** reheeon;
part of town: **barrio [m]**
barrreeo
argument **disputa [f]**
deesspoota; to have an
argument: **discutir**
deesskooteer
arm **brazo [m]** bratho
around **alrededor de**
alrededor de
arrivals **llegadas** lyegadass
to arrive **llegar** lyegar
art **arte [m]** arte; or
(school subject) **dibujo [m]**
deebooho; art school:
escuela de bellas artes
esskooela de belyass
artess; art gallery: **museo
de arte [m]** moosseo de
arte
artist **artista [m/f]**
arteessta
as **como** como, or 'as ... as'
e.g. 'as tall as': **tan ... como**
tan komo; as usual: **como
siempre** komo ssyempre
ashtray **cenicero [m]**
theneethero
Asia **Asia** Asseea
to ask (a question)
preguntar pregoontar, or
(for something) **pedir**
pedeer, or (to ask out)
invitar eenbeetar
aspirin **aspirina [f]**
asspeereena
assistant **dependiente
[m/f]** dependyente
asthma **asma [m]** assma
at (time) **a las** a lass; or
(place) **en** en; or (at X's
place) **en casa de** en kassa
de

apple **la manzana**
el rabillo rabeelyo

la cáscara
kasskara

el corazón
korathon

la pepita pepeeta

to attack **atacar** atakar
attractive **atractivo/a**
atrakteebo/a
audience **público [m]**
poobleeko
August **agosto** agossto
Australia **Australia**
Aoosstraleea
Australian **australiano/a**
aoostraleeano/a
author **autor/a** aootor/a
autumn **otoño** otonyo
average (noun) **promedio
[m]/ media [f]** promedeeo
medeea; or (adj) **mediano/a**
medeeano/a
avocado **aguacate [m]**
agooakate
to avoid **evitar** ebeetar
away **a** a; it's 3km away:
está a tres kilómetros
essta a tress keelometross
awful **horrible [m/f]**
horrreeble

baby **bebé [m]** bebe;
babysitter: **servicio de
canguros [m]** serbeetheeo
de kangooross
back **parte de atrás [f]**
parte de atrass; or (part of
body) **espalda [f]** esspalda

63

backpack *mochila [f]* *motsheela*

backpacker *mochilero/a* *motsheelero/a*

bad *malo/a/os/as* *malo/a/oss/ass;* not bad: **no está mal** *no essta mal;* really bad: **malísimo** *maleessemo;* too bad!: **¡Qué pena!** *Ke pena*

badge *insignia [f]* *eenseegneea,* or **chapa [f]** *tshapa;* small badge: **pin [m]** *peen*

badminton *bádminton [m] badmeenton*

bag *bolso [m] bolsso*

baggage *el equipaje ekeepahe*

baker´s *panadería [f] panadereea*

balcony *balcón [m] balkon*

ball *pelota [f] pelota;* **balón [m]** *balon*

ballet *ballet [m] ballet*

banana *plátano [m] platano*

band *grupo [m] groopo*

bank *banco [m] bangko*

bar *bar [m] bar;* counter: **mostrador [m]** *mosstrador*

bargain *ganga [f] ganga*

baseball *béisbol [m] beyeesbol*

basketball *baloncesto [m] balonthessto*

bat *bate [m] bate;* tennis: **raqueta [f]** *raketa*

bath *baño [m] banyo*

bathroom *cuarto de baño [m] kooarto de banyo*

battery *pila [f] peela;* car: **batería [f]** *batereea*

to be *ser/estar ser/esstar;* or (to be hot/hungry/X years old) **tener** *tener;* or (for weather) **hacer** *ather*

beach *playa [f] playa*

beans *judías [f] hoodeeas;* green beans: **judías verdes [f]** *hoodeeass berdess*

bear (animal) **oso [m]** *osso*

beard *barba [f] barba*

beat *ritmo [m] reetmo*

beautiful *bonito/a boneeto/a*

because *porque porke;* because of: **por** *por*

to become *volverse bolbersse*

bed *cama [f] kama;* double bed: **cama de matrimonio [f]** *kama de matreemoneeo;* bed and breakfast: **cama y desayuno, pensión [f]** *kama ee dessayoono, penseeon*

bee *abeja [f] abeha*

bedroom *dormitorio [m] dormeetoreeo*

beetle *escarabajo [m] esskarabaho*

beef *carne de vaca [f] karne de baka*

beer *cerveza [f] therbetha;* on tap: **caña [f]** *kanya*

before *antes antess*

beggar *mendigo [m] mendeego*

begin (to begin) **comenzar** *komenthar*

beginner *principiante [m/f] preentheepeeante*

beginning *principio [m] preentheepeeo*

behind *detrás detrass*

Belgium *Bélgica Belcheeka*

below *abajo abaho*

belt *cinturón [m] theentooron*

bend *curva [f] koorba*

beside *al lado de al lado de*

best *el mejor/la mejor el/ la mehor;* or (it's the best) **lo mejor** *lo mehor*

better *mejor mehor;* it is better to: **es mejor ...** *ess mehor ...*

between *entre entre*

big *grande [m/f] grande*

band   grupo (m)

el guitarrista geetarrreessta

la batería batereea

el batería batereea

el teclista tekleessta

la guitarra geetarrra

el saxo* saksso

el saxofonista sakssofoneessta

el cantante kantante

el sintetizador seenteteethadorr

el micrófono meekrofono

bike **bicicleta [f]**
beetheekleta; racing
bike: **bicicleta de
carreras [f]** *betheekleta
de karrrerass;* mountain
bike: **bicicleta de
montaña [f]**
*betheekleta de
montanya;* by bike: **en
bici** *en beethee*
biker **ciclista [m/f]**
theekleessta
bill **cuenta [f]** *kwenta*
bin **basura [f]** *bassoora*
binoculars **prismáticos
[m]** *preessmateekoss*
biodegradable
biodegradable
byodegradable
bird **pájaro [m]** *paharo*
birthday **cumpleaños [m]**
koompleanyoss; happy
birthday: **feliz cumpleaños**
feleeth koompleanyoss
biscuit **galleta [f]** *galyeta*
bit (of cake) **trozo [m]**
trotho; a bit tired: **un poco
cansado** *oon poko
kanssado*
to bite **morder** *morder* or
(insect) **picar** *peekar*
bitter **amargo/a** *amargo/a*
black **negro/a** *negro/a*
blanket **manta [f]** *manta*
to bleed **sangrar** *ssangrar*
blind **ciego/a** *thyego/a*
blister **ampolla [f]**
ampolya
bloke **tío [m]** *teeo,* **tipo
[m]** *teepo*
blond **rubio/a** *roobeeo;* the
blond guy/girl: **el rubio/la
rubia** *el roobeeo/ la
roobeea*
blood **sangre [f]** *ssangre;*
blood pressure: **tensión
arterial [f]** *tensseeon
artereeal*

bike **bicicleta (f)**
el **manillar** *maneelyar*
el **sillín** *seelyen*

la **rueda**
rooeda

la **cadena**
kadena

el **pedal** *pedal*

la **bomba** *bomba*

el **freno** *freno*

las **marchas** *martshass*

blue **azul** *athul*
to board (ship etc.)
embarcarse *embarkarsse*
boarding pass **tarjeta de
embarque [f]** *tarheta de
embarke*
to boast **presumir**
pressoomeer
boat (big boat) **barco [m]**
barko; or (small boat) **barca
[f]** *barka*
body **cuerpo [m]** *kooerpo*
boiled **cocido/a** *kotheedo/a*
bone **hueso** *ooesso;* fish
bone: **espina [f]** *esspeena*
book **libro [m]** *leebro*
to book **reservar**
resserbar; booked up:
completo/a *kompleto/a*
bookshop **librería [f]**
leebrereea
boot (shoe) **bota [f]** *bota*
bored (to be bored) **estar
aburrido** *esstar
aboorrreedo;* or (to get
bored) **aburrirse**
aboorrreersse
boring **aburrido/a**
aboorrreedo/a

to borrow **pedir prestado**
pedeer presstado
boss **jefe/a** *hefe/a*
both **ambos/as**
*amboss/ass;*or **los/las dos**
loss/lass doss
bottle **botella [f]** *botelya;*
bottle opener: **sacacorchos
[m]** *sakakortshoss*
bottom **la parte inferior
[f]** *la parte eenfereeor,* or
(river, pool, glass) **fondo
[m]** *fondo,* or (bum) **culo
[m]** *koolo*
bowl **cuenco [m]** *kwenko*
bowling **bolos [m]** *boloss*
boxer shorts **calzoncillos
[m]** *kalthontheelyoss*
box office **taquilla [f]**
takeelya
boy **chico [m]** *tsheeko,* or
(young boy) **niño [m]**
neenyo
boyfriend **novio** *nobeeo*
bra **sujetador [m]**
suhetador
brakes **frenos [m]** *frenoss*
brave **valiente [m/f]**
balyente
bread **pan [m]** *pan;*
wholemeal bread: **pan
integral [m]** *pan eentegral*
to break **romper** *romper;*
breakfast **desayuno [m]**
dessayoono
breast **pecho [m]** *petsho*
breath **aliento [m]**
alyento; out of breath: **sin
aliento** *seen alyento*
to breathe **respirar**
resspeerar
bridge **puente [m]** *pwente*
bright (clever) **inteligente
[m/f]** *enteleehente;* or
(colour) **vivo [m]** *beebo*
brilliant **genial,
fantástico** *heneeal,
fantassteeko*

to bring (person) **llevar** *lyebar;* thing: **traer** *traer*

Britain **Gran Bretaña** *gran bretanya*

broke **sin blanca** *seen blanka*

broken **roto/a** *roto/a*

brother **hermano** *ermano*

brown **marrón** *marrron* tanned: **moreno/a** *moreno/a*

bruise **cardenal [m]** *kardenal*

brush **cepillo [m]** *thepelyo;* paintbrush: **pincel [m]** *peenthel*

bug **microbio [m]** *meekrobeeo;* insect: **insecto [m]** *enssekto*

building **edificio [m]** *edeefeetheeo*

bull **toro [m]** *toro*

bump **chinchón [m]** *tsheentshon;* to bump into something: **chocar contra** *tshokar kontra;* to bump into someone by chance: **encontrarse con** *enkontrarsse kon*

to bunk off **largarse/ abrirse/ pirarse** *largarsse/ abreersse/ peerarsse*

to burn **quemar** *kemar*

to burst **explotar** *ekssplotar*

bus **autobús [m]** *aotobooss;* bus station: **estación de autobuses [f]** *esstatheeon de aootoboossess;* bus stop: **parada de autobús [f]** *parada de aootobooss;* to take the bus: **coger el autobús** *coher el aotobooss*

busy **ocupado/a** *okoopado/a*

but **pero** *pero*

butcher's **carnicería [f]** *karneethereea*

butter **mantequilla [f]** *mantekeelya*

butterfly **mariposa [f]** *mareepossa*

button **botón [m]** *boton*

to buy **comprar** *komprar*

by (near) **cerca de** *therka de;* saved by someone: **por** *por;* or (by my/ your/ him/ herself) **solo/a** *ssolo/a*

bye **adiós/ hasta luego** *adeeoss/ assta looego*

café **cafetería [f]** *kafetereea*

cake **pastel [m]** *passtel;* cake shop: **pastelería [f]** *passtelereea;* it's a piece of cake: **está chupado*** *essta choopado*

calculator **calculadora** *kalkooladora*

to call **llamar** *lyamar;* to be called: **llamarse** *lyamarsse*

calory **caloría [f]** *kaloreea;* low calorie: **bajo en calorías** *baho en kaloreeass*

camcorder **cámara de vídeo [f]** *kamara de beedeo*

camera **cámara fotográfica [f]** *kamara fotografeeka*

to camp **acampar** *akampar;* to go camping: **ir de camping** *eer de kampeeng*

camera **cámara fotográfica (f)**

el carrete *karrete*

el flash *flassh*

el zoom *thoom*

el objetivo *obheteebo*

la tapadera *tapadera*

el parasol *parassol*

campsite **camping [m]** *kampeeng*

can **lata [f]** *lata;* can opener: **abridor [m]** *abreedor*

can **poder** *poder;* to know how to: **saber** *saber*

candle **vela [f]** *bela*

canoe **canoa [f]/piragua [f]** *kanoa/peeragooa;* to go canoeing: **ir en canoa** *eer en kanoa*

cap **gorra [f]** *gorrra*

capital **capital [f]** *kapeetal*

captain **capitán [m]** *kapeetan*

car **coche [m]** *kotshe;* car park: **aparcamiento [m]** *aparkamyento*

card **postal [f]** *posstal;* credit card: **tarjeta de crédito [f]** *tarheta de kredeeto;* a game of cards: **partida de cartas[f]** *parteeda de kartass*

care (I don't care!) **¡Me da igual!** *me da eegooal* **¡No me importa!** *no me eemporta*

career **carrera [f]** *karrrera*
careful **prudente**
proodente; to be careful:
tener cuidado *tener*
kooeedado
carnival **carnaval [m]**
karnabal
carrot **zanahoria [f]**
thanaorreea
to carry **llevar** *lyebar*
cartoon **dibujos animados**
[m] *deeboohoss*
aneemadoss
case (in case) **en caso de**
en kasso de
cash **dinero efectivo/**
metálico *deenero*
efekteebo/ metaleeko; to
pay cash: **pagar en**
efectivo/en metálico
pagar en efekteebo/en
metaleeko; cash dispenser:
cajero automático [m]
kahero aootomateeko
cassette **casete [m]/ cinta**
[f] *kassete/ theenta;*
cassette player: **casete [m]**
kassete
castle **castillo [m]**
kastoolyo
casual **casual** *kassooal*
cat **gato [m]** *gato*
to catch **coger** *koher*

cathedral **catedral [f]**
katedral
Catholic **católico/a**
katoleeko/a
cauliflower **coliflor [f]**
coleeflor
cave **cueva [f]/ caverna [f]**
kooeba/ kaberna
caving **espeleología [f]**
esspeleoloheea
CD **CD [m]/ compact disc**
[m]/ disco compacto [m]
thee de/ kompakt deesk/
deesko kompakto; CD
player: **CD [m]** *thee de*
to celebrate **celebrar**
thelebrar
cellar **sótano [m]** *ssotano;*
for wine: **bodega [f]**
bodega
cemetery **cementerio [m]**
thementereeo
centre **centro [m]** *thentro*
century **siglo [m]** *seeglo*
cereal **cereales [m]**
therealess
chair **silla [f]** *sseelya;* with
arms: **sillón [m]** *seelyon*
champion **campeón/a**
kampeon/a
championship
campeonato [m]
kampeonato

chance (accident)
casualidad [f]
cassooaleedath
opportunity: **oportunidad**
[f] *oportooneedath;* risk:
riesgo [m] *rrrryessgo;* by
chance: **de casualidad** *de*
kassooaleedath
change **cambio [m]**
kambeeo; money: **cambio**
[m]/ suelto [m] *kambeeo/*
ssooelto
to change **cambiar**
kambeear
changing-room **probador**
[m] *probador*
channel **canal [m]** *kanal;*
the Channel: **el canal de la**
Mancha *el kanal de la*
Mantsha; the Channel
tunnel: **el túnel de la**
Mancha *el toonel de la*
Mantsha; the Channel
Islands: **las islas**
Anglonormandas *lass*
eesslass Anglonormandass
chaos **caos [m]** *kaoss*
chap* **tío*/tipo* [m]** *teeo*
teepo
character **caracter [m]**
karakter; person in cartoon
etc: **personaje [m]**
personahe

campsite **el camping**

la tienda de campaña **la caravana** *karabana*
la caravana *tyenda de kampanya*
karabana
la hamaca *amaka*
el mazo *matho*
la estaca *esstaka*
los servicios[m] *sserbeetheooss*
la cantimplora *kanteemplora* **el camping gas** *kampeeng gass*
la recepción *retheptheeon*

67

climbing *escalada (f)*
or *alpinismo (m)*

las rocas
rokass

los mosquetones
mossketoness

el alpinista
alpeeneessta

el casco
kassko

la correa
korrrea

la magnesia
magnesseea

la bolsa de
magnesia
*bolssa de
magnesseea*

el cinturón de
escalada
*theentooron de
esskalada*

las botas de
escalada
*botass de
esskalada*

la cuerda
kooerda

---

charity *institución
benéfica [f]
eenssteetootheeon
benefeeka*
charter flight *vuelo
charter [m] booelo
tsharter*
charts *los cuarenta
principales [m] loss
kooarenta preentheepaless*
to chat *charlar tsharlar* or
(to chat up) **ligar con** *leegar
kon*
cheap *barato/ a/ os/ as
barato/ a/ oss/ ass*
cheaper *más barato/ a/ os/
as mass barato/ a/ oss/ ass*
to cheat *hacer trampa
ather trampa*
to check (a fact, date)
verificar *bereefeekar,* or (a
passport, ticket) **controlar**
kontrolar; to check in
(luggage) **facturar el
equipaje** *faktoorar el
ekepahe*
check-in (at airport)
facturación de equipajes
*factooratheeon de
ekeepahess*
check-out (cash register)
caja [f] *kaha*
cheeky *descarado/a
desskarado/a*
cheers *salud salood*
cheer up! *¡anímate!
aneemate*
cheese *queso [m] kesso*
chemist's *farmacia [f]
farmatheea*
cheque *cheque [m] tsheke*
cheque book *talonario de
cheques [m] talonareeo de
tshekess*
cherry *cereza [f] theretha*
chest *pecho [m] petsho*
chewing gum *chicle [m]
tsheekle*

---

chicken *pollo [m] polyo*
child *niño/a neenyo/a*
chips *patatas fritas [f]
patatass freetass*
chocolate *chocolate [m]
tshokolate;* hot chocolate:
chocolate caliente [m]
tshokolate kalyente
choice *elección [f]
elektheeon*
choir *corazón [m]
korathon*
to choose *elegir eleheer*
chop *chuleta [f] tshooleta*
Christian *cristiano/a
kreesteeano/a*
Christmas *Navidad [f]
Nabeedath*
to chuck (throw) **tirar**
teerar, or (finish with a
boy/girlfriend) **dejar a** *dehar
a*
church *iglesia [f]
eeglesseea*
cider *sidra [f] seedra*
cigarette *cigarrillo [m]
theegarrreelyo*
cinema *cine [m] theene*
circus *circo [m] theerko*
city *ciudad [f] theeoodath*
classical *clásico/a
klasseeko/a*
clean *limpio/a leempeeo/a*
clever *inteligente [m/f]
eenteleehente* or (cunning)
astuto *asstooto* or (to be
gifted) **tener talento** *tener
talento*
cliff *acantilado [m]
akanteelado*
to climb *escalar esskalar*
climber *alpinista [m/f]
alpeeneessta*
climbing *escalada [f]/
alpinismo [m] esskalada/
alpeeneessmo*
cloakroom *guardarropa
[m] gooardarrropa*

close **cerca de** *therca de*, or (feeling) **íntimo** *eenteemo*, or (as in close friend) **amigo íntimo** *ameego eenteemo*; close by: **muy cerca** *mooy therka*
to close **cerrar** *therrar*
closed **cerrado/a** *therrado/a*
clothes **ropa [f]** *rrropa*
cloud **nube [f]** *noobe*
club **club [m]** *cloob*; night club: **discoteca [f]** *deesskoteka*
clubbing (to go clubbing) **salir de marcha** *saleer de martsha*
coach **autobús [m]** *aootobooss*; or (trainer) **entrenador [m]** *entrenador*
coast **costa [f]** *kossta*
coat **abrigo [m]** *abreego*
code **código [m]** *kodeego*; phoning: **prefijo [m]** *prefeeho*
co-ed (school) **mixta** *meekssta*
coffee **café [m]** *kafe*; black coffee: **café solo [m]** *kafe ssolo*; with milk: **café con leche [m]** *kafe kon letshe*; a decaffeinated: **descafeinado [m]** *desskafeynado*
coin **moneda [f]** *moneda*
cold **frío** *freeo*; chilled: **helado** *elado*; to be cold (person): **tener frío** *tener freeo*; it is cold (weather): **hace frío** *athe freeo*; to have cold feet: **entrarle miedo** *entrarle myedo*
cold (illness) **resfriado** *rrressfreeado*; to have a cold: **estar constipado/a** *esstar konsteepado/a*
to collect **coleccionar** *kolektheeonar*

colour **color [m]** *kolor*
to come **venir** *beneer*; to come back: **volver** *bolber*; to come in: **entrar** *entrar*
comfortable **cómodo** *komodo*; to be/feel comfortable: **encontrarse a gusto** *enkontrarsse a goosto*
comic book **tebeo [m]** *tebeo*
common **común [m/f]** *komoon*
compass **brújula [f]** *broohoola*
competition **concurso [m]** *konkoorsso*; people: **competencia [f]** *kompetentheea*
to complain **quejarse** *keharsse*
completely **completamente** *kompletamente*
compulsory **obligatorio** *obleegatoreeo*
computer **ordenador [m]** *ordenador*; computer studies: **informática [f]** *enformateeka*
concert **concierto [m]** *kontheeyerto*
condom **condón [m]** *kondon*
to confuse **confundir** *konfoondeer*
congratulations **enhorabuena** *enhorabooena*
connection **correspondencia [f]/ enlace [m]** *korrresspondentheea/ enlathe*
conservation **preservación [f]** *presserbatheeon*
constipated **estreñido/a** *esstrenyeedo/a*

consulate **consulado [m]** *konsoolado*
to contact **ponerse en contacto** *ponersse en kontakto*
contact lens **lentillas [f]** *lenteelyass*; soft/hard lens: **lentillas duras/blandas** *lenteelyass doorass/ blandass*; cleansing/rinsing solution: **líquido limpiador de lentillas** *leekeedo leempeeador de lenteelyass*
contemporary **contemporáneo/a** *kontemporaneo/a*
to continue **continuar** *konteenooar*
contraceptive **anticonceptivo [m]** *anteekonthepteebo*
conservation **conservación [f]** *konsserbatheeon*
to cook **cocinar** *kotheenar*
cool (relaxed) **tranquilo/a** *trankeelo/a*; trendy: **moderno/a** *moderno/a*, or **guay*** *gooay*
to cope **arreglárselas** *arrreglarsselass*; to face up to: **enfrentarse con** *enfrentarsse kon*
to copy **copiar** *kopeear*
cork **corcho [m]** *kortsho*
corkscrew **sacacorchos [m]** *ssakakortshoss*
corner **esquina [f]** *esskeena*
correct **correcto/a** *korrrecto/a*
Corsica **Córcega** *Korthega*
cosmopolitan **cosmopolita** *kossmopoleeta*
cost **costar** *kosstar*
cotton **algodón [m]** *algodon*; cotton wool: **algodón hidrófilo [m]** *algodon heedrofeelo*

country **país** [m] *paeess;*
countryside: **campo** [m]
kampo
course **curso** [m] *koorsso;*
meal: **plato** [m] *plato;* first
course: **primer plato** [m]
preemer plato; of course:
por supuesto *por*
soopooessto
court (tennis, squash)
pista [f]/ **cancha** [f]
peesta/ kantsha
cousin **primo/a** *preemo/a*
to cover **cubrir** *koobreer*
cow **vaca** [f] *baka*
coward **cobarde** [m/f]
kobarde
to crack **venirse abajo/
darse por vencido**
*beneersse abaho/ darsse
por bentheedo;* to crack a
joke: **contar un chiste**
kontar oon tsheesste; to
crack up: **morirse de risa**
moreersse de reessa
cramp **calambre** [m]
kalambre
crazy **loco/a** *loko/a;* to
drive crazy: **volver loco/a**
bolber loko/a; to be crazy:
estar loco/a por *esstar
loko/a por;* you must be
crazy: **¿estás loco/a?**
esstass loko/a
credit card **tarjeta de
crédito** [f] *tarheta de
kredeeto*
creepy **horripilante/ que
pone la carne de gallina**
*orrreepeelante/ ke pone la
karne de galyeena*
cricket **criquet** [m] *kreeket*
or (insect) **grillo** [m]
greelyo
crime **crimen** [m] *kreemen*
crisis **crisis** [f] *kreesseess*
crisps **patatas fritas** [f]
patatass freetass

to criticize **criticar**
kreeteekar
cross (angry) **enfadado/a**
enfadado/a; sign: **cruz** [f]
krooth
to cross **cruzar** *kroothar*
crossing (by ferry etc)
traversía [f] *trabersseea*
crossroads **cruce** [m]
kroothe
crossword **crucigrama** [m]
krootheegrama
cruel **cruel** [m/f] *krooel*
crush (I've got a crush on
him/her) **estoy perdido/a
por él/ella** *esstoy
perdeedo/a por el/elya*
to cry **llorar** *lyorar*
cucumber **pepino** [m]
pepeeno
cult **culto** [m] *coolto*
cultural **cultural** *cooltooral*
culture **cultura** [f]
cooltoora
cup **taza** [f] *tatha*
cupboard **armario** [m]
armareeo
curious **curioso/a**
kooreeosso/a
custom **costumbre** [f]
kosstoombre
customer **cliente/a**
klyente/a
customs **aduana** [f]
adooana
to cut **cortar** *kortar*

to dance **bailar** *baeelar*
dancer (ballet etc)
bailarín/a *baeelareen;* **or**
(flamenco) **bailaor/a**
baeelaor/a
dangerous **peligroso/a**
peleegrosso/a
to dare **atreverse**
atrebersse; challenge:
desafiar *dessafeear*

dark **oscuridad** [f]
osskooreedath; or (colour)
oscuro *osskooro;* it is dark:
es de noche *ess de notshe*
date **fecha** [f] *fetsha,* or
(meeting) **cita** [f] *theeta;*
date of birth: **fecha de
nacimiento** *fetsha de
natheemyento;* up to date:
actualizado/a
aktooaleethado/a; out of
date: **caducado/a**
kadookado/a
day **día** [m] *deea;* the next
day: **el próximo día** [m] *el
proksseemo deea;* the day
before: **el día antes** [m] *el
deea antess;* day off: **día
libre** [m] *deea leebre*
dead **muerto/a** *mooerto/a*
deaf **sordo/a** *ssordo/a*
dear **querido/a** *kereedo/a*
decaffeinated
descafeinado [m]
desskafeynado
December **diciembre**
deetheeyembre
to decide **decidir**
detheedeer
deck (on boat) **cubierta** [f]
coobyerta; deck chair:
tumbona [f] *toombona*
deep **profundo/a**
profoondo/a
degree (temperature)
grado [m] *grado;*
(university) **licenciatura** [f]
leethentheeatoora
delicatessen **charcutería
fina** [f] *tsharrkootereea
feena*
delicious **delicioso/a**
deleetheeosso/a
democracy **democracia** [f]
demokratheea
demonstration
manifestación [f]
maneefesstatheeon

denim (denims) **pantalón vaquero** *pantalon bakero*
dentist **dentista [m/f]** *denteesta*
deodorant **desodorante [m]** *dessodorante*
department store **grandes almacenes [m]** *grandess almatheness*
departure **salida [f]** *ssaleeda*; departure lounge: **sala de embarque [f]** *ssala de embarke*
to depend **depender** *depender*
deposit **depósito [m]** *deposseeto*
depressing **deprimente [m/f]** *depreemente*
to describe **describir** *desskreebeer*
desk **escritorio [m]** *esskreetoreeo*
dessert **postre [m]** *posstre*
detail **detalle [m]** *detalye*
detour **desviación [f]** *dessbeeatheeon*
diabetic **diabético/a** *deeabeteeko/a*
dialect **dialecto [m]** *deealekto*
dialling tone **señal para marcar [f]** *senyal para markar*
diarrhoea **diarrea [f]** *deearrea*
diary **agenda [f]** *ahenda*, or (private book) **diario [m]** *deeareeo*
dice **dado [m]** *dado*
dictionary **diccionario [m]** *deektheeonareeo*
diesel **gasoil [m]** *gassoeel*
diet **régimen [m]** *reheemen*; to go on a diet: **ponerse a dieta** *ponersse a dyeta*

different **diferente [m/f]** *deeferente*
difficult **difícil [m/f]** *deefeetheel*
dining room **comedor [m]** *komedor*
dinner (evening) **cena [f]** *thena*; (midday) **comida [f]** *komeeda*
direction **dirección [f]** *deerektheeon*
director **director/a** *deerektor/a*
dirty **sucio/a** *sootheeo/a*; or (rude) **grosero/a** *grossero*; to get dirty: **ensuciarse** *ensootheearsse*; to have a dirty mind: **ser un pervertido** *ser oon perberteedo*
disabled **incapacitado/a** *eenkapatheetado/a*; **físico** *feeseeko*; **incapacitado/a** *eenkapatheetado/a*; **mental** *mental*
disadvantage **desventaja [f]** *dessbentaha*

diving **el buceo**

disappointed **desilusionado/a** *desseeloosseeonado/a*
disaster **desastre [m]** *dessasstre*
disk jockey **pinchadiscos [m]** *peentshadeesskoss*
disco **discoteca [f]** *deeskoteka*
discount **descuento [m]** *desskooento*
discrimination **discriminación [f]** *desskreemeenatheeon*
to discuss **discutir** *deeskooteer*
disgusting **asqueroso/a, repugnante** *asskerosso/a, repoognante*
dish **plato [m]** *plato*
disk (computer) **disquete [m]** *deeskete*
distance **distancia [f]** *deesstantheea*; in the/from a distance: **desde lejos** *dessde lehoss*
to dive **bucear** *boothear*

las aletas *uleiass*

el cinturón de plomo *theentooron de plomo*

la botella de oxígeno *botelya de oksseegeno*

el chaleco estabilizador *tshaleko esstabeeleethador*

la buceadora *bootheeadora*

las gafas de buceo *bootheo*

el descompresor *desskompressor*

el traje de buceo *trahe de bootheo*

el tubo de respiración *toobo de resspeeratheeon*

la consola *konssola*

71

diving *buceo [m]* bootheo; scuba diving: **buceo con botellas de oxígeno [m]** bootheo kon botelyass de oksseeheno; diving board: **trampolín [m]** trampoleen

divorced *divorciado/a* deebortheeado/a

dizzy *estar mareado/a* esstar mareado/a

to do *hacer* ather; to do up: **abrochar** abrotshar

doctor *médico [m/f]* medeeko

dodgy (dubious) *raro/a* rraro/a; risky: **arriesgado** arrryessgado

dog *perro [m]* perro

dole (on the dole) **en el paro** en el paro

door *puerta [f]* pooerta

double *doble [m/f]* doble

down to go down: **bajar** bahar; to be/feel down: **estar deprimido/a** esstar depreemeedo/a

to draw (picture) *dibujar* deeboohar

dream *sueño [m]* sooenyo

dress *vestido [m]* besteedo

to dress *vestirse* besteersse

drink *bebida [f]* bebeeda; let's go for a drink: **vamos a tomar algo** bamoss a tomar algo

to drink *beber* beber

to drive *conducir* kondootheer; to go by car: **ir en coche** eer en kotshe

driver *conductor [m]* kondooktor

to drop *dejar caer* dehar kaer; let go of: **soltar** ssoltar; to drop in: **pasar por** passar por; to drop off: **dejar** dehar; to drop out: **retirarse** reteerarsse

drug *droga [f]* droga; drug addict: **drogadicto/a** drogadeekto/a

drunk *borracho/a* borrratsho/a

to get drunk *emborracharse* emborrratsharsse

dry *seco/a* seko/a

to dry *secar* sekar

dubbed *doblado/a* doblado/a

dump *vertedero [m]* bertedero; dull/awful place: **lugar desagradable [m]/ tugurio [m/f]** loogar dessagradable/ toogooreeo; to be down in the dumps: **verlo todo negro** berlo todo negro

dungarees *mono [m]/ peto [m]* mono/peto

during *durante* doorante

duty-free *libre de impuestos* leebre de eempooesstoss

dying (to be dying to) **morirse por** moreersse por; to be dying of hunger/thirst: **morirse de hambre/sed** moreersse de ambre/ssed

each *cada* kada; each one: **cada uno/a** kada oono/a

ear *oído [m]* oeedo

early *temprano* temprano

earphones *auriculares [m]* aooreekoolaress

east *este [m]* esste

Easter *Semana Santa [f]* ssemana ssanta

easy *fácil* fatheel

easy-going *tranquilo/a* trankeelo/a

to eat *comer* komer

EC *CE Comunidad Europea [f]* komooneedath eooropea

ecology *ecología [f]* ekoloheea

education *educación [f]* edookatheeon; higher education: **enseñanza superior [f]** ensenyantha soopereeor

egg *huevo [m]* ooebo

elbow *codo [m]* kodo

election *elección [f]* elektheeon

electric *eléctrico/a* elektreeko/a

electricity *electricidad [f]* elektreetheedath

egg *el huevo*

el huevo cocido/duro ooebo kotheedo/dooro

el huevo frito ooebo freeto

los huevos revueltos ooeboss rebooeltoss

el huevo escalfado ooebo esskalfado

el huevo en cáscara ooebo en kasskara

la yema yema

la clara klara

la cáscara kasskara

la huevera ooebera

elevator **ascensor [m]**
assthenssor
e-mail **e-mail [m]** *e maeel*
embarrassing **embarazoso**
embarathosso; how
embarrassing!: **¡qué**
vergüenza! *ke*
bergooentha
embassy **embajada [f]**
embahada
emergency **emergencia [f]**
emerhentheea; emergency
exit: **salida de emergencia**
[f] *ssaleeda de*
emerhentheea
empty **vacío/a** *batheeo/a*
end **fin [m]** *feen* or (of
road) **final [m]** *feenal*
engine **motor [m]** *motor*
England **Inglaterra**
eenglaterrra
English **inglés/inglesa**
eengless/eenglessa; in
english: **en inglés** *en*
eengless
to enjoy yourself
divertirse *deeberteersse*
enough **bastante**
basstante; I've had
enough!: **¡basta!** or **¡estoy**
harto/a! *bassta, esstoy*
arto/a
entertainment guide
guía del ocio [f] *geea del*
otheeo
envelope **sobre [m]** *sobre*
environment
medio ambiente [m]
medeeo ambyente
epileptic **epiléptico**
epeelepteeko; epileptic fit:
ataque epiléptico [m]
atake epeelepteeko
equal **igual** *eegwal*
erotic **erótico/a** *eroteeko/a*
escalator **escalera**
mecánica [f] *esskalera*
mekaneeka

essential **esencial**
essentheeal
EU **UE Unión Europea [f]**
ooneeon eooropea
Eurocheque **eurocheque**
[m] *eoorotsheke*
Europe **Europa** *eooropa;*
eastern/western Europe:
Europa del este/ del oeste
eooropa del esste/ del
oesste
European **europeo/a**
eooropeo/a
evening **tarde [f]** *tarde*
everybody **todo el mundo**
todo el moondo
everything **todo** *todo*
everywhere **por todos**
sitios *por todoss sseeteeoss*
to exaggerate **exagerar**
ekssaherar
exam **exámen [m]**
ekssamen
example **ejemplo [m]**
ehemplo; for example: **por**
ejemplo *por ehemplo*
excellent **excelente**
ekssthelente
except **excepto** *ekssthepto*
excess (baggage) **exceso**
de equipaje [m]
ekssthesso de ekeepahe;
fare: **suplemento [m]**
sooplemento
exchange **cambio [m]**
kambeeo; exchange holiday:
intercambio [m]
eenterkambeeo; foreign
exchange office: **oficina de**
cambio [f] *ofeetheena de*
kumbeeo; exchange rate:
tipo de cambio [m] *teepo*
de kambeeo
excited **entusiasmado/a**
entoosseeassmado/a
to get excited
entusiasmarse
entoosseeassmarsse

exciting **emocionante**
emotheeonante
excuse **excusa [f]**
eksskoossa; excuse me:
perdone *perdone*
exercise **ejercicio [m]**
ehertheetheeo
exhausted **agotado/a**
agotado/a
exhibition **exposición [f]**
ekssposseetheeon
exit **salida [f]** *saleeda*
expensive **caro/a** *karo/a*
experience **experiencia [f]**
ekssperyentheea
to explain **explicar**
eksspleekar
to explore **explorar**
ekssplorar
extra **suplementario**
sooplementareeo
eye **ojo [m]** *oho*
fabulous **fabuloso**
faboolosso
face **cara [f]** *kara*
to fail (exam) **suspender**
ssoosspender
to faint **desmayarse**
dessmayarsse
fair **justo** *hoossto*
faithful **fiel** *fyel*
to fall **caer** *kaer;* to fall for:
enamorarse de
enamorarsse de; a trick:
dejarse engañar *deharsse*
enganyar; to fall out: **reñir**
con *renyeer kon*
family **familia [f]**
fameeleea
famous **famoso/a**
famosso/a; well-known:
conocido/a *konotheedo/a*
fan **fan [m/f]** *fan;*
enthusiast: **entusiasta [m/f]**
entoosseeassta
to fancy **gustar** *goostar;*
do you fancy? **¿te apetece?**
te apetethee

fantastic **fantástico** *fantassteeko*

far **lejos** *lehos*

fare **tarifa [f]** *tareefa;* full fare: **tarifa completa [f]** *tareefa kompleta;* reduced fare: **tarifa reducida [f]** *tareefa redootheeda*

farm **granja [f]** *granha*

fashion **moda [f]** *moda*

fashionable **de moda** *de moda*

fast **rápido** *rapeedo;* quickly: **rápidamente** *rapeedamente*

fat (on meat) **grasa [f]** *grassa;* large: **gordo/a** *gordo/a;* to get fat: **engordar** *engordar*

father **padre [m]** *padre*

favourite **favorito/a** *faboreeto/a*

February **febrero** *febrero*

fed (to be fed up) **estar harto/a de** *esstar arto/a de*

to feel (as in to feel happy/ good) **sentirse** *ssenteersse* or (as in to feel hot/hungry) **tener** *tener;* to feel like: **apetecer** *apetether*

feminist **feminista [m/f]** *femeeneessta*

ferry **ferry [m]** *ferry*

fever **fiebre [f]** *fyebre*

few **unos pocos** *oonoss pokoss*

fig **higo [m]** *eego*

fight **pelea [f]** *pelea;* organized fight: **combate [m]** *kombate*

figure (as in to have a good figure) **tener buen tipo** *tener booen teepo*

to fill **rellenar** *relyenar;* to fill up: **llenar** *lyenar*

film (in cinema) **película [f]** *peleekoola;* in camera: **carrete [m]** *karrrete*

to find **encontrar** *enkontrar;* to find out: **informarse** *enformarsse;* discover: **descubrir** *desskoobreer*

fine (penalty) **multa [f]** *moolta,* or (OK) **bien** *byen*

finger **dedo [m]** *dedo*

to finish **terminar** *termeenar*

fire **fuego [m]** *fooego;* fire place: **chimenea [f]** *tsheemenea;* fire brigade: **bomberos [m]** *bombeross;* fire exit: **salida de emergencia [f]** *saleeda de emerhentheea*

fireworks **fuegos artificiales [m]** *fwegoss arteefeethealess*

first **el primero/la primera** *preemero/preemera;* at first: **al principio** *al preentheepeeo*

first aid **primeros auxilios [m]** *preemeross aooksseeleeoss;* first aid kit: **botiquín [m]** *boteekeen*

fish **pescado [m]** *pesskado;* fisherman: **pescador [m]** *pesskador*

fishing **pesca [f]** *pesska;* to go fishing: **ir de pesca** *eer de pesska*

fit (tantrum) **ataque [m]** *atake;* physically fit: **en forma** *en forma;* good-looking: **guapo/a** *gooapo/a;* to be in fits of laughter: **troncharse de risa** *trontsharsse de reessa*

to fit **ir bien** *eer byen;* does it fit? **¿te va bien?** *te ba byen;* it fits me well: **me va bien** *me ba byen*

to fix **reparar** *rrreparar;* to fix a date/time: **fijar una fecha/hora** *feehar oona fetsha/ora*

fizzy **con gas** *kon gass*

flat **piso [m]** *peesso;* not round: **plano/a** *plano/a;* tyre: **pinchada** *peentshada*

flavour **sabor [m]** *ssabor*

flea market **rastro [m]** *rasstro*

flight **vuelo [m]** *booelo;* flight attendant: **azafata [f]** *athafata*

flirt **ligón/a** *leegon/a*

to flirt **ligar** *leegar*

floor **piso [m]** *peesso*

flop **fracaso [m]** *frakasso*

flower **flor [f]** *flor*

flu **gripe [f]** *greepe*

fluently **con soltura** *kon soltoora*

fly **mosca [f]** *mosska*

first aid kit **el botiquín**

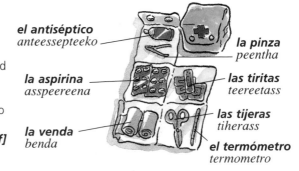

el antiséptico *anteessepteeko*

la pinza *peentha*

la aspirina *asspeereena*

las tiritas *teereetass*

las tijeras *tiherass*

la venda *benda*

el termómetro *termometro*

to fly **volar** *bolar;* to go by plane: **ir en avión** *eer en abeeon*
foal **potro** *[m] potro*
to follow **seguir** *segeer*
food **comida** *[f] komeeda;* food-poisoning.
intoxicación alimentaria *[f] eentoksseekatheeon aleementareea*
foot **pie** *[m] pye;* on foot: **a pie** *a pye;* to put your foot in it: **meter la pata**

frame (as in picture, bike) **cuadro** *[m] kooadro;* or (glasses) **montura** *[f] montoora*
France **Francia** *Frantheea*
to freak out (lose your cool) **flipar/ alucinar** *fleepar/ alootheenar*
freckles **pecas** *[f] pekass*
free **libre** *[m/f] leebre;* no charge: **gratis** *[m/f] gratees*
to freeze (food) **congelar** *konhelar;* it's freezing: **está**

from **de** *de;*
front (of car/train/dress) **delantera** *[f] delantera;* of building: **fachada** *[f] fatshada;* in front of: **delante de** *delante de*
fruit **fruta** *[f] froota*
full **lleno/a** *lyeno;* hotel,etc.: **completo/a** *kompleto/a;* I'm full: **estoy lleno/a** *esstoy lyeno/a*
fun **divertido/a** *deeberteedo/a;* to have fun:

football **fútbol** *[m]*

American football **fútbol americano** *[m]*

el portero *portero*
el hincha *eentsha*
las hombreras *ombrerass*
el casco *kassko*
la animadora *aneemadora*
la rejilla *rehilya*
la portería *portereea*
el balón *balon*
el futbolista *foolbooleessia*
el árbitro *arbeetro*
el crampón *krampon*
la camiseta *kameesseta*

meter la pata
football **fútbol** *[m] footbol;* American football: **fútbol americano** *[m] footbol amereekano*
for **para** *para*
forbidden **prohibido** *proheebeedo*
foreigner **extranjero/a** *eksstranhero/a*
forest **bosque** *[m] bosske*
to forget **olvidar** *olbeedar*
to forgive **perdonar** *perdonar*
fork **tenedor** *[m] tenedor*
fountain **fuente** *[f] fooente*

helando *essta elando*
French **francés/a** *franthess/a;* in French: **en francés** *en franthess;* French fries: **patatas fritas** *[f] patatass freetass*
fresh **fresco/a** *fressko/a*
Friday **viernes** *byerness*
fridge **frigorífico** *[m] freegoreefeeko*
fried **frito** *freeto*
friend **amigo/a** *ameego/a*
friendly **simpático/a** *seempateeko/a*
frightened (to be frightened) **tener miedo** *tener myedo*

divertirse *deeberteersse;* just for fun: **en broma** *en broma;* to make fun of: **burlarse de** *boolarsse de*
funfair **feria** *[f] fereea*
funny **gracioso/a** *gratheeosso/a;* **extraño/a** *eksstranyo/a*
fuss (to kick up a fuss) **armar un lío** *armar oon leeo*
gallery **galería** *[f] galereea*
game **juego** *[m] hooego* or (football, hockey, tennis) **partido** *[m] parteedo;* or (cards) **partida** *[f] parteeda*
garage **garage** *[m] garahe*

garden **jardín [m]** *hardeen*
garlic **ajo [m]** *aho*
gas **gas [m]** *gass*
gate (in airport) **puerta [f]** *pooerta*
gear (car, bike) **marcha [f]** *martsha*
general (in general) **en general** *en heneral*
generous **generoso/a** *henerosso/a*
geography **geografía [f]** *heografeea*
German **alemán/a** *aleman/a*
Germany **Alemania** *Alemaneea*
to get (buy) **comprar** *komprar;* or (fetch) **ir a buscar** *eer a boosskar;* or (bring) **traer** *traer;* to get/take a train/taxi: **coger** *koher;* or (understand) **entender** *entender; or (to get away)* **escapar** *esskapar;* to get off (bus, train) **bajarse** *baharsse;* to get on (bus, train) **montar** *montar;* to get along/on with: **llevarse bien con** *lyebarsse byen kon;* to get up: **levantarse** *lebantarsse*
girl (little) **niña [f]** *neenya;* or (adult/young) **chica [f]** *tsheeka*
girlfriend **novia [f]** *nobeea*
to give **dar** *dar,* or (gift) **regalar** *regalar,* or (to give back) **devolver** *debolber,* or to give up (smoking,etc.): **dejar de** *dehar de,* or (to give way) **ceder el paso** *theder el passo*
glass **vaso [m]** *basso*
glasses **gafas [f]** *gafass*
glove **guante [m]** *gooante*

go (turn) **vuelta [f]** *booelta;* your go: **te toca** *te toka;* who's go is it?: **¿a quién le toca?** *a kyen le toka;* go-cart: **kart [m]** *kart*
to go **ir** *eer,* or (leave) **irse/ marcharse** *eersse/ martsharsse;* go ahead!: **¡venga!** *benga;* to go away: **irse** *eersse;* to go back: **volver** *bolber;* to go in: **entrar** *entrar;* to go out: **salir** *saleer*
goal (sport) **gol [m]** *gol*
goalkeeper **portero [m]** *portero*
God **Dios** *Deeoss*
good **bueno/a** *booeno/a;* or (weather) **buen tiempo** *booen tyempo;* good-looking: **guapo/a** *gooapo/a;* good morning: **buenos días** *booenoss deeyass;* good afternoon: **buenas tardes** *booenass tardess;* good night: **buenas noches** *booenass notshess*
goodbye **adiós** *adeeoss*
gooseberry (to play gooseberry) **sujetar la vela** *soohetar la bela*
gossip **cotilleo [m]** *koteelyeo;* person: **cotilla [m/f]** *koteelya*
to gossip **cotillear** *koteelyear*
government **gobierno [m]** *gobyerno*
graffiti **pintada [f]/ grafiti [m]** *peentada/ grafeetee*
gram **gramo [m]** *gramo*
grandfather **abuelo [m]** *abooelo*
grandmother **abuela [f]** *abooela*
grant **beca [f]** *beka*

grapefruit **pomelo [m]** *pomelo*
grapes **uvas [f]** *oobass,* or (bunch of grapes) **racimo de uvas [m]** *ratheemo de oobass;* grape harvest: **cosecha de uvas [m]** *kosetsha de oobass*
grass **hierba [f]** *yerba*
grateful **agradecido/a** *agradetheedo/a*
great **estupendo/a, genial** *esstoopendo/a, heneeal*
green **verde [m/f]** *berde*
grey **gris [m/f]** *greess*
grilled **asado/a** *assado/a*
gross (coarse) **grosero/a** *grossero/a*
grotty **desagradable [m/f]** *dessagradable,* or (to feel grotty) **sentirse mal** *ssenteersse mal*
ground **suelo [m]** *sooelo;* on the ground: **en el suelo** *en el sooelo;* ground floor: **planta baja [f]** *planta baha*
group **grupo [m]** *groopo*
to grow **crecer** *krether*
to guess **adivinar** *adeebeenar*
guest **invitado/a** *eenbeetado/a*
guide **guía [f]** *geea*
guilty **culpable [m/f]** *koolpable*
guitar **guitarra [f]** *geetarrra*
guy **hombre [m]/ tío* [m]** *ombre/ teeo*
gym (gymnastics) **gimnasia [f];** *heemnasseea,* or (gymnasium) **gimnasio [m]** *heemnasseo*
gypsy **gitano/a** *heetano/a*
habit **costumbre [f]** *kosstoombre*

to haggle *regatear* *regatear*

hair (on head) *pelo [m]* *pelo*, or (on body) *vello [m]* *belyo*; hairstyle: *peinado [m]* *peynado*

hairdresser *peluquero/a* *pelookero/a*

half *mitad [f]* *meetad*, or (with numbers) *medio/a* *medeeo/a*; half a kilo: *medio kilo [m]* *medeeo keelo*; half an hour: *media hora [f]* *medeea ora*; a half bottle: *media botella [f]* *medeea botelya*; half asleep/dressed: *medio dormido/a, medio vestido/a* *medeeo dormeedo/a, medeeo bessteedo/a*; half time: *descanso [m]* *desskansso*

ham *jamón [m]* *hamon*

hamburger *hamburguesa [f]* *amboorgessa*

hand *mano [f]* *mano*; by hand: *a mano* *a mano*; handmade: *hecho a mano* *etsho a mano*; helping hand: *una mano [f]* *oona mano*

to hang (something up) *colgar* *kolgar*; to hang around/out (go somewhere often): *frecuentar* *frekooentar*; to hang up (phone): *colgar* *kolgar*

hang-glider *ala delta [f]* *ala delta*

hang-gliding *vuelo libre [m]* *booelo leebre*

hangover *resaca [f]* *ressaka*

to happen *pasar* *passar*

happy *feliz [m/f]* *feleeth*

hard *duro/a* *dooro/a*

hat *sombrero [m]* *ssombrero*

to hate *odiar* *odeear*

to have *tener* *tener* or, (a drink: *tomar algo* *tomar algo*; to have to: *tener que* *tener ke*

hayfever *fiebre del heno [f]* *fyebre del eno*

he *él* *el*

head *cabeza [f]* *kabetha*

health *salud [f]* *salood*; health foods: *alimentos naturales [m]* *aleementoss natooraless*

healthy *sano/a* *sano/a*

to hear *oir* *oeer*; to hear about: *oir hablar de* *oeer ablar de*

heart *corazón [m]* *korathon*; to be heart-broken: *partírsele el corazón* *parteerssele el korathon*

heating *calefacción [f]* *kalefaktheeon*

heavy *pesado/a* *pessado/a*

helicopter *helicóptero [m]* *eleekoptero*

hello *hola* *ola*

helmet *casco [m]* *kassko*

help *ayuda [f]* *ayooda*; help!: *¡socorro!* *ssokorrro*; to help: *ayudar* *ayoodar*; to help yourself: *servirse* *serbeersse*

her (her bag) *su [m/f]* *soo*; or "it's her" and after "of", "to", "with", etc.: *ella* *elya*; I see her: *la* *la*

here *aquí* *akee*; here is/are: *aquí está/n* *akee essta/n*

hi *hola* *ola*

hiccup *hipo [m]* *eepo*

to hide *esconder* *esskonder*; or (yourself) *esconderse* *esskondersse*

hi-fi *cadena [f]/ equipo de música [m]* *kadena/ ekeepo de moosseeka*

hair *el pelo*

los bucles *bookless*

el pelo liso *pelo leesso*

el pelo rizado *pelo reethado*

el secador *ssekador*

la espuma *esspooma*

el pelo corto *pelo korto*

la laca *laka*

el pelo largo *pelo largo*

pelirrojo *peleer-roho*

la gomina *gomeena*

el pelo castaño *pelo kasstanyo*

el pelo negro *pelo negro*

el cepillo *thepeelyo*

el peine *peyne*

el pasador *passador*

el pelo rubio *pelo roobeeo*

77

high **alto/a** *alto/a*
hiking (to go hiking) **hacer una excursión** *ather oona eksskoorsseeon*
hill **colina [f]** *koleena*
him (as in "it's him") and after "of", "to", "than", "with", **él** *el*; I see/know him: **lo** *lo*
Hindu **hindú [m/f]** *eendoo*
hippie **hippie [m/f]** *heepee*
his **su/sus** *ssoo/ssooss*
history **historia [f]** *eesstoreea*
hit **éxito [m]** *eksseeto*
to hit **golpear** *golpear*; to knock into: **chocar contra** *tshokar kontra*
to hitch **hacer autostop/ hacer dedo** *ather aootosstop/ ather dedo*
HIV positive **seropositivo/a** *sseroposseeteebo/a*
hobby **pasatiempo [m]/ afición [f]/ hobby [m]** *passatyempo/ afeetheeon/ hobby*
to hold **tener/ sostener** *tener/ ssosstener*
hole **agujero [m]** *agoohero*
holiday **vacaciones [f]** *bacatheeoness*; bank holiday: **día festivo [m]/ fiesta [f]** *deeya fessteebo/ fyessta;* holiday camp: **colonia de verano/ vacaciones [f]** *koloneea de berano/ bakatheeoness,* or (for children) **campamento [m]** *kampamento*
home **casa [f]** *kassa;* at my/your etc. home: **en mi/ tu casa** *en mee/too kassa*
homeless **sin techo/ vagabundo [m]** *seen tetsho/ bagaboondo*

homosexual **homosexual [m/f]** *omossekssooal*
honest **honesto/a, sincero/a** *onessto/a, seenthero/a*
honey **miel [f]** *myel*
to hope **esperar** *essperar*
horn **claxon [m]** *klaksson*
horoscope **horóscopo [m]** *orosskopo*
horrible **horrible** *orrreeble*
horror film **película de miedo [m]** *peleekoola de myedo*
horse **caballo [m]** *kabalyo*
hospital **hospital [m]** *osspeetal*
host **anfitrión** *anfeetreeyon*
hostess **anfitriona** *anfeetreeyona*
hot **caliente [m/f]** *kalyente;* spicy: **picante [m/f]** *peekante;* to be hot (person): **tener calor** *tener kalor;* it is hot (weather): **hace calor** *athe kalor*
hotel **hotel [m]** *otel*
hour **hora [f]** *ora*
house **casa [f]** *kassa*

hovercraft **aerodeslizador [m]** *aerodessleethador*
how **cómo** *komo;* how are you?: **¿qué tal?** *ke tal;* how much?: **¿cuánto/a?** *kooanto/a;* how many?: **¿cuántos/as** *kooantoss/ass*
to hug **abrazar** *abrathar*
human **humano/a** *oomano/a*
humour **humor [m]** *oomor*
hungry to be hungry: **tener hambre** *tener ambre*
hurry (to be in a hurry) **tener prisa** *tener preessa*
to hurry **darse prisa** *darsse preessa*
to hurt **doler** *doler*
hysterics (nervous fit) **histerismo [m]** *heesstereessmo;* laughter: **ataque de risa [m]** *atake de reessa*
I **yo** *yo*
ice **hielo [m]** *yelo;* ice cream: **helado [m]** *elado;* ice cube: **cubito de hielo [m]** *koobeeto de yelo;* ice rink: **pista de hielo [f]** *peessta de yelo*

horoscope
horóscopo (m)

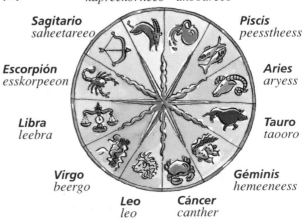

Capricornio *kapreekorneeo*
Acuario *akooareeo*
Sagitario *saheetareeo*
Piscis *peesstheess*
Escorpión *esskorpeeon*
Aries *aryess*
Libra *leebra*
Tauro *taooro*
Virgo *beergo*
Géminis *hemeeneess*
Leo *leo*
Cáncer *canther*

idea **idea [f]** *eedea*
idiot **idiota [m/f]** *eedeeota*
if **si** *see*
ill **enfermo/a** *enfermo/a*
illegal **ilegal [m/f]** *eelegal*
to imagine **imaginar**
emaheenar
immigrant **inmigrante**
[m/f] *eenmeegrante*
important **importante**
[m/f] *eemportante*
in **en** *en*; to be in: **estar en**
casa *esstar en kassa*; the
in-thing (in fashion): **de**
moda *de moda*
inclusive **todo incluido**
todo eenklooeedo
independent
independiente [m/f]
eendependyente
India **India** *eendeea*
infection **infección [f]**
eenfektheeon
information **información**
[f] *enformatheeon*
injection **inyección [f]**
eenyektheeon
injury **herida [f]** *ereeda*;
injury time: **tiempo extra**
[m] *tyempo oksstra*
innocent **inocente [m/f]**
eenothente
insect **insecto [m]**
eenssekto; insect bite:
picadura [f] *peekadoora*;
insect repellent:
insecticida [m]
enssekteetheeda
inside **dentro** *dentro*;
inside out: **al revés** *al*
rebess
to insist **insistir**
ensseessteer
instead of **en vez de** *en*
beth de
instructor **profesor/a,**
monitor/a *professor/a,*
moneetor/a

instrument **instrumento**
[m] *eensstroomento*
insult **insulto [m]**
eenssoolto
insurance **seguro [m]**
segooro
intercom **interfono [m]**
eenterfono
interested (to be interested
in) **interesarse por**
enteressarsse por
interesting **interesante**
[m/f] *enteressante*
international
internacional [m/f]
eenternatheeonal
internet **internet [f]**
enternet
interval (theatre) **descanso**
[m] *desskansso*
interview **entrevista [f]**
entrebeessta
to introduce (to person)
presentar *pressentar*
invitation **invitación [f]**
eenbeetatheeon
to invite **invitar** *eenbeetar*
Ireland **Irlanda** *eerlanda*
Irish **irlandés/a**
eerlandess/a
island **isla [f]** *eessla*
Italy **Italia** *etaleea*
jacket **chaqueta [f]**
tshaketa; bomber style:
cazadora [f] *kathadora*
jam **mermelada [f]**
mermelada
January **enero** *enero*
jazz **jazz [m]** *jass*
jealous **celoso/a** *thelosso/a*
jeans **vaqueros [m]**
bakeross
jellyfish **medusa [f]**
medoossa
jewellery **joyas [f]/**
bisutería [f] *hoyass/*
beesootereea
Jewish **judío/a** *joodeeo/a*

job **trabajo [m]** *trabaho*
to join **hacerse miembro/**
socio *hathersse*
myembro/sotheeo
joke **broma [f]** *broma*
to joke **bromear** *bromear*
judo **judo [m]** *joodo*
to juggle **hacer juegos**
malabares *ather hooegoss*
malabaress
juice **zumo [m]** *thoomo*
jukebox **máquina de**
discos [f] *makeena de*
deesskoss
July **julio** *hooleeo*
to jump **saltar** *saltar*
June **junio** *hooneeo*
junk **trastos viejos [m]**
trasstoss byehoss

instruments **los instrumentos**
(see also band picture)

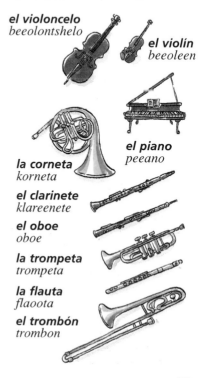

el violoncelo
beeolontshelo

el violín
beeoleen

el piano
peeano

la corneta
korneta

el clarinete
klareenete

el oboe
oboe

la trompeta
trompeta

la flauta
flaoota

el trombón
trombon

just (to have just done) **acabar de hacer** *akabar de ather*

to keep guardar *gooardar;* not to stop: **no parar de** *no parar de;* to keep an eye on: **vigilar** *beecheelar*

key llave [f] *lyabe*

keyboard teclado [m] *teklado*

kick patada [f] *patada*

kid niño/a *neenyo/a*

to kill matar *matar;* to kill yourself (laughing): **morirse de risa** *moreerse de reessa*

kilo kilo [m] *keelo*

kilometre kilómetro [m] *keelometro*

kind amable [m/f] *amable*

kiss beso [m] *besso*

to kiss besar *bessar;* one another: **besarse** *bessarsse*

kit (tools) **herramientas [f]** *errramyentass*

kitchen cocina [f] *kotheena*

kite cometa [f] *kometa*

knee rodilla [f] *rodeelya*

knickers bragas [f] *bragass*

knife cuchillo [m] *kootsheelyo*

to know (facts) **saber** *saber,* or (person, place) **conocer** *konother*

kosher conforme a la ley judaica *konforme a la ley hoodaeeka*

lager cerveza [f] *therbetha*

laid-back relajado/a *relahado/a*

lake lago [m] *lago*

lamb cordero [m] *kordero*

language idioma [m] *eedeeoma*

laptop ordenador portátil [m] *ordenador portateel*

laser láser [m] *lasser*

last el último/ la última *oolteemo/ oolteema;* at last: **por fin** *por feen*

late tarde *tarde*

Latin America América latina *amerekka lateena*

to laugh reirse *reyrsse* or (to have a laugh) **mondarse de risa** *mondarsse de reessa;* or (to laugh at) **reirse de** *reyrsse de;* or (to burst out laughing) **echarse a reir** *etsharsse a reyr*

launderette lavandería [f] *labandereea*

lazy perezoso/a *perethosso/a*

leaf hoja [f] *oha*

to learn aprender *aprender*

leather cuero [m] *kooero*

to leave dejar *dehar;* go away: **irse** *eersse;* to leave alone: **dejar en paz** *dehar en path*

left izquierda [f] *eethkeyerda;* on the left: **a la izquierda** *a la eethkeyerda;* left handed: **zurdo/a** *thoordo/a*

leg pierna [f] *pyerna*

lemon limón [m] *leemon*

to lend prestar *presstar*

leotard leotardo [m] *leotardo*

less menos *menoss*

lesson lección [f] *lektheeon*

letter carta [f] *karta*

lettuce lechuga [f] *letshooga*

liar mentiroso/a *menteerosso/a*

library biblioteca [f] *beebleeoteka*

jacket *la chaqueta*

jewellery *la bisutería*

la cazadora *kathadora*

los pendientes *pendyentess*

el cuello *kooelyo*

la chaqueta *tshaketa*

la manga *manga*

el botón *boton*

la cadena *kadena*

el collar *kolyar*

el broche *brotshe*

el pin *pin*

el anillo *aneelyo*

la hebilla *ebeelya*

la pulsera *poolssera*

el brazalete *brathalete*

kite *la cometa*

la canilla *kaneelya*

el cordón *kordon*

la cola *kola*

licence *licencia [f]*
leethentheea; driving
licence: **permiso de**
conducir [m] *permeesso de*
kondootheer
lie *mentira [f] menteera*
to lie *mentir menteer*
life *vida [f] beeda*
lifeguard *socorrista [m/f]*
sokorreessta
lifejacket *chaleco*
salvavidas [m] *tshaleko*
ssalbabeedass
lifestyle *modo de vida*
[m] modo de beeda
lift *ascensor [m]*
assthenssor
light *luz [f] luth;* not dark:
claro/a *klaro/a;* not heavy:
ligero/a *leegero/a*
lighter *mechero [m]*
metshero
like *como komo;* what's
he/she like?: **¿cómo es?**
komo ess
to like *gustar goostar;* I
like him/her: **me gusta** *me*
goossta; I'd like: **me**
gustaría *me goostareea*
likely *probable [m/f]*
probable; not likely!: **¡ni**
hablar! *nee ablar*
lilo *colchón de aire [m]*
koltshon de aeere
line *línea [f] leenea*
lip *labio [m] labeeo*
to listen *escuchar*
esskootshar

litre *litro [m]*
leetro
little *pequeño/a*
pekenyo; a little of: **un**
poco de *oon poko de*
live *en directo en deerekto*
to live *vivir beebeer;* to
live it up: **pegarse la gran**
vida *pegarsse la gran*
beeda
liver *hígado [m] eegado*
living room *salón [m]*
salon
loaded (with money)
forrado/a *forrrado/a*
loads of **montones de**
montoness de
to loathe *odiar odeear*
local (regional) **de la**
región *de la reheeon;*
in/from this part of town:
del barrio, vecino/a *del*
barreo, betheeno/a
to lock *cerrar con llave*
therrar kon lyabe
London *Londres londress*
lonely *solo/a solo/a*
long *largo/a largo/a;* a
long time: **mucho tiempo**
mootsho tyempo; how
long?: **¿cuánto tiempo?**
kooanto tyempo
loo *servicio [m]*
serbeetheeo
to look *mirar meerar;* to
look after: **cuidar** *kooeedar;*
to look for: **buscar**
boosskar; to look forward:
esperar con ansia *essperar*
kon anseea; to look like:
parecerse a *parethersse a*
to lose *perder perder*

lost *perdido/a perdeedo/a;*
to get lost: **perderse**
perdersse; get lost!: **¡vete**
a la porra/ mierda! *bete a*
la porra/ myerda; lost
property: **objetos perdidos**
[m] obhetoss perdeedoss
lots *mucho motsho*
loud *fuerte fooerte*
lousy *malísimo/a*
maleesseemo/a
love *amor [m] amor;* in
love: **enamorado/a**
enamorado/a; love life:
vida amorosa [f] beeda
amorossa; to make love:
hacer el amor *ather el*
amor
to love *querer kerer*
lovely (things) **precioso/a**
pretheeosso/a; people
guapo/a *gooapo/a*
low *bajo/a baho/a;* low
cut: **escotado/a**
esskotado/a
low-down (to get the low
down) **informarse**
eenformarsse
luck *suerte [f] sooerte;*
bad luck: **mala suerte [f]**
mala sooerte; **¡buena**
suerte! *booena swerte*
luckily *afortunadamente*
afortoonadamente
luggage *equipaje [m]*
ekeepahe; hand luggage:
equipaje de mano [m]
ekeepahe de mano
lunch *comida [f] komeeda*
lyrics *letra [f] letra*
machine *máquina [f]*
makeena

macho **macho [m]** *matsho*
mad **loco/a** *loko/a*
madam **señora [f]** *senyora*
magazine **revista [f]**
rebeessta
mail **correo [m]** *korreo*
to make **hacer** *ather;* earn:
ganar *ganar;* it makes me
ill/ jealous/ happy: **me pone
enfermo/a, celoso/a, feliz**
*me pone enfermo/a,
thelosso/a, feleeth*
to make up (invent)
inventa *eenbentar,* or (be
friends again) **hacer las
paces/ reconciliarse** *ather
lass pathess/
rekontheeleearsse*
make-up **maquillaje [m]**
makeelyahe
man **hombre [m]** *ombre*
to manage **arreglárselas**
arrreglarsselass; to
manage to: **lograr** *lograr*
many **muchos/a**
mootshoss/a; not many: **no
muchos/as** *no
mootshoss/ass*
map **mapa [m]** *mapa;* of
town: **plano [m]** *plano*
March **marzo** *martho*
margarine **margarina [f]**
marhareena
mark (stain) **mancha [f]**
mantsha; at school: **nota
[f]** *nota*
market **mercado [m]**
merkado
match (for a candle) **cerilla
[f]** *thereelya;* sport:
partido [m] *parteedo*
material **tela [f]** *tela*
maths **matemáticas [f]**
matemateekass
matter it doesn't matter: **no
importa** *no eemporta;*
what's the matter?: **¿qué
pasa?** *ke passa*

mature **maduro/a**
madooro/a
May **mayo** *mayo*
mayonaise **mayonesa [f]**
mayonessa
me (it's me) **soy yo** *soy yo;*
than me: **que yo** *ke yo;* of
me/to me: **a/de mí** *a/de
mee;* with me: **conmigo**
konmeego; he sees/knows
me: **me ve/ me conoce** *me
be/ me konothee*
meal **comida [f]** *komeeda*
to mean **querer decir**
kerer detheer; to mean to:
tener la intención de *tener
la eententheeon de*
meat **carne [f]** *karne*
media **medios de
comunicación [m]**
*medeeoss de
komooneekatheeon*
medicine (medication)
medicamento [m]
medeekamento
Mediterranean
Mediterráneo [m]
medeeterrraneo
medium (size) **mediana [f]**
medeeana; or (cooking)
**medio (ni muy hecho ni
poco hecho)** *medeeo (nee
mooy etsho nee poko etsho)*
to meet (by chance)
encontrarse *enkontrarsse;*
by arrangement: **quedar
con/ver** *kedar kon/ber*
melon **melón [m]** *melon;*
watermelon: **sandía [f]**
sandeeya
menu **carta [f]** *karta;* set
menu: **menú [m]** *menoo*
mess **desorden [m]**
dessorden
message **mensaje [m]**
menssahe
method **método [m]**
metodo

metre **metro [m]** *metro*
microwave **microondas
[m]** *meekroondass*
middle **medio [m]**
medeeo; in the middle of:
en medio de *en medeeo
de;* midnight: **medianoche
[f]** *medeeanotshe*
milk **leche [f]** *letshe;* milk-
shake: **batido [m]** *bateedo*
mind do you mind?: **¿te
importa?/ ¿te molesta?** *te
eemporta/ te molessta;*
don't mind: **no me
importa/ no me molesta**
*no me emporta/ no me
molessta;* it's all the same to
me: **me da igual** *me da
eegooal*
minute **minuto [m]**
meenooto
mirror **espejo [m]** *esspeho*
Miss **señorita [f]**
senyoreeta
to miss (train/bus) **perder**
perder; to long for: **echar
de menos** *etshar de
menoss;* I miss you: **te echo
de menos** *te etsho de
menoss;* he misses París:
echa de menos París *etsha
de menoss pareess*
mistake **error [m]** *error;*
to make a mistake:
equivocarse *ekebokarsse*
to mix (or to mix up)
mezclar *methklar;* or
muddle: **embrollar**
embrollar
mixed up (in your mind)
estar confuso/a *esstar
konfoosso/a*
to moan (complain)
quejarse *keharsse*
mobile phone **móvil [m]**
mobeel
model (fashion) **modelo
[m/f]** *modelo*

make-up *el maquillaje*

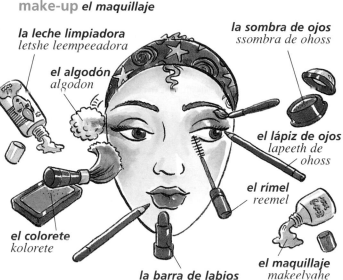

la leche limpiadora
letshe leempeeadora

el algodón
algodon

el colorete
kolorete

la barra de labios
barrra de labeeoss

la sombra de ojos
ssombra de ohoss

el lápiz de ojos
lapeeth de ohoss

el rímel
reemel

el maquillaje
makeelyahe

modern **moderno/a**
moderno/a
moment (in a moment)
dentro de un momento
[m] *dentro de oon*
momento; at the moment:
por el momento *por el*
momento
Monday **lunes [m]** *looness*
money **dinero [m]**
deenero; money-belt:
riñonera [f] *reenyonera*
month **més [m]** *mess*
monument **monumento**
[m] *monoomento*
mood (in a good/bad mood)
de buen/mal humor *de*
booen/mal oomor
moody **de humor**
cambiadizo, lunático/a *de*
oomor kambeeadeetho,
loonateeko/a
moon **luna [f]** *loona*
moped **vespa [f]** *besspa*
more **más** *mass*
morning **mañana [f]**

manyana
mosque **mezquita [f]**
methkeeta
mosquito **mosquito [m]**
moskeeto; mosquito bite:
picadura [f] *peekadoora;*
mosquito repellent:
repelente para insectos
[m] *repelente para*
eenssektoss
most (as in most handsome)
el/ la/ los/ las más *el/ la/*
loss/ lass mass; or (as in I
want the most, I like it the
most) **el que más** *el ke*
mass; most of the
time/people: **la mayoría de**
la mayoreea de; to make
the most of: **aprovechar al**
máximo *aprobetshar al*
maksseemo
mother **madre [f]** *madre*
moto **motor [m]** *motor*
motorbike **moto [f]** *moto*
motorway **autopista [f]**
aootopeessta

mountain **montaña [f]**
montanya
mouse (animal/computer)
ratón [m] *raton*
mouth **boca [f]** *boka*
to move **moverse**
mobersse; or (change
address) **mudarse**
moodarsse; move over!:
¡apártate! *apartate*
movie **película [f]**
peleekoola
movies **cine [m]** *theene*
Mr **señor [m]** *senyor*
Mrs **señora [f]** *senyora*
much **mucho** *mootsho*
mugged (to get mugged)
atracar/ asaltar *atrakar/*
assaltar
murder **asesinato [m]**
assesseenato
muscle **músculo [m]**
mooscoolo
museum **museo [m]**
mooseo
mushroom **champiñón**
[m] *tshampeenyon*
music **música [f]** *mooseeka*
musician **músico [m/f]**
mooseeko
Muslim **musulmán/a**
moosoolman/a
must (to have to) **tener**
que/ deber *tener ke/*
deber; I must: **tengo que/**
debo *tengo que/ debo*
mustard **mostaza [f]**
mosstatha
my **mi/mis [m/f]** *mee/mees*
naked **desnudo/a**
dessnoodo/a
name **nombre [m]**
nombre; last name:
apellido [m] *apelyeedo;*
what's your name?: **¿cómo**
te llamas?/¿cómo se
llama? *komo te lyamass/*
komo sse lyama

napkin **servilleta [f]**
serbeelyeta
narrow **estrecho/a**
esstretsho/a
nasty **desagradable [m/f]**,
malo/a *dessagradable,*
malo/a
national **nacional [m/f]**
natheeonal
nationality
nacionalidad [f]
natheeonaleedath
natural **natural [m/f]**
natooral
nature **naturaleza [f]**
natooraletha
naughty **malo/a** *malo/a*
near **cerca de** *therka de*
nearest **el/la más**
cercano/a *el/la mass*
therkano/a
nearly **casi** *kassee*
necessary **necesario/a**
netheessareeo/a
neck **cuello [m]** *kooelyo*
to need **necesitar**
nethesseetar
neighbour **vecino/a**
betheeno/a
neighbourhood **barrio**
[m] *barrreeo*
nerve **nervio [m]** *nerbeeo;*
nerve-racking: **exasperante**
[m/f] *ekssassperante;* to
get on someone's nerves:
poner nervioso/a *poner*
nerbeeosso/a; what a
nerve!: **¡qué cara!** *ke kara*
nervous (to be/feel nervous)
estar nervioso/a *esstar*
nerbeeosso/a; to have
butterflies: **tener los**
nervios de punta *tener*
loss nerbeeoss de poonta
never **nunca** *noonka;* never
mind!: **¡no importa!** *no*
eemporta; too bad: **¡qué**
pena! *ke pena*

new **nuevo/a** *nooebo;* New
Year: **Año nuevo [m]** *anyo*
nooebo; New Zealand:
Nueva Zelanda *nooeba*
thelanda
news **noticias [f]**
noteetheeass; news stand:
quiosco [m]/ puesto de
periódicos [m] *keeossko/*
pooessto de pereeodeekoss
newsagent's **estanco [m]**
esstanko
newspaper **periódico [m]**
pereeodeeko
next **próximo/a**
proksseemo/a; next to: **al**
lado de *al lado de*
nice (likeable) **simpático/a**
sseempateeko/a; nice and...
(as in nice and cold) **bien**
byen
nickname **apodo [m]/**
diminutivo [m] *apodo/*
deemeenooteebo
night **noche [f]** *notshe;*
last night: **anoche** *anotshe*
nightmare **pesadilla [f]**
pessadeelya
no **no** *no;* no
entry/smoking: **prohibido**
entrar/fumar *proheebeedo*
entrar/foomar; no way!: **¡ni**
hablar! *nee ablar*
nobody **nadie** *nadye;*
nobody else: **nadie más**
nadye mass
noise **ruido [m]** *rooeedo*
normal **normal [m/f]**
normal
north **norte [m]** *norte;*
north of: **al norte de** *al*
norte de
nose **nariz [f]** *nareeth*
nosy **entrometido/a,**
curioso/a *entrometeedo/a,*
kooreeosso/a; to be nosy:
ser cotilla [m/f] *sser*
koteelya

not **no** *no*
note (money) **billete [m]**
beelyete
notebook **libreta [f]**
leebreta
nothing **nada** *nada;*
nothing else: **nada más**
nada mass
nought **cero** *thero*
novel **novela [f]** *nobela*
November **noviembre**
nobyembre
now **ahora** *ahora*
nowhere **en ninguna**
parte *en neengoona parte*
nuclear **nuclear** *nooklear*
number **número [m]**
noomero
nurse **enfermero/a**
enfermero/a
nuts **frutos secos [m]**
frootoss ssekoss
nutter (crazy person)
chiflado/a *tsheeflado/a*
obnoxious **odioso/a**
odeeosso/a
obscene **obsceno**
obsstheno
obsession **obsesión [f]**
obssesseeon
obvious **obvio/evidente**
obeeo/ ebeedente
o'clock **en punto** *en*
poonto
October **octubre** *oktoobre*
odd **extraño** *eksstranyo;*
the odd one out: **excepción**
[f] *eksstheptheeon*
of **de** *de*
off switched off:
apagado/a *apagado/a*
offended **ofendido/a**
ofendeedo/a
to offer **ofrecer** *ofrether*
office **oficina [f]**
ofeetheena
official **oficial [m/f]**
ofeetheeal

often *a menudo a menoodo;* how often?: *¿cuántas veces? kooantass bethess*

oil *aceite [f] atheyte*

OK *de acuerdo de akooerdo,* I'm OK. *estoy bien esstoy byen;* it's OK: *está bien/vale essta byen/bale*

old *viejo/a byeho/a;* how old are you?: *¿cuántos años tienes? kooantoss anyoss tyeness;* old-fashioned: *pasado de moda passado de moda*

olive *aceituna [f] atheytoona*

omelette *tortilla [f] torteelya*

on *en/sobre/encima de en/sobre/entheema de;* switched on: *encendido/a enthendeedo/a;* on Sundays: *los domingos loss domeengoss;* to be on (film): *poner poner*

one-way *de dirección única de deerektheeon oonooka*

onion *cebolla [f] thebolya*

only *sólo ssolo;* only daughter/son: *hija única/ hijo único eeha ooneeka/ eeho ooneeko*

open *abierto/a abyerto/a;* in the open air: *al aire libre al aeere leebre*

to open *abrir abreer*

opera *ópera [f] opera*

opinion *opinión [f] opeeneeon*

opportunity *oportunidad [f] oportooneedath*

opposite (facing) *enfrente de enfrente de;* not the same: *lo contrario lo kontrareeo*

optician's *óptico [m] opteeko*

optimistic *optimista [m/f] opteemeessta*

or *o o*

orange (fruit) *naranja [f] naranha;* or (colour) *naranja [m] naranha*

orchestra *orquesta [f] orkessta*

order *orden [m] orden;* to order: *pedir pedeer*

ordinary *ordinario/a ordeenareeo/a*

to organize *organizar organeethar*

original *original [m/f] oreeheenal*

other *otro/a otro/a;* the other one: *el otro/la otra el otro/la otra*

otherwise *si no see no*

our *nuestro/a/os/as nooesstro/a/oss/ass*

out (to be out) *no estar (en casa) no esstar (en kassa);* out of order: *estropeado esstropeado;* sign: *no funciona no foontheeona*

outdoor *exterior/ al aire libre eksstereeor/ al aeere leebre*

outrageous *atroz [m/f] atroth*

outside *fuera fooera*

oven *horno [m] orno*

over (not under) *por encima de por entheema de;* over here: *por aquí por akee;* over there: *por allí por alyee*

nuts *los frutos secos*

la nuez *nooeth*

la nuez de Brasil *nooeth de Brasseel*

la almendra *almendra*

el pistacho *peestatsho*

el anarcado *anarkado*

el cacahuete *kakaooete*

el cascanueces *kasskanooethess*

el coco *koko*

la avellana *abelyana*

85

overdraft **en descubierto** *en desskoobyerto*
overrated **supervalorado/a** *sooperbalorado/a*
to overtake **adelantar** *adelantar*
to owe **deber** *deber*
own (on your own) **solo/a** *ssolo/a*
owner **propietario/a** *propyetareeo/a*
to pack (bags) **hacer las maletas** *ather lass maletass*
package tour **viaje organizado [m]** *beeahe organeethado*
padlock **candado [m]** *kandado;* on bike: **cadena [f]** *kadena*
page **página [f]** *paheena*
pain (to be a pain/nuisance) **ser molesto/a, fastidioso/a** *sser molessto/a, fassteedyosso/a*
to paint **pintar** *peentar*
palace **palacio [m]** *palatheeo*
pan (saucepan) **cazo [m]/ cacerola [m]** *catho/catheerola;* frying: **sartén [f]** *ssarten*
panic **pánico [m]** *paneeko*
paper **papel [m]** *papel*
paperback (book) **libro en rústica [m]** *leebro en roossteeka*
parachute **paracaídas [m]** *parakaeedass*
parcel **paquete [m]** *pakete*
parents **padres [m]** *padress*
park **parque [m]** *parke*
to park **aparcar** *aparkar*
parking space **aparcamiento [m]** *aparkamyento*

part **parte [f]** *parte;* or (for bike,etc) **pieza [f]** *pyetha;* to take part: **participar** *parteetheepar*
party **fiesta [f]** *fyessta;* or (political) **partido [m]** *parteedo*
to party **hacer una fiesta/festejar** *ather oona fyessta/fesstehar*
pass (for travel) **bono [m]** *bono;* ski pass: **pase [m]** *passe*
to pass **pasar** *passar,* or (exam) **aprobar** *aprobar*
passenger **pasajero/a** *passahero/a*
passport **pasaporte [m]** *passaporte*
pasta **pasta [f]** *passta*
path **sendero [m]** *sendero*
patient **paciente [m/f]** *pathyente*
pattern **diseño [m]** *deessenyo*
pavement **acera [f]** *athera*
to pay **pagar** *pagar;* to pay back: **devolver** *debolber*
peace **paz [f]** *path*
peaceful **tranquilo/a** *trankeelo/a*
peach **melocotón [m]** *melokoton*
peanut **cacahuete [m]** *kakahooete*
pear **pera [f]** *pera*
peas **guisantes [m]** *geessantess*
pedestrian **peatón [m]** *peaton;* pedestrian crossing: **paso de peatones [m]** *passo de peatoness*
pen **bolígrafo [m]** *boleegrafo;* pen pal: **amigo por correspondencia [m]** *ameego por corrresspondentheea*
pencil **lápiz** *lapeeth*

people **gente [f]** *hente*
pepper **pimienta [f]** *peemeyenta;* vegetable: **pimiento [m]** *peemeyento*
perfect **perfecto/a** *perfekto/a*
performance **representación [f]** *repressentatheeon;* cinema: **sesión [f]** *ssesseeon*
perhaps **quizás** *keethass*
period (menstruation) **regla [f]** *regla*
person **persona [f]** *perssona*
petrol **gasolina [f]** *gassoleena;* lead-free petrol: **gasolina sin plomo [f]** *gassoleena seen plomo;* petrol-station: **gasolinera [f]** *gassoleenera*
pharmacy **farmacia [f]** *farmatheea*
philosophy **filosofía [f]** *feelosofeea*
phobia **fobia [f]** *fobeea*
phone **teléfono [m]** *telefono;* phone booth: **cabina [f]** *kabeena;* phone call: **llamada [f]** *lyamada*
to phone **llamar** *lyamar;* to phone back: **volver a llamar/ llamar de vuelta** *bolber a lyamar/ lyamar de booelta*
photo **foto [f]** *foto*
photographer **fotógrafo [m]** *fotografo*
to pick **elegir** *eleheer;* to pick up, gather: **recoger** *rekoher*
picnic **picnic [m]** *peekneek*
picture (drawing) **dibujo [m]** *deebooho;* painting: **cuadro [m]** *cooadro*
pie (meat/ vegetable/ sweet) **pastel [m]** *passtel*
piece **trozo [m]** *trotho*

pig **cerdo [m]** *therdo*
pigeon **paloma [f]** *paloma*
pill **píldora [f]** *peeldora;*
to be on the pill: **tomar la
píldora** *tomar la peeldora*
PIN **número personal [m]**
noomero personal
pinball **flipper [m]**
fleepper
pineapple **piña [f]** *peenya*
pink **rosa** *rossa*
pity (it's a pity!) **¡es una
pena!** *ess oona pena*
pizza **pizza [f]** *peetsa*
place **sitio [m]** *seeteeo;*
at/to my/your place: **en/a
mi/tu casa** *en/a/mee/too
kassa*
plan **plan [m]** *plan*
plane (aircraft) **avión [m]**
abeeon
plant **planta [f]** *planta*
plaster (for cut/blister)
venda [f] *benda;* cast:
escayola [f] *esskayola*
plastic **plástico [m]**
plassteeko
plate **plato [m]** *plato*
play (in theatre) **obra [f]**
obra
to play **jugar** *hoogar*
player **jugador/a**
hoogador/a
please **por favor** *por fabor*
plug (for water) **tapón [m]**
tapon; for electrics:
enchufe [m] *entshoofe*
plum **ciruela [f]** *theerooela*
pocket **bolsillo [m]**
bolseelyo; pocket-money:
dinero de bolsillo [m]
deenero de bolseelyo
poem **poema [m]** *poema*
to point **indicar** *endeekar;*
with a finger: **señalar**
senyalar
police **policía [f]**
poleetheea; police officer:

phone booth *la cabina*

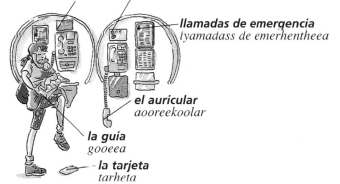

el teléfono de tarjeta
telefono de tarheta

el teléfono de monedas
telefono de monedass

llamadas de emergencia
lyamadass de emerhentheea

el auricular
aooreekoolar

la guía
gooeea

la tarjeta
tarheta

agente [m]/policía [m]
ahente/ poleetheea; police-
station: **comisaría [f]**
komeessareea
polite **cortés [m/f]** *kortess*
politics **política [f]**
poleeteeka
pollution **contaminación
[f]** *kontameenatheeon*
poor **pobre** *pobre*
popular **popular** *popoolar*
pork **cerdo [m]** *therdo*
posh **elegante [m/f]**
elegante
positive **positivo/a**
poseeteebo/a; sure:
seguro/a *segooro/a*
possible **posible** *poseeble*
post **correo [m]** *korrreo;*
post-box: **buzón [m]**
buthon; post-office:
Correos *korrreoss*
postcard **postal [f]** *posstal*
poster **cartel [m]/póster
[m]** *kartel/posster*
potato **patata [f]** *patata;*
mashed potato: **puré de
patatas [m]** *poore de
patatass*
pound **libra [f]** *leebra*

practical **práctico**
prakteeko
to practise (sport) **entrenar**
entrenar, or (instrument)
ensayar *enssayar*
prawn **gamba [f]** *gamba*
to prefer **preferir** *prefereer*
pregnant **embarazada**
embarathada
to prepare **preparar**
preparar
present **regalo [m]** *regalo*
to pretend **fingir** *feengeer*
pretty (things) **bonito/a**
boneeto/a, or (person)
guapo/a *gooapo/a*
price **precio [m]** *pretheeo*
printer (machine)
impresora [f] *eempressora*
private **privado/a**
preebado/a
prize **premio [m]** *premeeo*
problem **problema [m]**
problema
programme
programa [m] *programa*
progress **progreso [m]**
progresso
promise **promesa [f]**
promessa

picnic *el picnic*

el banco banko

el disco deessko

la basura bassoora

el queso kesso

el agua agooa

el pan pan

la sandía sandeea

las uvas oobass

la nevera nebera

el termo termo

el salchichón ssaltsheetshon

el sacacorchos ssakortshoss

el paño panyo

la panera panera

la navaja nabaha

---

proof **prueba [f]** *prooeba*
prostitute **prostituta [f]** *prossteetoota*
protect (to protect) **proteger** *proteher*
Protestant **protestante [m/f]** *protesstante*
proud **orgulloso/a** *orgoolyosso/a*
psychological **psicológico** *psseekoloheeko*
public **público/a** *poobleeko/a*
to pull **tirar** *teerar;* to pull someone's leg: **tomarle el pelo** *tomarle el pelo*
to punch **dar un puñetazo** *dar oon poonyetatho*
puncture to have a puncture: **tener un pinchazo** *tener oon peentshatho*
to punish **castigar** *kassteegar*

puppy **cachorro [m]** *katshorrro*
pure **puro/a** *pooro/a*
purpose **propósito [m]** *proposseeto*
purse **monedero[m]/ cartera [f]** *monedero/ kartera*
to push **empujar** *empoohar*
to put **poner** *poner;* to put away: **guardar** *gooardar;* to put off: **posponer** *possponer;* to discourage: **disuadir** *deesooadeer;* to put on clothes: **ponerse** *ponersse;* to put someone up: **alojar** *alohar;* to put up with: **soportar** *ssoportar*
puzzle **puzzle [m]** *puthle*
quality **calidad [f]** *kaleedath*
quantity **cantidad [f]** *kanteedath*

to quarrel **reñir** *renyeer*
quarter **cuarto [m]** *kooarto*
question **pregunta [f]** *pregoonta*
queue **cola [f]** *kola*
to queue **hacer cola** *ather kola*
quick **rápido/a** *rapeedo/a*
quickly **rápidamente** *rapeedamente*
quiet **tranquilo/a** *trankeelo/a;* not loud: **bajo/a** *baho/a;* to be/keep quiet: **callarse** *kalyarsse*
quite **bastante** *basstante;* I quite agree: **estoy de acuerdo** *esstoy de akooerdo*
race **carrera [f]** *karrera*
racist **racista** *ratheessta*
racket **raqueta [f]** *raketa*
radiator **radiador [m]** *radeeador*
radio **rádio [f]** *radeeo;* radio cassette player: **casete [m]** *kassete*
raft **balsa [f]** *balssa*
railway **ferrocarril [m]** *ferrrokarrreel;* Spanish railways: **RENFE**
rain **lluvia [f]** *lyoobeea;* it's raining: **está lloviendo** *essta lyobyendo*
rape **violación [f]** *beeolatheeon*
rare **raro/a** *raro/a;* barely cooked: **poco hecho/a** *poko etsho/a*
rash **irritación [f]** *eerrreetatheeon*
raspberry **frambuesa [f]** *frambooessa*
raw **crudo/a** *kroodo/a*
razor **maquinilla de afeitar [f]** *makeeneelya de afeytar;* razor blade: **cuchilla [f]** *kootsheelya*

reaction **reacción [f]**
reaktheeon
to read **leer** *leer*
ready **preparado/a**
preparado/a
real **verdadero/a,**
auténtico/a *berdadero/a,*
aootenteeko/a
to realize **darse cuenta**
darsse kooenta
really **ciertamente/**
verdaderamente
thyertamente/
berdaderamente; extremely:
terriblemente
terrreeblemente
reason **razón [f]** *rathon*
recent **reciente** *rethyente*
reception **recepción [f]**
retheptheeon
recipe **receta [f]** *retheta*
to recognize **reconocer**
rekonother
to recommend
recomendar *rekomendar*
record (sport) **récord [m]**
rekord
to record **grabar** *grabar*
red **rojo** *roho;* to blush:
ponerse rojo/a *ponersse*
roho/a
reduced (in sales) **rebajas**
[f] *rebahass*
refund **devolución [m]**
debolootheeon
to refuse **negarse**
negarsse
region **región [f]** *recheeon*
registered (post,letter)
certificado/a
therteefeekado/a; luggage:
facturado *faktoorado*
regular **regular** *regoolar;*
usual: **habitual** *abeetooal*
rehearsal **ensayo [m]**
enssayo
to relax **relajarse**
relaharsse

relaxed **relajado/a**
relahado/a
relief **alivio [m]** *aleebeeo*
religion **religión [f]**
releeheeon
to remember **acordarse**
de/recordar *akordarsse de/*
rekordar
remote **remoto/a**
remoto/a; remote control:
mando a distancia [m]
mando a deesstantheea
to rent **alquilar** *alkeelar;*
for rent: **se alquila** *se*
alkeela
to repair **reparar** *reparar*
to repeat **repetir**
repeteer
reply **respuesta [f]**
resspooessta
to reply **contestar**
kontesstar
rescue **rescate [m]**
resskate
to rescue
rescatar/salvar
resskatar/ssalbar
research
investigación [f]
eenbessteegatheeon
reservation **reserva**
[f] *resserba*
reserved **reservado/a**
resserbado/a
responsible
responsable [m/f]
ressponssable
rest (break) **descanso**
[m] *desskansso;*
remainder: **resto [m]**
ressto
to rest **descansar**
desskanssar
restaurant
restaurante [m]
resstaoorante
result **resultado [m]**
resooltado

return **vuelta [f]** *booelta;*
ticket: **ida y vuelta** *eeda ee*
booelta
revenge **venganza [f]**
bengantha; to get your
revenge: **vengarse**
bengarsse
to reverse **dar marcha**
atrás *dar martsha atrass;*
to reverse the charges
(phone): **llamar a cobro**
revertido *lyamar a kobro*
reberteedo
rice **arroz [m]** *arroth*
rich **rico/a** *reeko/a*
ride (to go for a ride –
bike/car) **ir a dar una**
vuelta en la bici/el coche
eer a dar oona booelta en
la beethee/el kotshe; to
take someone for a ride
(trick): **tomar el pelo** *tomar*
el pelo

rain *la lluvia*

el arco iris
arko eereess

el paraguas
paragooass

el charco
tsharko

el impermeable
eempermeable

la gota de lluvia
gota de lloobeea

la bota de caucho
bota de kaootsho

rider (horse) *jinete [m/f]*
heenete
riding equitación [f]
ekeetatheeon
right (correct) *correcto*
korrekto; fair: *justo*
hoossto; not left: *derecha*
[f] deretsha; you are right:
tienes razón tyeness
rathon; on the right: *a la*
derecha a la deretsha;
right away: *enseguida*
enssegeeda; right-of-way:
prioridad [f] preeoreedath
to ring llamar *lyamar*
riot disturbio [m]
deesstoorbeeo; to have a
riot: *pasárselo bomba*
passarsselo bomba
to rip rasgar/ romper
rassgar/ romper
ripe maduro/a *madooro/a*
risk riesgo [m] *ryessgo*
river río [m] *reeo*
road carretera [f]
karrretera; in town: *calle*
[f] kalye; road map: *mapa*
de carreteras [m] mapa de
karrreterass

rock (boulder) *canto*
rodado kanto rodado; rock
face: *roca [f] roka*; music:
rock [m] rock
roll (bread) *bollo [m] bolyo*
roller blades patines [m]
pateeness
romance romance [m]
romanthe
romantic romántico/a
romanteeko/a
roof tejado [m] *tehado*;
roof rack: *baca [f] baka*
room habitación [f]
abeetatheeon; single/double
room: *habitación*
individual/ doble [f]
abeetatheeon
eendeebeedooal/ doble
rope cuerda [f] *kooerda*
rotten (off) *podrido/a*
podreedo/a; mean, unfair:
horrible horrreeble
round (drinks) *ronda [f]*
ronda; shape: *redondo/a*
redondo/a
roundabout glorieta [f]
gloryeta
route ruta [f] *roota*

to row remar *remar*
to rub frotar *frotar*; to rub
it in: *insistir eenseesteer*; to
rub out: *borrar borrrar*
rubber band goma [f]
goma
rubbish basura [f]
basoora; rubbish bin: *cubo*
de la basura [f] koobo de
la bassoora; to talk rubbish:
decir tonterías detheer
tontereeass
rude mal educado/a *mal*
edookado/a; crude:
grosero/a grossero/a
rugby rugby [m] *roogby*
ruins ruinas [f] *rooeenass*
rule regla [f] *regla*
rumour rumor [m] *roomor*
to run correr *korrrer*; to
run away: *escaparse*
esskaparsse; to run out:
expirar/vencer
eksspeerar/benther
rush hour hora punta [f]
ora poonta
sad triste *treesste*
safe seguro/a *segooro/a*;
for valuables: *caja fuerte*
[f] kaha fooerte
safety seguridad [f]
segooreedath; safety
belt: *cinturón de*
seguridad [m]
theentooron de
segooreedath; safety
pin: *imperdible [m]*
eemperdeeble
sailing (boat) *barco*
de vela [m] barko de
bela; to go sailing:
navegar nabegar
salad ensalada [f]
enssalada; fruit salad:
ensalada de fruta [f]
enssalada de froota;
green salad: *ensalada*
verde [f] enssalada

riding *la equitación*

la cola kola

los pantalones de montar
pantaloness de montar

la silla
seelya

la chaqueta de montar
tshaketa de montar

el casco de montar
kassko de montar

la brida breeda

las riendas
ryendass

la fusta
foossta

el estribo
esstreebo

la cincha
theentsha

las botas de montar
botass de montar

berde; mixed salad:
ensalada mixta [f]
enssalada meekssta; salad
dressing: **vinagreta [f]**
beenagreta
salami **salchichón [m]/**
salami [m] *saltsheetshon/*
salamee
sale (for sale) **se vende** *se*
bende
sales (reduced prices)
rebajas [f] *rebahass*
salmon **salmón [m]**
ssalmon
salt **sal [f]** *ssal*
same **el mismo/la misma**
meessmo/meessma
sand **arena [f]** *arena*
sandal **sandalia [f]**
ssandaleea
sandwich **sandwich [m]**
sandweetsh
sanitary towel
compresa [f] *kompressa*
sarcastic **sarcástico/a**
ssarkassteeko/a
Saturday **sábado [m]**
sabado
sauce **salsa [f]** *ssalssa*
sausage **salchicha [f]**
ssaltsheetsha
to save **salvar** *ssalbar;*
money: **ahorrar** *aorrar*
savoury (not sweet)
salado/a *ssalado/a*
to say **decir** *detheer*
scared (to be scared) **tener**
miedo *tener myedo;* scared
stiff: **muerto/a de miedo**
mooerto/a de myedo
scarf **bufanda [f]**
boofanda; square: **fular**
[m] *foolar*
scary **de miedo** *de myedo*
scenery **paisaje [m]**
paeessahe
school (primary) **escuela**
primaria [f] *esskooela*

sailing boat *el barco de vela*

el mástil
massteel

el velero
belero

la botavara
botabara

el camarote
kamarote

el spinnaker *speenaker*

la vela mayor
bela mayor

el barco de
vela *barko*
de bela

el ancla
ankla

el bote
bote

el remo *remo*

el chaleco salvavidas
tshaleko salbabeedass

el
foque
foke

la boya *boya*

el timón
teemon

la caña del
timon
canya del
teemon

el cabo de la vela
mayor *kabo de la*
bela mayor

preemareea; secondary:
escuela secundaria [f]
esskooela sekoondareea;
high school: **instituto de**
enseñanza media [m]
eenssteetooto de
ensenyantha medeea
science **ciencia [f]**
thyentheea
scissors **tijeras [f]**
teeherass
score **tanteo [m]** *tanteo*
to score a goal **marcar un**
gol *markar oon gol;* point:
marcar un tanto *markar*
oon tanto
Scotland **Escocia**
esskotheea
Scottish **escocés/a**
esskothess/a
to scratch (yourself)
rascarse *rasskarsse*
to scream **gritar** *greetar*

screen **pantalla** *pantalya*
scruffy **desaliñado/a**
dessaleenyado/a
sculpture **escultura [f]**
esskooltoora
sea **mar [m]** *mar*
seafood **mariscos [m]**
mareesskoss
seasick (to be seasick) **estar**
mareado/a *esstar*
mareado/a
season **estación/**
temporada [f] *esstatheeon*
temporada; season ticket:
(transport) **bono**
transporte [m] *bono*
transsporte
seat **asiento [m]** *assyento;*
chair: **silla [f]** *seelya*
second (time) **segundo**
[m] *segoondo;* second-
hand: **de segunda mano**
de segoonda mano

secret **secreto/a** *sekreto/a*
secretary **secretario/a** *sekretareeo/a*
to see **ver** *ber;* to see again: **volver a ver** *bolber a ber;* see you soon: **hasta luego/ hasta pronto** *assta looego/ assta pronto*
to seem **parecer** *parether*
selfish **egoísta [m/f]** *egoeessta*
self-service **autoservicio [m]/ self-service [m]** *aootosserbeetheeo/ self-serbees*
to sell **vender** *bender*
to send **enviar** *enbeear*
sense **sentido [m]** *senteedo;* it doesn't make sense: **no tiene sentido** *no tyene ssenteedo*
sensible **razonables** *rathonabless*
sensitive **sensible** *senseeble*
September **septiembres** *sseptyembress*
serious **serio/a** *sereeo/a*
service **servicio [m]** *serbeetheeo*
sewing **costura [f]** *kosstoora*
sex (gender) **sexo [m]** *sekkso;* intercourse: **relaciones sexuales [f]** *relatheeoness sekssooaless*
sexist **sexista [m/f]** *seksseessta*
sexy **sexy** *sekssee*
shade **sombra [f]** *ssombra;* in the shade: **a la sombra** *a la ssombra*
shame **vergüenza [f]** *bergooentha;* what a shame!: **¡qué pena!** *ke pena*
shampoo **champú [m]** *tshampoo*

shape **forma [f]** *forma*
to share **compartir** *komparteer*
shattered **agotado/a** *agotado/a*
to shave **afeitarse** *afeytarsse*
shaving cream **crema de afeitar [f]** *krema de afeytar;* foam: **espuma de afeitar [m]** *esspooma de afeytar*
she **ella** *elya*
sheet **sábana [f]** *sabana*
shirt **camisa [f]** *kameessa*
shock **susto [m]/shock [m]** *ssoossto/sshok*
shoe **zapato [m]** *thapato;* athletics shoes: **zapatos de deporte [m]** *thapatoss de deporte*
shop **tienda [f]** *tyenda*
shopping (to go shopping for clothes) **ir de compras** *eer de komprass;* for groceries **hacer la compra** *ather la kompra;* shopping centre: **centro comercial [m]** *thentro komertheeal;* window shopping: **ir de escaparates/ ir a mirar escaparates** *eer de esskaparatess/ eer a meerar esskaparatess*
short **corto/a** *korto/a;* short cut: **atajo [m]** *ataho;* short sighted: **miope** *myope*
shorts **pantalones cortos [m]** *pantaloness kortoss*
shoulder **hombro [m]** *ombro*
to shout **gritar** *greetar*
show **espectáculo [m]** *esspektakoolo*
to show **mostrar** *mosstrar;* to show off: **presumir** *presoomeer*
shower **ducha [f]** *dootsha*

shut **cerrado/a** *therrado/a;* shut up!: **¡cállate!** *kalyate*
shy **tímido/a** *teemeedo/a*
sick **enfermo/a** *enfermo/a;* to be sick (vomit): **vomitar** *bomeetar;* to feel sick: **estar mareado/a** *esstar mareado/a;* to be sick of: **estar harto de** *esstar arto de*
side **lado [m]** *lado,* or (of hill) **ladera [f]** *ladera*
sightseeing **visita turística [f]** *beesseeta tooreesteeka*
sign (with hand) **firma [f]** *feerma;* on road: **señal [f]** *senyal*
signature **firma [f]** *feerma*
Sikh **sic** *seek*
silence **silencio [m]** *seelentheeo*
silly **tonto/a** *tonto/a*
simple **simple** *seemple*
since **desde** *dessde*
to sing **cantar** *kantar*
singer **cantante [m/f]** *kantante*
single (ticket) **de ida** *de eeda;* unmarried: **soltero/a** *ssoltero/a*
Sir **señor** *senyor*
sister **hermana [f]** *ermana*
to sit down **sentarse** *ssentarsse*
sitting down **sentado/a** *ssentado/a*
size **talla [f]** *talya*
skate **patín [m]** *pateen*
skate board **monopatín [m]** *monopateen*
skating (ice-skating) **patinaje sobre hielo [m]** *pateenahe sobre yelo;* roller skating: **patinaje sobre ruedas [m]** *pateenahe sobre rooedass*
to ski **esquiar** *esskeear*

skiing **esquí [m]** *esskee;*
water skiing: **esquí
acuático [m]** *esskee
akooateeko;* to go skiing: **ir
a esquiar** *eer a esskeear;*
ski resort: **estación de
esquí [f]** *esstatheeon de
esskee*
skin **piel [f]** *pyel*
skirt **falda [f]** *falda*
skiver **irresponsable/
frescales* [m/f]**
*eerrressponssable/
fresskaless*
sky **cielo [m]** *thyelo*
slang **argot [m]** *argot*
to sleep **dormir** *dormeer;*
to sleep in (lazy): **quedarse
en la cama** *kedarsse en la
kama;* to sleep in (late):
quedarse dormido/a
kedarsse dormeedo/a; to
sleep with someone:
acostarse con alguien*
akostarsse kon algeeyen
sleeper (on train) **litera [f]**
leetera
sleeping bag **saco de
dormir [m]** *sako de
dormeer*
slice **rodaja [f]** *rodaha*
to slip **resbalar**
ressbalar
slob **dejado/a**
dehado/a
slow **lento/a** *lento/a*
slowly **despacio**
desspatheeo
sly **astuto/a**
asstooto/a
small **pequeño/a**
pekenyo/a
smart (cunning)
listillo/a
leessteelyo/a, or
(elegant) **elegante**
elegante
smell **olor [m]** *olor*

to smell **oler** *oler,* or (to
stink) **oler mal** *oler mal*
smile **sonrisa [f]** *sonreesa*
to smile **sonreir** *ssonreyr*
to smoke **fumar** *foomar;*
smoking sign: **fumadores**
foomadoress; non-
smoking: **no fumadores**
no foomadoress
snack **bocado [m]/
snack [m]** *bokado/
ssnack*
snail **caracol [m]** *karakol*
snake **serpiente [f]**
serpyente
sneaky **astuto/a**
asstooto/a
to sneeze **estornudar**
esstornoodar
to sniff **aspirar/ inhalar**
asspeerar/ eenalar
snobbish **esnob [m/f]**
essnob
snore **roncar** *ronkar*
snow **nieve [f]** *nyebe;*
snowball: **bole de nieve
[f]** *bole de nyebe*
so **tan** *tan;* or (as in "so
you see I could have
gone") **así que** *asseeke;*
so-so **asi así** *assee assee*

soaking **empapado/a**
empapado/a
soap **jabón [m]** *habon;*
soap-opera: **telenovela [f]/
culebrón [m]** *telenobela/
koolebron*

to ski **esquiar**

el teleférico *telefereeko*
la telesilla *teleseelya*
el trineo *treeneo*
el surf *soorf*
la pista *peessta*
el deslizador *dessleethador*
la cinta *la theenta*
las gafas *gafass*
fuera de pista *fooera de peessta*
el guante *gooante*
el teleski *teleskee*
el traje de esquiar *trahe de esskeear*
el palo de esquiar *palo de esskear*
la riñonera *rinyonera*
el pase *passe*
el plumas *ploomass*
las mallas *malyas*
le ski *skee*
el montículo *montekoolo*
la fijación *fihatheeon*
las botas de esquiar *botass de esskeear*

sob (to sob) **sollozar**
ssolyothar
soccer fútbol [m] *footbol*
society sociedad [f]
sothyedath
sock calcetín [m]
kaltheteen
socket (electrical) **enchufe
[m]** *entshoofe*
soft blando/a *blando/a;*
soft drink: **bebida sin
alcohol [f]** *bebeeda seen
alkohol*
software software [m]
software
soldier soldado [m]
soldado
solid sólido/a *soleedo/a*
some un poco de *oon
poko de;* some of them:
algunos/as *algoonoss/ass;*
some people: **alguna
gente/ cierta gente**
*algoona hente/ thyerta
hente*
somebody alguien *algyen;*
somebody else: **alguien
más** *algyen mass*
something algo *algo*
something else: **algo más**
algo mass
sometimes a veces
abethess
**somewhere en alguna
parte** *en algoona parte;*
somewhere else: **en otra
parte** *en otra parte*
son hijo [m] *eeho*
song canción [f]
kantheeon
soon pronto *pronto*
sorry (excuse me/forgive
me) **perdón** *perdon;* I'm
sorry: **lo siento** *lo syento*
sort clase [f]/tipo [m]
classe/ teepo
sound sonido [m]
ssoneedo

soup sopa [f] *ssopa*
south sur [m] *soor;* south
of: **al sur de** *al soor de*
**South America América
del Sur/Sudamérica**
*amereeka del
soor/soodamereeka*
**souvenir recuerdo
[m]/souvenir [m]**
rekooerdo/soobeneer
space espacio [m]
esspatheeo; room: **sitio [m]**
seeteeo
Spain España *esspanya*
Spanish español/española
esspanyol/esspanyola
spare (extra) **de sobra** *de
sobra;* spare part: **pieza de
repuesto [f]** *pyetha de
repooessto;* spare time:
tiempo libre [m] *tyempo
leebre*
to speak hablar *ablar*
speaker (loudspeaker)
altavoz [m] *altaboth*
special especial [m/f]
esspetheeal
speciality especialidad [f]
esspetheealeedath
speed velocidad [f]
belotheedath; at full speed:
a toda velocidad *a toda
belotheedath*
to spend (money) **gastar**
gasstar, or (time) **pasar**
passar
spice especia [f]
esspetheea
spicy picante [m/f]
peekante
spider araña [f] *aranya*
spinach espinacas [f]
esspeenakass
to spit escupir *esskoopeer*
to split (divide) **repartir**
reparteer; leave: **largarse**
largarsse; to split up:
separarse *ssepararsse*

to spoil (damage)
estropear *esstropear;* ruin:
arruinar *arrooenar*
spoiled (child) **mimado/a**
meemado/a
**spontaneous
espontáneo/a**
esspontaneo/a
spoon cuchara [f]
kootshara
sport deporte [m]
deporte; sports centre:
centro deportivo [m]
thentro deporteebo
sporty deportivo/a
deporteebo/a
spot (pimple) grano [m]
grano; place: **sitio [m]/
lugar [m]** *seeteeo/ loogar*
sprain esguince [m]
essgeenthee
spring (season) **primavera
[f]** *preemabera;* or (water)
manantial [m] *mananteeal*
square (in town) **plaza [f]**
platha; not trendy:
carroza/carca [m/f]
karrotha/ karka
squash (game) **squash [m]**
sskooassh
stadium estadio [m]
esstadeeoo
stairs escaleras [f]
esskalerass
stamp sello [m] *selyo*
to stand (bear) **soportar**
ssoportar; I can't stand: **no
soporto** *no ssoporto;* (not
sit) **estar de pie** *esstar de
pye;* (to stand up) **ponerse
de pie** *ponersse de pye;* (to
stand up for) **defender**
defender
stand-by (ticket, passenger)
lista de espera [f] *leessta
de esspera*
star (in sky/film) **estrella [f]**
esstrelya

start **principio [m]**
preentheepeeo; of race:
salida [f] *saleeda*
starter *(first course)*
entremeses [m]
entremessess
station (train/ underground/
radio) **estación [f]**
esstatheeon
to stay **quedarse**
kedarsse
steak **filete [m]** *feelete*
to steal **robar** *robar*
steep **empinado/a**
empeenado/a
step (footstep) **paso [m]**
passo, or (stair) **escalón [m]**
esskalon
stepbrother **hermanastro**
ermanasstro
stepfather **padrastro**
padrasstro
stepmother **madrastra**
madrasstra
stepsister **hermanastra**
ermanasstra
stereo (personal stereo)
walkman [m] *walkman*
stereotype **estereotipo[m]**
esstereotoopo
to stick (glue) **pegar** *pegar*
stiff **liso** *leesso;* to be/feel
stiff: **tener agujetas** *tener*
agoohetass
still (even now) **todavía**
todabeea; or (not moving)
inmóbil *eenmobeel*
to sting **picar** *peekar*
stingy (not generous)
tacaño/a *takanyo/a*
to stink **oler mal** *oler mal*
to stir **mover** *mober;* or
(cause trouble) **provocar un**
escándalo *probokar oon*
esskandalo
stomach **estómago [m]**
esstomago; or (tummy)
barriga [f] *barrreega*

stone **piedra [f]** *pyedra*
to stop **parar** *parar,* or
(prevent) **impedir**
eempedeer
storm **tormenta [f]**
tormenta
story **historia [f]**
eestoreea, or (plot)
argumento [m]
argoomento, or (in
newspaper) **artículo [m]**
arteekoolo
straight (not curved)
derecho/a *deretsho/a;* or
(directly) **directamente**
deerektamente, or (not gay),
heterosexual [m/f]
eterossekssooal; straight
ahead: **todo recto** *todo*
rekto
strange **extraño/a**
eksstranyo/a
stranger **extranjero/a**
eksstranhero/a
strawberry **fresa [f]** *fressa*
street **calle [f]** *kalye* or
(high/main road) **calle**
principal [f] *kalye*
preentheepal
strength **fuerza [f]**
fooertha
stress **tensión [f]**
tensseeon
strict **estricto/a**
esstreekto/a
strike (stop work) **huelga**
[f] *ooelga*
string **cuerda [f]** *kooerda*
striped **a rayas** *a rayass*
strong **fuerte [m/f]** *fooerte*
stubborn **cabezota [m/f]**
kabethota
stuck (unable to move)
bloqueado/a *blokeado/a;*
stuck up: **presumido/a**
presoomeedo/a
student **estudiante [m/f]**
esstoodeeante

to study **estudiar**
esstoodeear
stuff (things) **cosas [f]**
kosass
stunning **alucinante***
[m/f] *alootheenante;* she´s
stunning: **es imponente/**
alucinante *ess*
eemponente/ alootheenante
stupid **estúpido/a**
esstoopeedo/a; to act
stupid: **hacer el tonto**
ather el tonto; a stupid
thing: **una tontería** *oona*
tontereea
subconsciously
inconscientemente
eenkonssthyentemente
subject **sujeto [m]** *sooheto*
subtle **sutil [m/f]** *sooteel*
suburbs **afueras [f]**
afooerass
to succeed **tener éxito**
tener eksseeto
success **éxito [m]** *eksseeto*
such **tal/tan** *tal/tan*
suddenly **de repente** *de*
repente
suede **ante [m]** *ante*
to suffer **sufrir** *soofreer*
sugar **azúcar [m]** *athookar*
to suggest **sugerir**
soohereer
suit **traje [m]** *trahe*
to suit **sentar bien** *sentar*
byen; it suits you: **te sienta**
bien *te syenta byen*
suitcase **maleta [f]** *maleta*
summer **verano [m]**
berano; summer camp:
campamento de verano
[m] *kampamento de*
berano
sun **sol [m]** *sol;* sun block:
protección total [f]
protektheeon total; sun
cream: **leche bronceadora**
[f] *letshe brontheadora*

to sunbathe **tomar el sol**
tomar el ssol
sunburned (to be/get
sunburned) **quemarse**
kemarsse
Sunday **domingo [m]**
domeengo
sunglasses **gafas de sol**
[f] *gafass de ssol*
sunny **soleado/a**
ssoleado/a
sunset **puesta de sol [f]**
pooessta de ssol
sunstroke **insolación [f]**
enssolatheeon
supermarket
supermercado [m]
soopermerkado
superstitious
supersticioso/a
soopersteetheeosso/a
supper **cena [f]** *thena*
supplement
suplemento [m]
sooplemento
to suppose **suponer**
sooponer
supposed to **supuesto/a**
soopooessto/a
sure **seguro/a** *seegooro/a*

to surf **hacer surf/hacer
surfing** *ather soorf/ather
soorfeeng;* Internet:
navegar por la Internert
nabegar por la eenternert
surprise **sorpresa [f]**
ssorpressa
suspense **suspense [m]**
soospensse
to swallow **tragar** *tragar*
to swap **cambiar/
intercambiar** *kambeear/
eenterkambeear*
to swear **jurar** *hoorar*
swearword **palabrota [f]**
palabrota
sweat **sudor [m]** *soodor*
to sweat **sudar** *soodar*
sweater **jersey [m]** *herssey*
sweatshirt **sudadera [f]**
soodadera
sweet **caramelo [m]**
karamelo; or (sugary) **dulce
[m/f]** *doolthe;* or (cute)
mono/a, lindo/a *mono/a,
leendo/a*
to swim **nadar** *nadar;* or
(to go swimming/to go for a
dip) **ir a bañarse** *eer a
banyarsse*

swimming **natación [f]**
natatheeon; swimming
pool: **piscina [f]**
peesstheena; swimming
costume/trunks: **bañador
[m]** *banyador*
Switzerland **Suiza**
sooeetha
swollen **hinchado/a**
eentshado/a
synagogue **sinagoga [f]**
seenagoga
table **mesa [f]** *messa;* table
football: **futbolín [m]**
footboleen; **table tennis:
ping-pong [m]/tenis de
mesa [m]** *peeng-pong/
teneess de messa*
tacky (shoddy) **cutre* [m/f]**
kootre
to take **tomar/coger**
tomar/koher; or (to lead)
llevar *lyebar*
to take away **llevarse**
lyebarsse
to take off **quitarse**
keetarsse, or (plane)
despegar *desspegar;* to
take part: **participar**
parteetheepar

to sunbathe *tomar el sol*   to surf *hacer surfing*

la toalla *toalya*
la arena *arena*
la sombrilla *ssombreelya*
la duna *doona*
la tumbona *toombona*
el mar *mar*
el surfista *soorfeesta*
el biombo *beeombo*
la tabla de surf *tabla de soorf*
la leche bronceadora *letshe brontheadora*
la visera *veessera*
las gafas de sol *gafass de ssol*
la hamaca *amaka*
la ola *ola*
el colchón de aire *coltshon de aeere*
la pamela *pamela*

96

take away (food) **comida para llevar** *komeeda para lyebar*
to talk **hablar** *ablar*
talkative **hablador/a** *ablador/a*
tall **alto/a** *alto/a*
tampon **tampón [m]** *tampon*
tan **bronceado [m]** *brontheado*
tanned **moreno/a** *moreno/a*
tap **grifo [m]** *greefo*
tape (cassette) **cinta [f]** *theenta*
tart **tarta [f]** *tarta*
to taste (something) **probar** *probar*
taxi **taxi [m]** *takssee;* taxi stand: **parada de taxis [f]** *parada de taksseess*
tea (drink) **té [m]** *te;* afternoon snack: **merienda [f]** *meryenda;* evening meal: **merienda-cena [f]** *meryenda-thena*
to teach **enseñar** *ensenyar*
teacher **profesor/a** *profesor/a*

team **equipo [m]** *ekeepo;* to be part of a team: **formar parte de un equipo** *formar parte de oon ekeepo*
tear (in tears) **llorando** *lyorando;* to burst into tears: **ponerse a llorar** *ponersse a lyorar*
to tease **tomar el pelo/ hacer rabiar** *tomar el pelo/ ather rabeear;* to be joking: **bromear** *bromear*
teenager **adolescente [m/f]** *adolessthente*
telephone **teléfono [m]** *telefono*
television **televisión [f]/ tele [f]** *telebeesseeon/ tele;* on television: **en la tele** *en la tele;* cable TV: **televisión por cable [f]** *telebeesseeon por kable;* digital TV: **televisión digital [f]** *telebeesseeon deeheetal*
to tell **decir** *detheer;* or (to recount) **contar** *kontar;* to tell off: **regañar, echar la bronca*** *reganyar, etshar la bronka*

temperature **temperatura [f]** *temperatoora;* to have a temperature: **tener fiebre** *tener fyebre*
temporary **temporal/ provisional** *temporal/ probeeseeonal*
tennis **tenis [m]** *teneess*
tent **tienda [f]** *tyenda*
term (school or university) **trimestre [m]** *treemesstre;* beginning of term: **el comienzo del curso escolar** *el komyentho del koorsso esskolar*
terrible **terrible** *terreeble*
terrific **estupendo/a** *esstoopendo/a*
to terrify **aterrorizar** *aterrroreethar*
terrorism **terrorismo [m]** *terrroreessmo*
test (school) **exámen [m]** *ekssamen*
textbook **libro de texto [m]** *leebro de tekssto*
Thames (river) **el Támesis** *el tamesseess*
than **que** *ke* or (with numbers) **de** *de*
to thank **dar las gracias** *dar lass gratheeass*
thankful (for) **agradecido/a por** *agradetheedo/a por*
thank you **gracias** *gratheeass*
that **ese/esa** *esse/essa,* or (that over there) **aquel/ aquella** *akel/akelya,* or (that one) **ése/ésa** *esse/essa,* or (that one over there) **aquél/ aquella** *akel/akelya*
to thaw (food) **descongelar** *desskonhelar*
the **el/la/los/las** *el/la/loss/lass*

to swim *nadar*

el gorro de baño *gorrro de banyo*

de espaldas *de esspaldass*

el manguito/el brazalete *mangeeto/brathalete*

el bañador *banyador*

el crawl *krawl*

el flotador *flotador*

la brazada *brathada*

el bañador *banyador*

el biquini *beekeenee*

las bermudas *bermoodas*

theatre **teatro [m]** *teatro*

their **su** *soo*

them (as in "I see/know them) **los/las** *loss/lass*, or (as in "it's them" and after "of", "than", "to" and "with" etc) **ellos/ellas** *elyoss/elyass*

what time is it?
¿qué hora es?

las nueve y cuarto *las nooebe ee kooarto*

las tres (en punto) *las tress*

las ocho menos diez *las otsho menoss dyeth*

las once y veinte *las onthe ee beinte*

la una menos cuarto *la oona menoss kooarto*

las diez y media *las dyeth ee medeea*

mediodía/ medianoche *medeeo deeya/ medeeanotshe*

theme **tema [m]** *tema*; theme park: **parque de atracciones [m]/ parque temático [m]** *parke de atraktheeoness/ parke temateeko*

then **entónces** *entonthess*

therapy **terapia [f]** *terapeea*

there **allí** *alyee*; there is/are: **hay** *ay*

thermometer **termómetro [m]** *termometro*

these **estos/estas** *esstoss/esstass*; these ones: **éstos/éstas** *esstoss/esstass*

they **ellos/ellas** *elyoss/elyass*

thick (liquid, soup) **espeso/a** *espesso/a*, or (book) **grueso/a** *grooesso/a*, or (stupid) **torpe [m/f]** *torpe*

thief **ladrón/ladrona** *ladron/ladrona*

thin **delgado/a** *delgado/a*

thing **cosa [f]** *kossa*

things **cosas [f]** *kossass*

to think **pensar** *penssar*

thirsty (to be thirsty) **tener sed** *tener sseth*

this **este/esta** *esste/essta*; this one: **éste/ ésta** *esste/essta*

those **esos/esas** *essoss/ essass*; those over there **aquellos/aquellas** *akelyoss/akelyass*; those ones: **ésos/ésas** *essoss/essass*; those ones over there **aquéllos/ aquéllas** *akelyoss/ akelyass*

thread **hilo [m]** *heelo*

threat **amenaza [f]** *amenatha*

thrill **emoción [f]** *emotheeon*; cold: **escalofrío [m]** *esskalofreeo*

thriller **thriller [m]** *threeler*; **película de acción [f]** *peleekoola de aktheeon*

throat **garganta [f]** *garganta*; sore throat: **dolor de garganta [m]** *dolor de garganta*

through **por/ a través de** *por/ a trabess de*; to go through: **cruzar** *kroothar*

to throw **lanzar** *lanthar*; to throw away: **tirar** *teerar*; to throw up: **vomitar** *bomeetar*

thug **granuja [m/f]** *granooha*

Thursday **jueves [m]** *hooebess*

ticket **billete [m]/ ticket [m]** *beelyete/ teekket*; ticket machine: **distribuidora de billetes [f]** *deesstreebooeedora de beelyetess*; ticket office: **taquilla [f]** *takeelya*; ticket collector: **revisor [m]** *rebeessor*; ticket stamping machine: **distribuidora automática de sellos [f]** *deesstreebooeedora aootomateeka de selyoss*

to tickle **hacer cosquillas** *ather kosskeelyas*

tide **marea [f]** *marea*

to tidy up **ordenar** *ordenar*

to tie **atar** *atar*

tights **medias [f]** *medeeass*

time (hour) **hora [f]** *ora*; (occasion) **vez [f]** *beth*; on time: **puntual [m/f]** *poontooal*; to have time: **tener tiempo** *tener tyempo*; what time is it?: **¿qué hora es?** *ke ora ess*

timetable **horario [m]** *orareeo*

tin (can) **lata [f]** *lata;* tin opener: **abrelatas [m]** *abrelatass*

tinted (hair) **teñido** *tenyeedo;* glass: **matizado** *mateethado*

tiny **diminuto/a** *deemeenooto/a*

tip (end) **punta [f]** *poonta* or (money) **propina [f]** *propeena*

tired **cansado/cansada** *kanssado/kanssada*

tissue (hanky) **pañuelo de papel [m]** *panyooelo de papel*

to **a** *a*

toast **tostada [f]** *tosstada*

today **hoy** *oy*

together **juntos/as** *hoontoss/hoontass*

toilet **servicio/s [m]** *sserbeetheeo/ss;* toilet paper: **papel higiénico [m]** *papel eehyeneeko*

toll **peaje [m]** *peahe*

tomato **tomate [m]** *tomate;* tomato sauce: **salsa de tomate [f]** *ssalssa de tomate*

tomorrow **mañana** *manyana;* the day after tomorrow: **pasado mañana** *passdo manyana*

tongue **lengua [f]** *lengooa*

tonight **esta noche** *essta notshe*

too (too much) **demasiado** *demasseeado,* or (also) **también** *tambyen*

tool **herramienta [f]** *herrramyenta*

tooth **diente [m]** *dyente*

toothbrush **cepillo de dientes [m]** *thepeelyo de dyentess*

toothpaste **dentrífico [m]** *dentreefeeko*

top (bottle) **tapón [m]** *tapon;* or (not bottom, item of clothing) **parte de arriba [f]** *parte de arrreeba*

topless **topless [m]** *topless;* to sunbathe topless: **tomar el sol haciendo topless** *tomar el sol hathyendo topless*

torch (for pocket) **linterna [f]** *leenterna;* or (flaming) **antorcha [f]** *antortsha*

to touch **tocar** *tokar;* to touch wood: **tocar madera** *tokar madera*

tour (day trip) **excursión [f]** *eksskoorsseeon;* or (concerts) **gira [f]** *heera;* package tour: **viaje organizado [m]** *beeahe organeethado*

tourist **turista (m/[f]** *tooreessta;* tourist office: **oficina de turismo [f]** *ofeetheena de tooreessmo*

touristy **turístico/a** *tooreessteeko/a*

towards **hacia** *atheea*

towel **toalla [f]** *toalya*

town **ciudad [f]** *theeoodath;* town centre: **centro de la ciudad [m]** *thentro de la theeoodath;* or (old town) **casco viejo [m]/ parte antigua [f]** *kassko byeho/ parte anteegooa;* town hall: **ayuntamiento [m]** *ayoontamyento*

toy **juguete [m]** *hoogete*

traffic **tráfico [m]** *trafeeko;* traffic jam: **atasco [m]** *atassko;* traffic lights: **semáforos [m]** *ssemafoross*

trail (route) **camino/ sendero [m]** *kameeno/sendero*

train **tren [m]** *tren*

to train (sport) **entrenar** *entrenar;* training course: **curso de formación [m]** *koorsso de formatheon*

trainers **zapatillas de deporte [f]** *thapateelyass de deporte*

tramp **vagabundo [m]** *bagaboondo*

tools *las herramientas*

la caja de herramientas *caha de herrramyentass*

el martillo *marteelyo*

el destornillador de estrella *desstorneelyador de esstrelya*

el destornillador *desstorneelyador*

el tornillo *torneelyo*

las tenazas *tenathass*

el clavo *klabo*

la llave inglesa *lyabe eennglessa*

la llave *lyabe*

train *el tren*

el panel de salidas *panel de ssaleedass*

el panel de llegadas *panel de lyegadass*

la taquilla *takeelya*

el tren *tren*

el bar *bar*   **el vagón** *bagon*

no fumadores *no foomadoress*

el vagón-restaurante *vagon resstaoorante*

la litera *leetera*

el carro *karrro*

el jefe de estación *hefe de esstatheeon*

to translate traducir *tradootheer*
to travel viajar *beeahar*
travel agency **agencia de viajes [f]** *ahentheea de beeahess*
traveller **viajero/a;** *beeahero/a;* traveller's cheque: **cheque de viaje** *tsheke de beeahe [m]*

tree **árbol [m]** *arbol*
trendy (person) **moderno/a** *moderno/a;* or (clothes) **a la última** *a la oolteema*
trip (long) **viaje [m]** *beeahe,* or (short) **excursión [f]** *eksskoorsseeon*
triple **triple** *treeple;* triplets: **trillizos/as** *treelyeethoss/ass*
trolley (for baggage/ shopping) **carro [m]** *karrro*
trouble **problemas [m]** *problemass*
trousers **pantalones [m]** *pantaloness*
true **verdadero/a** *berdathero/a*
to trust **confiar** *konfeear*
truth **verdad [f]** *berdath*
to try **intentar** *eententar*
T-shirt **camiseta [f]** *kameesseta*
Tuesday **martes [m]** *martess*
tuna **atún [m]** *atoon*
tunnel **túnel [m]** *toonel*
to turn **girar** *heerar;* to turn around/back: **dar la vuelta/volver** *dar la booelta/bolber;* to turn down (music/heat): **bajar** *bahar;* to turn off (light/TV): **apagar** *apagar;* to turn on (light/TV): **encender** *enthender*
to turn up (music/heat) **subir** *soobeer,* or (to arrive) **llegar** *lyegar*
twin (brother/sister) **gemelo/a** *hemelo/a*

typical **típico/a** *teepeeko/a*
tyre **rueda [f]** *roeeda;* tyre pressure: **presión de las ruedas [f]** *presseeyon de lass rooedass*
ugly **feo/a** *feo/a*
umbrella **paraguas [m]** *paragooass*
unbelievable **increíble** *eenkreyble*
under **debajo de** *debaho de*
underground (trains) **metro [m]** *metro*
to understand **entender/ comprender** *entender/komprender*
underwear **ropa interior [f]** *ropa eentereeor*
unemployed person: **parado/a** *parado/a;* out of work: **en el paro** *en el paro*
unemployment **paro [m]** *paro*
unfortunately **desafortunadamente** *dessafortoonadamente*
United States **Estados Unidos [m]** *Esstadoss Ooneedoss*
university **universidad [f]** *ooneeberseedath*
unusual (rare) **raro/a** *raro/a;* original: **original** *oreeheenal*
up (to go up/walk up) **subir** *soobeer*
uptight **nervioso/a** *nerbeeosso/a*
urgent **urgente [m/f]** *oorhente*
us **nosotros/as** *nossotross/ass*
to use **utilizar/usar** *ooteeleethar/oossar*
used (to be used to) **estar acostumbrado/a** *esstar akoosstoombrado/a*

useful **útil** *ooteel*
useless (of no use) **inútil**
eenooteel; or (no good)
malo/a *malo/a*
usual (customary) **usual**
[m/f] *oossooal;* as usual:
como siempre *komo*
syempre
usually **normalmente**
normalmente
vacation **vacaciones [f]**
bakatheeoness
vaccination **vacuna [f]**
bakoona
valuables **objetos de valor**
[m] *obhetoss de balor*
vanilla **vainilla [f]**
baeeneelya
vegetable **verdura [f]**
berdoora
vegetarian **vegetariano/a**
behetareeano/a
vending machine
distribuidor automático
[m] *deesstreebooeedor*
aootomateeko
very **muy** *mooy;* very
much: **muchísimo**
mootsheeseemo
video **vídeo [m]**
beedeo,

view **vista [f]** *beessta;*
opinion: **opinión [f]**
opeeneeon
village **pueblo [m]**
pooeblo
vine **viña [f]** *beenya*
vineyard **viñedo [m]**
beenyedo
visit **visita [f]** *beesseeta*
to visit **visitar** *beesseetar*
vital **vital/esencial**
beetal/essentheeal
volleyball **voleibol [m]**
boleybol
vote **voto [m]** *boto*
wacky **chiflado/a,**
chalado/a *tsheeflado/a,*
tshalado/a
to waffle **meter el rollo/**
meter mucha paja* *meter*
el rolyo/ meter mootsha
paha
wage **sueldo [m]/ salario**
[m] *ssooeldo/ssalareeo*
waist **cintura [f]**
theentoora
waistcoat **chaleco [m]**
tshaleko
to wait **esperar** *essperar*
waiter **camarero [m]**
kamarero

waiting room **sala de**
espera [f] *ssala de esspera*
waitress **camarera [f]**
kamarera
to wake up **despertarse**
desspertarsse
Wales **País de Gales [m]**
paeess de galess
wall **pared [f]** *pareth*
walk **paseo [m]** *passeo*
to walk **andar** *andar*, or
(to go on foot) **ir a pie/ ir**
andando *eer a pye/ eer*
andando, or (to walk
around/about) **dar un**
paseo *dar oon passeo*
wallet **cartera [f]** *kartera*
walnut **nuez [f]** *nueth*
to want **querer** *kerer*
war **guerra [f]** *gerra*
wardrobe **armario [m]**
armareeo
warm (water) **templado/a**
templado/a; or (eg hands)
caliente *kalyente*
to warm up (things)
calentar *kalentar*, or
(people) **calentarse**
kalentarsse
warning **aviso [m]**
abeesso

water **el agua**

el agua mineral sin gas *agooa meeneral seen gass*

el cubito de hielo *coobeeto de yelo*

wine **el vino**

el vino blanco *beeno blanko*

el vino tinto *beeno teento*

el vino rosado *bino rosado*

la media botella *medeea botelya*

el jarro *harrro*

el agua mineral con gas *agooa meeneral kon gass*

la jarra *harrra*

un vaso de agua *basso de agooa*

el sacacorchos *sakakorthoss*

el tapón *tapon*

una copa de vino *kopa de beeno*

101

wart *verruga [f]*
berrrooga
to wash *lavar* labar, or
(yourself) *lavarse labarsse,*
or (to wash up) *lavar los
platos* labar loss platoss
washing (washing machine)
lavadora [f] labadora;
washing powder:
detergente [m]
deterhente; washing up:
platos [m] platoss;
washing-up liquid:
lavavajillas [m]
lababaheelyass
waste (of food/money etc)
desperdicio [m]
dessperdeetheeo; waste of
time: *pérdida de tiempo
[f]* perdeeda de tyempo
to waste (food/money)
desperdiciar
dessperdeetheear; or (time/
opportunity) *perder* perder
watch *reloj [m]* reloh
to watch (look at) *mirar*
meerar; or (keep an eye on)
vigilar beeheelar; watch
out!: *¡cuidado!* kooeedado
water *agua [m]* agooa;
waterfall: *cascada [f]*
kasskada
waterproof *impermeable*
eempermeable
wave (of hand) *señal [m]*,
or (on water) *ola [f]* ola

way (direction) *dirección
[f]* deerektheeon; or (route)
camino [m] kameeno; or
(manner) *manera [f]*
manera; or (to be/get in the
way) *molestar/estorbar*
molesstar/esstorbar; to get
one's own way: *salirse con
la suya* saleersse kon la
sooya; no way!: *¡ni hablar!*
nee ablar
we *nosotros/as*
nossotross/ass
weak *débil* debeel;
coffee/tea: *no muy fuerte*
no mooy fooerte
to wear *llevar* lyebar, or to
wear out (exhaust) *agotar*
agotar, or (overuse):
desgastar dessgasstar
weather *tiempo [m]*
tyempo; what's the weather
like?: *¿qué tiempo hace?*
ke tyempo athe; weather
forecast: *pronóstico del
tiempo [m]/ tiempo [m]*
pronossteeko del tyempo/
tyempo
Web site *página web [f]*
paheena web
wedding *boda [f]* boda
Wednesday *miércoles*
myerkoless
week *semana [f]* semana
weekend *fin de semana
[m]* feen de semana

weight *peso* pesso; to lose
weight: *adelgazar*
adelgathar; to put on
weight: *engordar* engordar
welcome *bienvenido/a*
byenbeneedo/a; you're
welcome!: *¡de nada!* de
nada
well *bien* byen; well-
behaved: *bien educado/a*
byen edookado/a; well-
cooked: *bien hecho/muy
hecho* byen etsho/mooy
etsho; well-known:
conocido/a konotheedo/a;
to be well: *estar bien*
esstar byen
west *oeste [m]* oesste
wet *mojado/a* mohado/a
what *qué* ke
wheel *rueda [f]* rooeda;
steering wheel: *volante [m]*
bolante
wheelchair *silla de ruedas
[f]* seelya de rooedass
when *cuándo* kooando
where *donde* donde
which *cuál/cuales*
kooal/kooaless; which
bike?: *¿qué bici?* ke
beethee
while (during) *mientras*
myentrass
white *blanco/a* blanko/a
who *quién* keeyen; whose:
de quién de keeyenn

weather
el tiempo

está
lloviendo
*essta
lyobyendo*

está nublado
essta nooblado

hace sol
athe sol

está nevando
essta nebando

whole **entero/a** *entero/a*
why **¿por qué?** *por ke*
wide **ancho/a** *antsho/a*
widow **viuda [f]** *beeooda*
widower **viudo [m]** *beeoodo*
wild (not tame) **salvaj** *salbah*
to win **ganar** *ganar*
wind **viento [m]** *byento*
window **ventana [f]** *bentana*, or (shop) **escaparate [m]** *esskaparte*
windscreen **parabrisas [m]** *parabreessass*; windscreen wiper: **limpiaparabrisas [m]** *leempeeaparabreessass*
windsurfer (board) **tabla de windsurfing** *tabla de weendsoorfeeng*, or (person) **windsurfista [m/f]** *weendsoorfeessta*
wine **vino [m]** *beeno*
winner **ganador/a** *ganador/a*
winter **invierno [m]** *eenbyerno*
wish **deseo [m]** *desseo*; best wishes (in a letter). **saludos cordiales** *saloodoss kordeealess*; Christmas: **Feliz Navidad** *feleeth nabeedath*; birthday: **Felicidades** *feleetheedadess*
to wish **desear** *dessear*
with **con** *kon*

without **sin** *seen*
witty **ingenioso** *inheneeosso*
wolf **lobo [m]** *lobo*
woman **mujer [f]** *mooher*
wonderful **maravilloso/a** *marabeelyosso/a*
wood **madera [f]** *madera*
wool **lana [f]** *lana*
word **palabra [f]** *palabra*; words (of song): **letra [f]** *letra*
work **trabajo [m]/ curro* [m]** *trabaho/ koorro*
to work **trabajar/currar*** *trabahar/koorrrar*; or (to function) **funcionar** *foontheeonar*
world **mundo [m]** *moondo*; World Wide Web: **World Wide Web [f]** *world waeed web*; out of this world: **maravilloso/a** *marabeelyosso/a*
worried **preocupado/a** *preokoopado/a*
to worry **preocuparse** *preokooparsse*
worse **peor** *peor*
worth (to be worth) **valer** *baler*
wrist **muñeca [f]** *moonyeka*
to write **escribir** *esskreebeer*
writer **escritor/a** *esskreetor/a*

wrong (incorrect) **falso/a** *falsso/a*; unfair: **injusto/a** *eenhoossto/a*; to be wrong/mistaken: **estar equivocado/a** *esstar ekeebokado/a*; what's wrong?: **¿qué pasa?** *ke passa*
to yawn **bostezar** *bosstethar*
year **año [m]** *anyo*
yellow **amarillo** *amareelyo*
yes **sí** *see*
yogurt **yogur [m]** *yogoor*
you (as in "you like him") **te/le/os/les** *te/le/oss/less*; or (as in "it's you" and after "and", "than") **tú/ usted/ vosotros-as/ ustedes** *too/ ossted/ bossotross-ass/ oosstedess*; or (after "for") **tí/ usted/ vosotros-as/ustedes** *tee/ oossted/ bossotross-ass/oosstedess*; or (as in "he knows you") **te/lo-a/os/los-as** *te/lo-a/oss/loss-ass*
young **jóven** *hoben*
your (to friend) **tu/ tus/ vuestro-a-os-as** *too/ tooss/ booesstro-a-oss-ass*; polite form: **su/sus** *ssoo/ssooss*
youth hostel **albergue juvenil [m]** *albergooe hoobeneel*
zip **cremallera [f]** *kremalyeera*

hay tormenta *ay tormenta*

hace frío *athe freeo*

hace calor *athe kalor*

hace viento *athe byento*

a *to*
a menudo *often*
a propósito *on purpose*
a través de *through*
a veces *sometimes*
abajo *below*
abanico [m] *fan*
abaratar *to lower the price (of)*
abarrotado/a (de gente) *jam-packed, very crowded*
abasto* (dar abasto) *to cope, to keep up*
abecedario [m] *alphabet*
abejas [f] *bees*
abeto [m] *fir tree*
abierto/a *open, open-minded*
abogado/a *lawyer*
abrazar *to hug*
abrebotellas [m] *bottle opener*
abridor [m] *can opener*
abrigo [m] *coat*
abril *April*
abrir *to open*
abrochar *to fasten (belt, shirt, etc)*
abuela [f] *grandmother*
abuelo [m] *grandfather*
aburrido/a *boring*
aburrirse *to get bored;* **estar aburrido/a:** *to be bored;* **ser aburrido/a:** *to be boring*
acabar *to finish;* **acabar de hacer algo:** *to have just done something*
acaecer *to happen, occur*
acampar *to camp*
acantilado [m] *cliff*
accidente [m] *accident*
aceite [m] *oil*
aceituna [f] *olive*
acento [m] *accent*

aceptar *to accept*
acercarse *to get/come near*
acontecimiento [m] *event*
acordarse *to remember*
acostarse *to go to bed*
actor [m] *actor*
actriz [f] *actress*
Acuario *Aquarius*
acuerdo [m] *agreement;* **estar de acuerdo:** *to agree*
adelantar *to overtake*
adelgazar *to lose weight, to get thin*
adicto/a *addict*
adiós *goodbye, bye*
adivinar *to guess*
adolescente [m/f] *teenager*
adorar *to love, to adore*
aduana [f] *customs*
adulto/a *adult*
adversario/a *opponent*
aerobic [m] *aerobics*
aerodeslizador [m] *hovercraft*
aerolínea [f] *airline*
aeropuerto [m] *airport*
afeitadora [f] *razor*
afeitarse *to shave*
afortunadamente *luckily*
afueras [f] *suburbs*
Africa *Africa*
agencia de viajes [f] *travel agency*
agenda [f] *diary*
agarrar *to grab*
agosto *August*
agotado/a *exhausted, shattered*
agotarse *to run out*
agradable *nice*
agradar *to please*
agradecer *to thank*

agradecido/a *grateful*
agresivo/a *aggressive*
agricultor/a *farmer*
agua [f] *water;* **agua mineral sin gas/con gas:** *still/sparkling mineral water*
aguacate [m] *avocado*
aguja [f] *needle*
agujero [m] *hole*
ahí *there*
ahora *now;* **ahora mismo:** *straight/right away*
aire [m] *air;* **al aire libre:** *in the open air;* **aire acondicionado [m]:** *air-conditioned*
aislado/a *isolated*
ajedrez [m] *chess*
al lado de *next to*
albaricoque [m] *apricot*
albergue juvenil [m] *youth hostel*
álbum [m] *album*
alcohol [m] *alcohol*
alcohólico/a *alcoholic*
alegre *cheerful*
alemán/alemana *German*
Alemania *Germany*
alergia [f] *allergy;* **alergia al polen:** *hayfever*
aleta [f] *flipper (diving)*
alfiler [m] *pin*
alfombra [f] *rug*
algo *something*
algodón [m] *cotton, cotton wool*
alguien *somebody*
algún/a/os/as *some, any*
alicates [m] *pliers*
aliento [m] *breath;* **sin aliento:** *out of breath*
alivio [m] *relief*
allí *there;* **por allí:** *over there*
almendra [f] *almond*
almohada [f] *pillow*

alojamiento [m] *accommodation*

alojar *to put someone up*

alpinismo [m] *mountaineering*

alpinista (m/f) *rock climber*

alquilar *to rent, to hire*

alrededor de *around*

altavoces [m] *loudspeaker*

alto/a *tall, high*

amable *kind*

amar *to love*

amargo/a *bitter*

amarillo *yellow*

ambos/as *both*

ambulancia [f] *ambulance*

amenaza [f] *threat*

América *America*

americano/a *American*

amigo/a *friend*

amistad [f] *friendship*

amor [m] *love;* **hacer el amor:** *to make love*

ampolla [f] *blister*

anacardo [m] *cashew nut*

añadir *to add*

ancho/a *wide*

ancla [m] *anchor*

andar *to walk*

anfitrión/a *host*

anillo [m] *ring*

animarse *to cheer up*

aniversario [m] *anniversary*

año [m] *year*

anoche *last night*

antes (de) *before;* **anteayer:** *the day before yesterday*

antibiótico [m] *antibiotic*

anticonceptivo [m] *contraceptive*

antiguo/a *old, antique*

antiséptico [m] *antiseptic*

anudar *to knot*

anular *to cancel*

anuncio [m] *advertisement;* **anuncios por palabras [m]:** *classified ads*

apagado/a *(switched) off*

apagar *to switch off*

aparcamiento [m] *car park, parking*

aparcar *to park*

apartamento [m] *flat*

apasionante *exciting*

apellido [m] *surname*

apetito [m] *appetite*

apodo [m] *nickname*

apostar *to bet*

apoyar *to support*

aprender *to learn*

apretar *to tighten/ press*

aprovecharse de *to take advantage of;* **¡que aproveche!:** *enjoy your meal!*

aproximadamente *approximately*

aquel/aquella *that (adj);* **aquellos/aquellas** *those ones (pronoun)*

aquí *here*

árabe *Arab*

araña [f] *spider*

árbitro [m] *umpire*

árbol [m] *tree*

arcoiris [m] *rainbow*

arena [f] *sand*

Argelia *Algeria*

argot [m] *slang*

argumento [m] *(reasoning) argument*

Aries *Aries*

armario [m] *cupboard, wardrobe*

arreglárselas* *to cope*

arroz [m] *rice*

arruinar *to ruin*

arte [m] *art*

artesanía [f] *craftship*

artículo [m] *article*

artista [m/f] *artist*

asado/a *grilled*

asaltar *to get mugged*

ascensor [m] *lift*

asegurarse *to make sure*

asesinato [m] *murder*

Asia *Asia*

asma [m] *asthma*

aspirina [f] *aspirin*

asqueroso/a *disgusting, revolting*

astuto/a *cunning*

asuntos [m] *business*

atacar *to attack, to get mugged*

atajo [m] *shortcut*

atar *to tie*

atasco [m] *traffic jam*

atención [f] *attention*

atractivo/a *attractive*

atrapar *to catch*

atreverse *to dare*

atroz [m/f] *outrageous*

atún [m] *tuna*

audiencia [f] *audience*

aumentar *to increase*

auricular [m] *phone receiver*

auriculares [m] *earphones*

Australia *Australia*

australiano/a *Australian*

autobús [m] *bus*

autocar [m] *coach*

automático/a *automatic*

autopista [f] *motorway*

autor/a *author*

autostopista [m/f] *hitch-hiker*

avanzar *to go/ move forwards*

avellana [f] *hazelnut*

aventurero/a *adventurous*
avería [f] *breakdown*
avión [m] *plane*
avisar *to warn;* **aviso [m]:** *warning*
avispa [f] *wasp*
ayer *yesterday*
ayuda [f] *help, aid*
ayudar *to help*
ayuntamiento [m] *town hall*
azafata [f] *flight attendant*
azúcar [m] *sugar*
azul *blue*

bacalao [m] *cod*
bailar *to dance*
bailarín/a *dancer*
baile [m] *dance*
bajar *to go/walk down, to lower*
bajarse *to get off*
bajo/a *low, short;* **abajo:** *down below, downstairs*
balcón [m] *balcony*
balde [m] *bucket*
ballet [m] *ballet*
balón [m] *ball*
baloncesto [m] *basketball*
balsa [f] *raft*
bañador [m] *swimsuit*
bañarse *to go for a swim, to take a bath*
banco [m] *bench, bank*
bandera [f] *flag*
bañador [m] *swimsuit*
baño [m] *bath*
bar [m] *bar*
baraja [f] *deck (of cards)*
baratillo [m] *second hand things/market*
barba [f] *beard*

barca [f] *boat (small)*
barco [m] *boat (big);*
barco de vela [m]: *sailing boat*
barra [f] *bar;* **barra de labios [f]:** *lipstick*
barrera [f] *gate*
barriga [f] *tummy, belly*
barrio [m] *neighbourhood*
bastante *quite, enough*
bastón [m] *stick for walking*
basura [f] *rubbish*
bata [f] *dressing gown*
bate [m] *bat*
batería [f] *battery, drums*
bebé [m] *baby*
beber *to drink*
bebida [f] *drink*
beca [f] *grant*
belga [m/f] *Belgian*
bermudas [f] *bermuda shorts*
besar *to kiss*
beso [m] *kiss*
biblioteca [f] *library*
bicho [m] *bug;* **¿qué bicho te ha picado?:** *what's the matter with you?/what's got into you?;* **bicho raro:** *weird person;* **mal bicho:** *nasty piece of work*
bicicleta/bici [f] *bike*
bien *well;* **estar bien:** *to be well;* **bien frío/a:** *nice and cold*
bienvenida [f] *welcome, reception*
bienvenido/a *welcome*
bigote [m] *moustache*
billete [m] *ticket, note*
biquini [m] *bikini*
blanco/a *white*
blando/a *soft*
boca [f] *mouth*

bocado [m] *snack or bit (of bridle)*
boda [f] *wedding*
bodega [f] *cellar for wine*
bolígrafo [m] *pen*
bollo [m] *small baguette*
bolos [m] *bowling*
bolsa [f] *carrier bag;* **la Bolsa:** *Stock Exchange*
bolsillo [m] *pocket*
bolso [m] *handbag*
bomba [f] *bomb, pump*
bomberos [m] *fire brigade*
bombilla [f] *lightbulb*
bondadoso/a *caring*
bonito/a *nice, pretty (things)*
bono transporte [m] *season ticket*
borracho/a *drunk*
borrar *to rub out, to erase*
bosque [m] *forest*
bostezar *to yawn*
bota [f] *boot;* **bota de goma [f]:** *welly;* **botas de montar:** *riding boots*
botavara [f] *sailing boom*
bote de vela [m] *sailing dinghy*
botella [f] *bottle*
botiquín [m] *first aid box*
botón [m] *button*
boya [f] *buoy*
bragas [f] *knickers*
bravo/a *brave*
braza [f] *breast-stroke*
brazaletes [m]/ manguitos [m] *armband (for swimming)*
brazo [m] *arm*
brida [f] *bridle (for riding)*
brillar *to shine*
brocha [f] *paintbrush*

broche [m] *brooch*
brocheta [f] *kebab*
broma [f] *joke*
bromear *to joke*
bronceado [m] *tan*
brújula [f] *compass*
bruto/a *thug*
buceador/a *diver*
bucear *to dive*
buceo [m] *diving, scuba diving*
buen (hace buen tiempo) *it's fine weather*
buenas noches *good night*
buenas tardes *good afternoon/good evening*
bueno/a *good*
bufanda [f] *scarf*
búho [m] *owl*
burlarse de *to make fun of...*
burrada [f]* *loads*
burro [m] *donkey*
buscar *to look for*

caballeros [m] *gentlemen*
caballo [m] *horse*
cabeza [f] *head*
cabezota *stubborn*
cabina [f] *cabin, phone booth*
cabra [f] *goat*
cacahuete [m] *peanut*
cacerola [f] *saucepan*
cacto [m] *cactus*
cada *each*
cada uno/a *each one*
cadena [f] *chain, hi-fi system*
caducado/a *no longer valid*
caerse *to fall*
café [m] *coffee, café*

solo: *black coffee;* **café con leche:** *white coffee*
caja [f] *box;* **caja de herramientas** [f]: *tool box*
caja fuerte [f] *safe (box for valuables)*
cajero [m] *cash dispenser*
calcetín [m] *sock*
calculadora [f] *calculator*
caldo [m] *broth*
calefacción [f] *heating*
calendario [m] *calendar*
calentar *to warm up*
calidad [f] *quality*
caliente [m/f] *hot*
callarse *to be/keep quiet, to shut up*
calle [f] *street*
callejón [m] *alleyway*
callos [m] *tripe*
calma [f] *calm*
calmarse *to cool/calm down;* **¡cálmate!:** *cool down!*
calor [m] *heat*
caloría [f] *calorie;* **bajo en calorías:** *low-calorie*
calzoncillos [m] *boxer shorts*
cama [f] *bed*
cámara de vídeo [f] *video camera*
cámara fotográfica [f] *camera*
camarero/a *waiter/waitress*
cambiar *to change*
cambio [m] *change, exchange;* **oficina de cambio** [f]: *foreign exchange office;* **tipo de cambio** [m]: *exchange rate;* **cambio de sentido** [m]/**media vuelta*** [f] *U-turn*
camino [m] *way, route*

camión [m] *lorry*
camisa [f] *shirt*
camiseta [f] *T-shirt*
campamento [m] *children's summer camp*
campeón/a *champion*
camping [m] *campsite*
camping gas [m] *camping stove*
campo [m] *countryside, football pitch*
caña del timón [f] *sailing tiller*
Canadá *Canada*
canal [m] *channel, TV channel;* **el canal de la Mancha:** *the Channel tunnel*
cancelar *to cancel*
Cáncer *Cancer*
canción [f] *song*
candado [m] *padlock*
canoa [f] *canoe*
cañón [m] *canon*
cansado/a *tired*
cantante [m/f] *singer*
cantar *to sing*
cantidad [f] *quantity;* **cantidades industriales*:** *tons, loads*
cantimplora [f] *water bottle*
canto [m] *boulder*
capital [f] *capital*
Capricornio *Capricorn*
cara [f] *face;* **cara a cara:** *face to face;* **poner buena cara:** *to look pleased;* **poner mala cara:** *to pull a long face;* **¡qué cara tienes!:** *what a cheek you've got!;* **jugar a cara o cruz:** *to toss a coin*
caracol [m] *snail*
caramelo [m] *sweet*
caravana [f] *camper van*
cárcel [f] *prison*

cardenal [m] *bruise*
carnaval [m] *carnival*
carne [f] *meat;* **carne de vaca:** *beef;* **carne asada [f]:** *roast meat;* **carnero [m]:** *mutton*
carnicería [f] *butcher's*
caro/a *expensive*
carrera [f] *carrier, race*
carrete [m] *film (for camera)*
carretera [f] *road;* **carretera de circunvalación [f]** *ring road, bypass*
carro [m] *chariot, trolley (shopping, luggage)*
carta [f] *letter, menu;* **carta de amor [f]:** *love letter*
cartel [m] *poster, notice*
cartera [f] *wallet*
casa [f] *house, home*
casarse *to marry*
cascada [f] *waterfall*
casco [m] *helmet, hoof*
casete [m] *cassette, cassette player*
casi *nearly*
caso [m] *case (occurrence)*
castaña [f] *chestnut*
castigar *to punish*
castillo [m] *castle*
catalejos [m] *binoculars*
catedral [f] *cathedral*
católico/a *Catholic*
causa [f] *cause*
caverna [f] *cave*
cazadora [f] *bomber style jacket*
cazuela [f] *pan*
CD [m] *CD, CD player*
cebolla [f] *onion*
cebra [f] *zebra*
ceder *to give in, to give way*

celebrar *to celebrate*
celoso/a *jealous*
cementerio [m] *cemetery*
cena [f] *supper*
cenar *to have supper*
cenicero [m] *ashtray*
centro [m] *centre;* **centro comercial:** *shopping centre;* **centro de la ciudad [m];** *city centre*
cepillar *to brush*
cepillo [m] *brush, hairbrush*
cera [f] *wax, pavement*
cerca *near*
cerdo [m] *pork, pig*
cereal [m] *cereal*
cerebro [m] *brain*
cereza [f] *cherry*
cero *zero*
cerrado/a *closed*
cerradura [f] *lock (on door, drawer, etc.)*
cerrar *to close;* **cerrar con llave:** *to lock*
cerveza [f] *beer;* **cerveza rubia [f]:** *lager;* **cerveza amarga [f]:** *bitter*
césped [m] *lawn;* **no pisar el césped:** *keep off the grass*
cesta [f] *basket*
chaleco [m] *waistcoat;* **chaleco salvavidas [m]:** *life jacket*
champiñón [m] *mushroom*
champú [m] *shampoo*
chándal [m] *track suit*
chaqueta [f] *jacket*
charco [m] *puddle*
charcutería [f] *meat (such as ham, salami, pate etc.) or shop selling them*
charlar *to chat*

cheque [m] *cheque*
cheque de viaje [m] *traveller's cheque*
chica [f] *girl*
chico [m] *boy*
chinchón [m] *bump*
chiste [m] *joke*
chocar contra *to bump into*
chocolate [m] *chocolate*
chuleta [f] *chop*
ciclista [m/f] *biker*
ciego/a *blind*
cielo [m] *sky*
ciencia [f] *science*
cierre [m] *closure, fastening*
cifras [f] *figures*
cigarro [m] or pito* [m] *cigarette*
cine [m] *cinema*
cinta [f] *tape;* **cinta adhesiva [f]:** *adhesive tape*
cintura [f] *waist*
cinturón [m] *belt*
circular *to move along*
ciruela [f] *plum*
cita [f] *date, appointment*
ciudad [f] *town, city*
clarinete [m] *clarinet*
claro/a *clear*
clásico/a *classical*
clavo [m] *nail*
claxon [m] *horn (car)*
cliente [m] *client*
climatizado/a *air-conditioned*
clip [m] *clip*
cobarde *coward*
cobrador *conductor (bus)*
cobro revertido *reversed charges (phone)*
coche [m] *car*
cocido [m] *stew with chickpeas*
cocido/a *boiled*

cocina [f] *kitchen, stove*
cocinar *to cook*
cocinero/a *cook, chef*
coco [m] *coconut*
código postal [m] *post code*
codo [m] *elbow*
cofre [m] *chest/ trunk/ box*
coger *to catch (e.g the bus)*
cojonudo/a *brilliant*
cola [f] *tail, queue;* **hacer cola:** *to queue*
colchón [m] *mattress*
coleccionar *to collect*
colegio [m] *school*
colgar *to hang up (things, telephone)*
coliflor [f] *cauliflower*
colina [f] *hill*
collar [m] *necklace*
color [m] *colour*
columna [f] *spine*
colorete [m] *blusher*
combatir *to fight*
comedia [f] *comedy*
comedor [m] *dining room*
comenzar *to start*
comer *to eat, to have lunch*
comestible [m] *foodstuffs*
cometa [f] *kite*
comida [f] *food, lunch, meal*
como siempre *as usual*
cómo *how*
como *like, as*
cómodo/a *comfortable*
compañía [f] *company, firm*
compartir *to share*
completo/a *full, booked up*
compra [f] *shopping*

comprar *to buy*
comprender *to understand*
común *common*
con *with*
con soltura *fluently*
concha [f] *shell*
concierto [m] *concert*
concurso [m] *contest, game show*
condón [m] *condom*
conducir *to drive*
conductor [m] *driver*
conejo [m] *rabbit*
confianza [f] *trust*
confitería [f] *confectionery*
conforme a la ley judaica *kosher*
confrontar *to confront*
confundir *to mix up, to confuse*
congelar *to freeze*
conejo [m] *rabbit*
congelar *to freeze*
conmigo *with me*
conocer *to meet, to know*
conocido/a *famous, well-known*
consejo [m] *advice*
consigna [f] *left-luggage office*
consola [f] *console*
constipado/a (estar constipada/o) *to have a cold*
construir *to build*
consulado [m] *consulate*
contagioso/a *contagious*
contaminación [f] *pollution*
contar *to tell (a story), to count*
contento/a *happy, pleased*
contestador

automático [m] *answering machine*
contigo *with you*
continuar *to follow, to carry on*
contra *against*
contrario *opposite*
controlar *to control*
copiar *to copy*
coquetear *to flirt*
corage [m] *bravery, courage*
corazón [m] *heart, apple core;* **tener el corazón partido:** *to be heart-broken*
corbata [f] *tie*
Córcega *Corsica*
cordero [m] *lamb*
coro [m] *choir*
correcto/a *correct*
corredor [m] *corridor, gallery*
correo [m] *post, mail*
Correos *post office*
correr *to run*
correspondencia [f] *connection (trains);* **amigo/a por correspondencia:** *pen pal*
corrida [f] *bullfight*
corriente *ordinary*
cortar *to cut*
corte [m] *cut, type of ice cream*
cortés *polite*
cortinas [f] *curtains*
corto/a *short (things);* **corto/a de miras:** *narrow-minded*
cosa [f] *thing*
cosas [f] *things, stuff*
coser *to sew*
cosmopolita *cosmopolitan*
costa [f] *coast*
costar *to cost*

costumbre [f] *custom, habit;* **estar acostumbrado/a:** *to be used to*
cotilla [m/f] *gossip (a person)*
cotillear *to gossip*
cotilleo [m] *gossip*
crecer *to grow*
creer *to believe*
cremallera [f] *zip*
crepe [m] *pancake*
criar *to bring up*
crin [f] *mane (of horse)*
crisis [f] *crisis*
cristal [m] *glass*
cristiano/a *Christian*
criticar *criticize*
crol [m] *crawl (swiming)*
cruce [m] *crossroads*
crucigrama [m] *crossword*
crudo/a *raw*
crujir *to crackle*
cruz [f] *cross*
cruzar *to cross, to go through*
cuaderno [m] *notebook*
cuadra [f] *stables*
cuadro [m] *picture*
¿cúal? *which (one)?*
cualquiera *any, anyone*
cuando *when*
cuánto *how much*
cuántos/as *how many*
cuarto [m] *quarter;* **las nueve y cuarto:** *quarter past nine*
cubierto/a *covered*
cubo [m] *bucket;* **cubo de la basura [m]:** *rubbish bin*
cubrecama [m] *bedspread*
cucaracha [f] *cockroach*
cuchara [f] *spoon*
cuchilla [f] *razor-blade*

cuchillo [m] *knife*
cuello [m] *collar, neck*
cuenco [m] *bowl*
cuenta [f] *bill*
cuento [m] *story*
cuerda [f] *string, rope*
cuero [m] *leather*
cuerpo [m] *body*
cueva [f] *cave*
cuidado [m] *care;* **tener cuidado:** *to be careful;* **¡cuidado!:** *watch out!*
cuidar *to look after*
culebrón [m]* *soap opera*
culpa [f] *guilt;* **es tu culpa:** *it's your fault*
culpable *guilty*
culto [m] *cult*
cultural *cultural*
cumpleaños [m] *birthday*
cuñado [m] *brother-in-law*
curar *to cure*
curioso/a *curious, odd, nosy*
currar* *to work*
curso de formación [m] *training (for a job)*
curva [f] *bend*

dado [m] *dice*
daño [m] *harm, damage*
dar asco *to disgust*
dar la bienvenida *to welcome*
dar *to give*
dardo [m] *dart*
darse cuenta *to realize*
darse prisa *to hurry*
De acuerdo *OK*
de pie *standing*
de prisa *quickly*
de repente *suddenly*

de *from, of*
debajo de *under*
deber *to have to, to owe*
deberes [m] *homework*
débil *weak*
debilidad [f] *weakness*
decepcionado/a *disappointed*
decidir *to decide*
decir *to say*
dedo [m] *finger*
defensa [f] *defence*
degustación [f] *tasting*
dejar *to let, to leave;* **dejar en paz:** *to leave alone;* **dejar caer:** *to drop*
delante de *in front of*
delgado/a *thin*
delicioso/a *delicious*
delirar *to be delirious*
demasiado *too much*
demasiados/as *too many*
democracia [f] *democracy*
demoler *to demolish*
dentera [f] *the shivers*
dentista [m/f] *dentist*
dentrífico [m] *toothpaste*
dentro *inside*
depender *to depend*
dependiente/a *shop assistant*
deporte [m] *sport*
deportivo/a *sporty*
depósito [m] *deposit, payment*
deprimente [m/f] *depressing*
deprimido/a *depressed*
deprisa *quickly*
derecha [f] *right;* **a la derecha:** *on the right*
derecho [m] *right, law;* **derechos humanos [m]:** *human rights*

derretirse to melt
derrochar to waste (resources)
desacierto [m] mistake
desafortunadamente unfortunately
desagradable [m/f] unpleasant
desaliñado/a scruffy
desaparecer to disappear
desastre [m] disaster; ¡qué desastre!: what a disaster!
desayuno [m] breakfast
descafeinado decaffeinated
descalzo/a barefoot
descansar to rest, to have a break
descanso [m] break, rest, interval, intermission
descapotable open top car
descaro [m] nerve, cheek
descifrar to decipher, to figure out
descompresor [m] (diving) regulator
describir to describe
descubrir to discover
descuento [m] discount
desde since
desear to wish
deseo [m] wish
deshacerse de to get rid of ...
desierto [m] desert
deslizar to slip, to slide
desmayarse to faint
desnudarse to undress
desnudo/a naked
desodorante [m] deodorant
desorden [m] mess
despacio slowly
despegar to take off

desperdiciar to waste (squander)
despertador [m] alarm clock
despertarse to wake up
despilfarrar to waste (money)
después after
destornillador [m] screwdriver
destrozar to bust (break)
destruir to destroy
desván [m] attic
desventaja [f] drawback, disadvantage
desviación [f] detour
detalle [m] detail
detener to stop
detergente [m] washing powder
detrás (de) behind
devolución [f] refund
devolver to pay back, to give back
día [m] day; **día libre** [m]: day off; **al día**: up-to-date
diabético/a diabetic
dialecto [m] dialect
diario [m] personal diary
diarrea [f] diarrhoea
dibujar to draw
dibujo [m] drawing; **dibujos animados** [m]: cartoons
diccionario [m] dictionary
diciembre December
diente [m] tooth
diferente [m/f] different
difícil difficult
dinero [m] money; **dinero efectivo/metálico**: cash
Dios god
diplomático/a diplomatic, tactful

dirección [f] direction, address
directo/a direct; **en directo**: live
director/a director
disco [m] disk, record
discutir to argue, to discuss
diseño [m] design, pattern
disputa [f] argument
disquete [m] floppy disk
distribuidor [m] distributor; **distribuidor automático** [m]: vending machine; **distribuidor de billetes** [m]: ticket machine
divertido/a fun, funny
divertirse to have fun
dividir (entre) to share (with)
divorciado/a divorced
doblar to dub (film), to fold
doble double
docena [f] dozen
documental [m] documentary
documento [m] document
dólar [m] dollar
dolor [m] ache, pain; **tener dolor de cabeza**: to have a headache
dolor de garganta [m]: sore throat
doloroso/a painful
domingo Sunday
donde where
dormir to sleep
dormitorio [m] bedroom
droga [f] drug
drogadicto/a drug addict
ducha [f] shower
dudar to hesitate

dulce *sweet (adj)*
dunas [f] *dunes*
durante *during*

echar de menos *to miss*
echar una mano *to give a hand*
ecología [f] *ecology*
edad [f] *age*
edificio [m] *building*
editor/a *editor*
edredón [m] *duvet*
educación [f] *education*
educado/a *polite*
egoísta *selfish*
ejercicio [m] *exercise*
el último/la última *last, latest*
él *he*
elástico/a *elastic*
elección [f] *election, choice*
eléctrico/a *electric*
elegante [m/f] *elegant*
elegir *to choose*
ella *she*
embajada [f] *embassy*
embalse [m] *reservoir*
embarazada *pregnant*
embarazoso *embarrassing*
embarque [m] *boarding;*
tarjeta de embarque [f]: *boarding pass/card*
emborracharse *to get drunk*
emergencia [f] *emergency*
emocionante *exciting*
empanada [f] *turnover*
empinado/a *steep*
empujar *to push*
en otra parte *somewhere else*

en *at, in*
enamorado/a *in love;*
estar enamorado/a: *to be in love*
enamorarse *to fall in love*
encantar *to like, to love*
encargarse de *to take care of*
encender *to light, to switch on*
enchufar *to plug in*
enchufe [m] *plug*
encima (de) *on top;* **por encima de:** *above*
encontrar *to find;*
encontrarse a gusto: *to feel comfortable;*
encontrarse con: *to meet with (someone)*
enero *January*
enfadado/a *upset, annoyed, angry*
enfadarse *to get angry*
enfermera [f] *nurse*
enfermo/a *ill, sick*
enfrente de *opposite*
engañar *to cheat*
engordar *to get fat, to put on weight*
enhorabuena *congratulations*
enlace [m] *connection (planes)*
enrollar *to roll up, to wind up*
ensalada [f] *salad;*
ensalada mixta [f]: *mixed salad*
ensayar *to rehearse*
ensayo [m] *rehearsal*
enseñar *to teach, to show*
entender *to understand*
entendido *understood*
entero/a *whole*
entónces *then*

entrada [f] *entrance;*
entrada gratis [f]: *free entry*
entre *between*
entrenamiento [m] *training (sport)*
entrenar *to train*
entrevista [f] *interview*
entusiasmado/a *excited*
entusiasta *enthusiast*
enviar *to send*
epiléptico *epileptic*
equipaje [m] *luggage*
equipo [m] *team*
equitación [f] *riding*
equivocado/a *wrong;*
estar equivocado/a: *to be wrong*
equivocarse *to make a mistake*
erótico/a *erotic*
error [m] *mistake*
escala [f] *stopover (on journey)*
escalada [f] *climbing, rock climbing*
escalar *to climb*
escaleras [f] *stairs;*
escaleras mecánicas [f]: *escalator*
escalofrío [m] *shiver*
escandaloso/a *scandalous, shocking*
escapar *to escape, run away*
escaño [m] *bench, seat*
escaparate [m] *shop window*
escarcha [f] *frost (covering)*
escarpado/a *steep*
escayola [f] *plaster*
escena [f] *scene*
escenario [m] *stage*
escocés/a *Scottish*
Escocia *Scotland*

esconder to hide
Escorpio Scorpio
escotado/a low-cut
escribir to write
escritor/a writer
escuchar to listen
escuela [f] school;
escuela de bellas artes
[f]: art school
ese/esa that (adj)
ése/ésa that one
(pronoun)
ésos/ésas those ones
(pronoun)
espacio [m] espace
espalda [f] back
España Spain
especia [f] spice
especialidad [f]
speciality
espectáculo [m] show
especular to speculate
espejo [m] mirror
espeleología [f]
caving
esperar to wait, to hope
espeso/a thick
espina [f] fish bone
espinacas [f] spinach
espíritu [m] spirit
esponja [f] sponge
espontáneo/a
spontaneous
espuma [f] foam,
mousse
esquiar to ski; **esquí**
náutico [m]: water-skiing
esquina [f] corner
estación [f] (**estación**
de trenes [f]) railway
station; **estación de**
autobuses [f]: bus station;
estación de esquí [f]: ski
resort; **estación de metro**
[f]: tube station
estadio [m] stadium
Estados Unidos United

States
estanco [m] shop (where
you can buy cigarettes,
stamps, phonecards, etc.)
estantería [f] shelf
estar constipado/a
to have a cold
estar to be; **estar en**
números rojos*: to be
overdrawn
estatua [f] statue
este east; **los países del**
este: eastern Europe
este/a this (adj)
éste/ésta
this one (pronoun)
esto this (pronoun)
estómago [m] stomach
estornudar to sneeze
estos/as these (adj)
éstos/éstas
these ones (pronoun)
estrechar la mano
to shake hands
estrecho/a narrow
estrella [f] star
estreñido/a constipated
estribo [m] stirrup
estropeado/a out of
order
estropear to damage, to
spoil
estudiante [m/f]
student
estudios [m] studies
estufa [f] heater, stove
estupendo/a terrific,
great
estúpido/a stupid
Europa Europe
evidente obvious
evitar to avoid
exagerado/a
exaggerated, over the top
exagerar to exaggerate
exámen [m] exam, test
exasperante [m/f]

nerve-racking
excedente [m] surplus
exceder to exceed
excelente excellent
excéntrico/a eccentric
excepción [f] exception
excepto except
exceso de equipaje
[m] excess baggage
excursión [f] day trip
éxito [m] success, hit
exótico/a exotic
experiencia [f]
experience
expirar to expire
explicar to explain
explotar to explode
exposición [f] exhibition
exterior outside
extranjero/a foreigner;
en el extranjero: abroad
extraño/a strange, odd,
weird
extraordinario/a
extraordinary

fábrica [f] factory
fabricar to manufacture
fácil easy
facturar to check in
(luggage)
falda [f] skirt
fallar to fail
falso/a false
falta [f] fault
faltar to be missing
familia [f] family
famoso/a famous
fantástico/a fantastic
farmacia [f] chemist's
shop, pharmacy
faro [m] headlight,
lighthouse
fascinante fascinating
fastidiar to annoy

fastidio [m] *nuisance*
fastidioso *annoying*
febrero *February*
fecha [f] *date (calendar)*
felicitar *to congratulate*
feliz *happy*
feminista *feminist*
fenomenal *brilliant*
feo/a *ugly*
feria [f] *funfair*
ferretería [f] *hardware shop*
ferrocarril [m] *railway*
festejar *to celebrate*
fideos [m] *noodles*
fiebre [f] *fever*
fiebre del heno [f] *hayfever*
fiel *faithful, loyal*
fiesta [f] *party;* **hacer una fiesta:** *to party*
fijación [f] *binding (ski)*
fijar *to fix*
filete [m] *steak*
filosofía [f] *philosophy*
fin [m] *end;* **fin de semana [m]:** *weekend*
fingir *to pretend*
fino/a *fine (adj)*
firma [f] *signature*
flash [m] *flash (camera)*
flauta [f] *flute*
flipper [m] *pinball*
flor [f] *flower*
flotar *to float*
fobia [f] *phobia*
fondo [m] *the bottom*
forma [f] *shape;* **en forma:** *fit*
forrado/a* *loaded (with money)*
foto [f] *photo*
fotógrafo [m] *photographer*
frambuesa [f] *raspberry*
francés/a *French*
Francia *France*

franela [f] *flannel*
freno [m] *brake*
fresa [f] *strawberry*
frescales* [m/f] *a skiver*
fresco/a *fresh, chilled*
frigorífico [m] *fridge*
frijol [m] *kidney bean*
frío [m] *cold*
frisbee *frisbee*
frito/a *fried*
frontera [f] *border*
fruta [f] *fruit*
frutería [f] *greengrocer's*
fuego [m] *fire;* **fuegos artificiales [m]:** *fireworks*
fuente [f] *fountain*
fuera *outside;* **fuera de:** *out of;* **fuera de juego:** *offside*
fuerte *strong, loud*
fuerte [m] *fort*
fumador/a *smoker*
fumadores *smoking;* **no fumadores:** *non-smoking*
fumar *to smoke*
funcionar *to work, function*
furioso/a *furious*
fútbol [m] *football;*
fútbol americano [m]: *American football*
futbolín [m] *table football*

gafas [f] *glasses (spectacles);* **gafas de sol [f]:** *sunglasses;* **gafas de esquiar [f]:** *ski goggles*
galería [f] *gallery*
galés/a *Welsh*
galleta [f] *biscuit*
gallina [f] *hen, chicken;* **ser un gallina*** *to be a coward*

gamba [f] *prawn*
ganador/a *winner*
ganar *to win, to earn*
ganga [f] *a bargain*
garganta [f] *throat*
gas [m] *gas;* **con gas:** *fizzy*
gasoil [m] *diesel*
gasolina [f] *petrol*
gasolinera [f] *petrol station*
gastado *spent, worn-out*
gastar *to spend, to use up*
gato [m] *cat*
gazpacho [m] *cold summery vegetable soup*
gel [m] *gel*
gemelo/a *twin brother/ sister*
Géminis *Gemini*
gemir *to groan*
género [m] *gender*
generoso/a *generous*
gente [f] *people*
geografía [f] *geography*
gimnasia [f] *gymnastics, exercise classes*
gimnasio [m] *gymnasium*
gira [f] *tour (music concert)*
girar *to turn*
giro en descubierto *overdraft;* **tener la cuenta en descubierto:** *to be overdrawn*
gitano/a *gipsy*
globo [m] *balloon*
glorieta [f] *roundabout*
glotón/a *greedy (for food)*
gobierno [m] *government*
gol [m] *goal (football)*
golpe [m] *blow*
golpear *to hit*

goma [f] *rubber, rubber band*
gordo/a *fat person*
gorra [f] *cap;* **de gorra*** *free;* **vivir de gorra:** *to be a sponger*
gota [f] *drop;* **gota de lluvia [f]:** *raindrop*
gracias *thank you*
gracioso/a *funny*
grado [m] *degree;* **licenciatura [f]** *(university degree)*
gramo [m] *gram*
granada [f] *pomegranate*
Gran Bretaña *Britain*
grande *big, large*
grandes almacenes [m] *department store*
granja [f] *farm*
grano [m] *spot*
grasa [f] *fat*
gratis *free*
Grecia *Greece*
grifo [m] *tap*
gripe [f] *flu*
gris *grey*
gritar *to yell, to shout, to scream*
grosella negra [f] *blackcurrant*
grosero/a *rude, gross*
grumo [m] *lump (in liquid)*
gruñon *grumpy*
grupo [m] *band, group*
guante [m] *glove*
guapo/a *good-looking, pretty, handsome (people)*
guardar *to keep, to put away*
guardarropa [m] *cloakroom*
guardia [m] *guard;* **guardia de tráfico [m]:** *traffic warden*

guerra [f] *war*
guía [f] *phone directory, guide*
guía del ocio [f] *entertainment guide*
guisado [m] *stew*
guisantes [m] *peas*
guitarra [f] *guitar*
guitarrista *guitarist*
gustar *to like;* **gustar a:** *to be fancied/liked by*

haber *to have*
habilidosa/o *crafty*
habitación [f] *room, bedroom;* **habitación doble:** *double room;* **habitación individual:** *single room*
hábito [m] *habit*
hablar *to speak, to talk*
hablador/a *chatterbox*
habladuría [f] *rumour, gossip*
hace *it's, ago;* **hace frío/calor:** *it's cold/hot;* **hace dos años:** *two years ago*
hacer *to do, to make*
hacer dedo *to hitchhike*
hacer el equipaje *to pack*
hacer el tonto *to act the fool, stupid*
hacer footing *jogging*
hacer fotos *to take photos*
hacerse el sueco *to act dumb*
hacerse pedazos *to fall to pieces*
hacerse *to become*
hacia *towards*
hacienda [f] *house, farm, ranch*

hamaca [f] *hammock*
hambre [m] *hunger;* **tener hambre:** *to be hungry*
harina [f] *flour*
harto/a (estar harto/a) *to be fed up*
hasta *until*
hasta luego *see you later*
hasta pronto *see you soon*
hay *there is/ there are;* **hay niebla:** *it's foggy*
hecho (muy hecho) *well cooked;* **hecho a mano:** *handmade*
helada [f] *frost (freezing)*
helado [m] *ice cream*
helar *to freeze*
helicóptero [m] *helicopter*
hemanastro [m] *stepbrother*
herida [f] *injury*
hermana [f] *sister*
hermanastra [f] *stepsister*
hermano [m] *brother*
hermoso/a *handsome*
héroe [m] *hero*
herradura [f] *horseshoe*
herramientas [f] *tools*
hielo [m] *ice*
hierba [f] *grass*
hija [f] *daughter*
hijo [m] *son*
hilo [m] *thread*
himno [m] *hymn*
hincha *football fan/ supporter*
hinchado/a *swollen*
hindú *Hindu*
hipo [m] *hiccup*
hipócrita *hypocrite*
hipopótamo [m] *hippopotamus*
historia [f] *history, story*

hoja [f] *leaf, sheet of paper*
hojear *to leaf through/ turn the pages of*
¡hola! *hello*
Holanda *Holland*
holgado/a *loose, baggy*
hombre [m] *man*
hombreras [f] *shoulder pads*
hombro [m] *shoulder*
homosexual *homosexual*
honesto/a *honest*
hora [f] *hour, time;* **puntual:** *on time;* **hora punta** [f]: *rush hour;* **¿qué hora es?:** *what time is it?;* **las tres:** *three o'clock*
horario [m] *timetable*
hormiga [f] *ant*
horno [m] *oven*
horóscopo [m] *horoscope*
horrible [m/f] *awful, horrible*
horror *horror*
hospedarse *to stay, lodge*
hospital [m] *hospital*
hostal [m] *small hotel*
hotel [m] *hotel*
hoy *today*
huelga [f] *strike*
hueso [m] *bone*
huevera [f] *egg cup*
huevo [m] *egg;* **huevo frito** [m]: *fried egg;* **huevo en cáscara** [m]: *soft-boiled egg;* **huevos revueltos** [m]: *scrambled eggs;* **huevo cocido/duro:** *hard-boiled egg;* **huevo escalfado:** *poached egg;* **huevos a punto de nieve:** *whipped egg whites*
huir *to run away*
humano/a *human*

humor [m] *humor, mood;* **de buen/mal humor:** *in a good/bad mood*

ida [f] *departure;* **de ida:** *single journey;* **billete de ida:** *single ticket;* **ida y vuelta:** *return journey;* **billete de ida y vuelta:** *return ticket*
idea [f] *idea*
idioma [m] *language, tongue;* **lengua materna** [f]: *mother tongue*
idiota *idiot*
iglesia [f] *church*
igual *equal, same;* **¡me da igual!:** *I don't care*
igualdad [f] *equality*
imaginar *to imagine*
imbécil *feeble-minded*
immigrante [m/f] *immigrant*
impedir *to prevent*
imperdible [m] *safety pin*
impermeable *waterproof (adj); raincoat (noun)*
importado/a *imported*
importante *important*
importar (importar un bledo/rábano) *to not care*
imposible *impossible*
impresionante *impressive*
impresora [f] *printer (machine)*
incapacitado/a *disabled*
incluído/a *included*
increíble *unbelievable*
India *India*
indigestión [f] *upset stomach*

indispensable *essential, vital*
infeliz *unhappy*
infierno [m] *hell*
información [f] *information*
informarse *to get information*
informática [f] *computing*
infusión [f] *herbal tea*
ingeniero/a *engineer*
ingenuo/a *naive*
Inglaterra *England*
inglés/a *English*
ingratitud [f] *ingratitude*
ingrediente [m] *ingredient*
iniciar *to initiate*
injuria [f] *an insult*
injusto/a *unfair*
inmadurez *immaturity*
inmóvil *still*
inscribirse *to register, to sign up for*
insecto [m] *bug (insect)*
insertar *to insert*
insignia [f] *badge*
insolación [f] *sunstroke*
insólito/a *offbeat*
insoportable *unbearable*
inspección [f] *inspection*
institución benéfica [f] *charity organization*
instrucciones [f] *user instructions*
instrumento [m] *instrument*
insulto [m] *insult*
intelectual *intellectual*
inteligente *intelligent*
intención [f] *intention*
intentar *to try*
intercambiar *to exchange, to swap*
interesante *interesting*
interfono [m] *intercom*

intermitente [m] *indicator*
internado [m] *boarding school*
interrogar *to interrogate, question*
inútil *useless*
investigación [f] *research*
invierno [m] *winter*
invitación [f] *invitation*
invitado/a *guest*
invitar *to invite*
inyección [f] *injection*
ir *to go;* **ir bien/mal:** *to go well/bad;* **irse:** *to leave*
ir de compras *to go shopping*
ir de marcha *to go clubbing*
ir más despacio *to slow down*
ira [f] *anger*
Irlanda *Ireland*
irlandés/a *Irish*
irse *to leave, to go away*
isla [f] *island;* **las islas Anglonormandas:** *the Channel Islands*
Italia *Italy*
IVA *VAT*
izquierda [f] *left*

jabón [m] *soap*
jactarse *to boast*
jamón [m] *ham*
jardín [m] *garden*
jarra [f] *jug*
jefe [m] *boss, leader;*
jefe de estación [m]: *station master*
jersey [m] *sweater*
jinete [m/f] *rider (on horse)*
jóven *young*

joyas [f] *jewellery*
jubilación [f] *retirement*
judía [f] *bean*
judío/a *Jewish*
judo [m] *judo*
juego [m] *game;* **video juegos [m]:** *video games;*
sala de juegos [f]/centro recreativo [m]: *amusement arcade*
jueves *Thursday*
jugador/a *player;*
jugador de fútbol [m]: *football player*
jugar *to play*
juguete [m] *toy*
julio *July*
junio *June*
junto a *next to*
juntos/as *together*
jurar *to swear*
justo/a *fair*

kilo [m] *kilo*
kilómetro [m] *kilometre*

la *the [f], her, it*
labio [m] *lip*
laca [f] *hair-spray*
lado [m] *side;* **al lado de:** *next to*
ladrar *to bark*
ladrón/a *thief*
lago [m] *lake*
lágrima [f] *tear*
lamentar *to regret*
lamer *to lick*
lámpara [f] *lamp*
lana [f] *wool*
langosta [f] *lobster*
lanzar *to throw*
lápiz [m] *pencil*
largo/a *long*

lata [f] *can, tin*
látigo [m] *whip*
lavabo [m] *wash basin, sink*
lavadora [f] *washing machine*
lavandería [f] *launderette*
lavaplatos [m] *dishwasher*
lavar *to wash*
lavarse *to wash yourself*
le *him*
lección [f] *lesson*
leche [f] *milk;* **leche bronceadora [f]:** *sun cream*
leche limpiadora [f] *make-up remover*
lechuga [f] *lettuce*
lechuza [f] *owl*
leer *to read*
lejos *far*
lentilla [f] *lentil, contact lens*
lento/a *slow*
Leo *Leo*
leotardo [m] *leotard*
les *them*
love *light*
levantarse *to get up*
libra [f] *pound (sterling)*
Libra *Libra*
libre *free;* **libre de impuestos (adj):** *duty-free*
librería [f] *bookshop*
libreta [f] *notebook*
libro [m] *book;* **libro en rústica/de bolsillo [m]:** *paperback book*
licencia [f] *licence*
licenciatura [f] *degree*
ligar con *to chat up*
ligar *to flirt*
ligero/a *light*
ligón/a *flirt*
lila *lilac, purple*

lima [f] *nail file*
limón [m] *lemon*
limpiaparabrisas [m] *windscreen wiper*
limpiar *to clean*
limpio/a *clean*
lindo/a *cute*
línea [f] *line, dialling tone*
linterna [f] *torch*
lío [m] *mess;* ¡**vaya lío!** *what a mess!*
lista de espera [f] *stand-by*
listo/a *clever;* **estar listo/a:** *to be ready*
litera [f] *sleeper, berth*
literatura [f] *literature*
litro [m] *litre*
llamada [f] *call, phone call*
llamar *to call, to ring, to phone*
llamarse *to be called*
llave [f] *key;* **llave inglesa [f]:** *adjustable spanner*
llegada [f] *arrival*
llegar a ser *to become*
llegar *to arrive*
llenar *to fill, to fill up*
lleno/a *full*
llevar *to take, to carry, to wear*
llevarse bien con *to get on/ along*
llorar *to cry*
llover *to rain;* **está lloviendo:** *it´s raining*
lluvia [f] *rain*
lo siento *I´m sorry*
loco/a *mad, crazy;* **estar loco/a-estar mal de la cabeza:** *to be out of one´s mind*
lograr *to manage to*
loncha [f] *slice*
loro [m] *parrot*

lubina [f] *sea bass*
lugar [m] *place*
luna [f] *moon*
lunes *Monday*
luz [f] *light*

macarrones [m] *macaroni*
macho *macho*
madera [f] *wood*
madrastra [f] *stepmother*
madre [f] *mother*
madrina [f] *godmother*
maduro/a *mature, ripe*
mal educado/a *rude*
mal *bad, wrong, badly*
maleta [f] *suitcase*
maletero [m] *car boot*
mañana [f] *morning*
mañana *tomorrow;* **pasado mañana:** *the day after tomorrow;* **mañana por la mañana:** *tomorrow morning;* **por la mañana:** *in the morning*
manatial [m] *spring (source of water)*
mancha [f] *stain*
mando a distancia [m] *remote control*
manera [f] *manner, way*
manga [f] *sleeve*
mangar* *to nick (steal)*
manifestación [f] *demonstration*
manilla [f] *handle*
manillar [m] *handlebars*
mano [f] *hand*
manta [f] *blanket*
mantequilla [f] *butter*
manzana [f] *apple*
mapa [m] *map;* **mapa de carreteras [m]:** *road map*

maquillaje [m] *make-up*
máquina [f] *machine*
maquinilla de afeitar [f] *razor*
mar [m] *sea*
maravilloso/a *wonderful*
marcar *to mark;* **marcar un gol:** *to score a goal*
marcha [f] *march;* **marcha atrás [f]:** *reverse gear;* **ir de marcha:** *to go out on the town, to have a wild time;* **marchoso/a** *raver;* **ser un marchoso/a:** *to be a raver*
marea [f] *tide*
mareo [m] *seasickness*
margarina [f] *margarine*
marido [m] *husband*
marinero [m] *sailor*
marioneta [f] *puppet*
mariposa [f] *butterfly*
mariscos [m] *seafood, shellfish*
marrón *brown*
Marruecos *Morocco*
martes *Tuesday*
martillo [m] *hammer*
marzo *March*
más *more*
máscara [f] *mask*
mástil [m] *mast*
matar *to kill*
matrimonio [m] *wedding*
mayo *May*
mayoría [f] *the majority*
mazo [m] *mallet*
mecánico [m] *mechanic*
mechero [m] *lighter*
media [f] *average, stocking*
medianoche [f] *midnight*
medias [f] *tights*
medicina [f] *medicine*
médico [m] *doctor*

medio [m] *middle, environment*

medio ambiente [m] *environment*

medio/a *half;* **son las diez y media:** *it´s half past ten;* **media botella [f]:** *half-bottle*

mediodía [m] *midday, noon*

medios de comunicación [m] *media*

Mediterráneo [m] *Mediterranean*

medusa [f] *jellyfish*

Méjico *Mexico*

mejilla [f] *cheek*

mejillón [m] *mussel*

mejor *better;* **el/la/lo mejor:** *the best;* **sentirse mejor:** *to feel better;* **es mejor...:** *it is better*

melocotón [m] *peach*

melón [m] *melon*

mendigar *to beg for*

mendigo/a *beggar*

menor *underage*

menos *less;* **al menos:** *at least;* **las ocho menos diez:** *ten to eight;* **la una menos cuarto:** *a quarter to one*

mentir *to lie*

mentira [f] *lie*

mentiroso/a *liar*

menú [m] *set menu*

mercado [m] *market*

merienda [f] *tea (afternoon snack)*

mermelada [f] *jam*

mes [m] *month*

mesa [f] *table*

metedura de pata [f] *blunder*

meter el rollo* *to waffle*

meter la pata *to blunder, to put your foot in it*

método [m] *method*

metro [m] *metre, underground, tube*

mezclar *to mix*

mezquita [f] *mosque*

mi/mis *my*

microbio [m] *bug, microbe*

micrófono [m] *microphone*

microondas [m] *microwave*

miedo [m] *fear;* **película de miedo [f]:** *scary/horror movie*

miel [f] *honey*

mientras *while*

miércoles *Wednesday*

mimado/a *spoiled (child)*

mío/a *mine*

miope *short-sighted*

míos/as *mine*

mirar *to look at;* **mirar fijamente:** *to stare*

mismo/a (el/la/lo mismo/a) *the same*

mitad [f] *half;* **mitad de precio:** *half-price*

mixto/a *mixed*

mochila [f] *backpack*

mochilero/a *backpacker*

moda [f] *fashion;* **a la moda:** *fashionable*

modelo [m/f] *model (fashion)*

moderno/a *trendy*

modo de vida [m] *lifestyle*

mogollón* [m] *a lot, much;* **mola mogollón:** *it´s great*

mojado/a *wet*

molar* *to like;* **me mola:** *I like it*

molestar *to bother, to annoy, to disturb*

molestia [f] *nuisance*

molesto *annoying*

molino [m] *windmill*

momento [m] *moment*

moneda [f] *coin*

monedero [m] *purse*

monitor/a *instructor*

mono [m] *overalls*

mono/a *cute*

montaña [f] *mountain*

montar *to ride*

montón* [m] *heap;* **un montón de:** *heaps/loads of*

monumento [m] *monument*;* **es un monumento:** *she is a beauty*

moral [f] *morale*

morcilla [f] *black pudding*

morder *to bite*

moreno/a *tanned, dark-haired*

morir *to die*

morriña [f] *homesickness*

morro* *mouth;* **estar de morros:** *to be in a bad mood;* **¡vaya morro!:** *what a cheek!*

mosca [f] *fly*

mosquito [m] *mosquito*

mostaza [f] *mustard*

mostrador [m] *counter*

mostrar *to show*

motivo [m] *motive, reason*

moto [f] *motorbike*

mover *to move*

muchos/as *many, a lot*

mudarse *to move house*

muelle [m] *quay*

muerto/a *dead*

mujer [f] *woman, wife*

multa [f] *fine*

multitud [f] crowd
Mundial [m] World Cup
mundo [m] world
muñeca [f] wrist, doll
murallas [f] city walls
músculo [m] muscle
museo [m] museum
músico musician
musulmán/a Muslim
muy very

nacer to be born
nacimiento [m] birth;
fecha de nacimiento [f]:
date of birth
nacionalidad [f]
nationality
nada nothing; **de nada:**
you're welcome; **no es
nada:** it doesn't matter
nadar to swim
nadie nobody
naipes [m] playing
cards
naranja [f] orange
nariz [f] nose
nata [f] cream, **nata
montada [f]:** whipped
cream
natación [f] swimming
natural natural
naturaleza [f] nature
navaja [f] penknife
navegación [f] sailing
navegar por Internet
to surf the net
Navidad [f] Christmas;
Feliz Navidad: Merry
Christmas
necesario/a necessary
necesidad [f] need
necesitar to need
negro black
nervio [m] nerve; **tener
nervio:** to have character;

**ser un manojo de
nervios:** to be a bundle of
nerves; **tener los nervios
de punta:** to have
butterflies
nevar to snow
nevera [f] cool box
niebla [f] fog
nieve [f] snow
niñez [f] childhood
niño/a child
no no, not
noche [f] night
nombrar to name
nombre [m] name
normalmente usually
norte [m] north
nosotros/as we
noticias [f] news
novela [f] novel
noviembre November
novio/a boy/girlfriend
nube [f] cloud
nuestro/a/os/as our
nuevo/a new; **de nuevo:**
again; **año nuevo [m]:**
new year; **Nueva Zelanda:**
New Zealand
número [m] number
nunca never

o or
oboe [m] oboe
obra [f] play (theater)
obras [f] roadworks
observar to observe
obturador [m] shutter
(camera)
ocio [m] leisure
octubre October
ocupado/a busy, engaged
ocuparse de to take care
of ...
odiar to hate, to loathe
odioso/a obnoxious,
hateful

oeste [m] west
ofendido/a offended
oficial official
oficina [f] office; **oficina
de turismo [f]:** tourist
office
ofrecer to offer
oído [m] ear (inner)
oir to hear
ojos [m] eyes
ola [f] wave
oler to smell; **oler mal:** to
stink
olor [m] smell
olvidar to forget
ombligo [m] belly
button
opinión [f] opinion
oportunidad [f] chance
óptico [m] optician's
optimista optimistic
opuesto opposite
orden [m] order
ordenador [m]
computer
ordinario/a ordinary
oreja [f] ear (outer)
organizar to organize
orgulloso/a proud
orquesta [f] orchestra
oscuro/a dark
ostra [f] oyster
otoño [m] autumn
otro/a other; **el otro/la
otra:** the other one

padrastro [m] stepfather
padre [m] father
padres [m] parents
padrino [m] godfather
pagar to pay
página [f] page
país [m] country
paisaje [m] scenery
pájaro [m] bird

palabra [f] *word*
palabrota [f] *swearword*
palacio [m] *palace*
palo [m] *stick*
palmear *to clap*
pamela [f] *sunhat for women*
pan [m] *bread;* **bollo [m]:** *small baguette;* **pan integral [m]:** *wholemeal bread*
panadería [f] *bakery*
panel [m] *board;* **panel de llegadas/salidas [m]:** *arrivals/departures board*
pánico [m] *panic*
pantalla [f] *screen*
pantalón de esquiar [m] *ski pants*
pantalón de montar [m] *jodhpurs*
pantalones [m] *trousers;* **pantalones cortos [m]:** *shorts*
pañuelo [m] *handkerchief*
papel [m] *paper;* **papel higiénico [m]:** *toilet paper*
papelería [f] *stationer's shop*
paquete [m] *parcel*
para *for*
parabrisas [m] *windcreen*
paracaídas [m] *parachute*
parada [f] *stop;* **parada de autobús [f]:** *bus stop;* **parada de taxis [f]:** *taxi stand*
parado/a *unemployed person*
paraguas [m] *umbrella*
parar *to stop*
parasol [m] *lens hood (camera)*
parecer *to seem*

parecerse *to look like*
pared [f] *wall*
paro [m] *unemployment;* **en el paro:** *unemployed*
párpado [m] *eyelid*
parque [m] *park*
parque de atracciones [m] *theme park*
parte [f] *part*
parte delantera [f] *front*
parte trasera [f] *back of a car, house,etc*
participar *to take part*
partido [m] *political party, or match (of game/sport)*
pasado/a de moda *old-fashioned*
pasaje [m] *passage (in street)*
pasajero/a *passenger*
pasaporte [m] *passport*
pasar *to pass, to happen;* **pasar de todo*:** *not to give a damn;* **yo paso*:** *count me out;* **no te pases*:** *don't over-do it;* **¿y qué pasa?:** *so what?;* **pasa de estudiar*:** *he/she isn't into studying*
Pascua [f] *Easter*
pase [m] *pass*
pasear *to go for a walk*
paseo [m] *walk, outing*
paso [m] *footstep*
pasta [f] *pasta*
pastel [m] *cake*
pastelería [f] *cake shop*
pastilla [f] *pill, tablet*
patada [f] *kick*
patatas fritas [f] *crisps, chips, French fries*
patético *pathetic*
patinar *to skate;*
patinaje sobre hielo [m]: *ice skating*

patines [m] *roller skates*
pato [m] *duck*
pavo [m] *turkey*
paz [f] *peace*
peaje [m] *toll*
peatones [m] *pedestrians*
pecas [f] *freckles*
pecho [m] *chest, breast*
pedal [m] *pedal*
pedido [m] *order*
pedir *to order, to ask;* **pedir prestado:** *to borrow*
pegatina [f] *sticker*
peinado [m] *hairstyle*
peine [m] *comb*
pelea [f] *fight*
pelear *to fight*
pelearse *to have a row*
película [f] *film*
peligroso/a *dangerous*
pelo [m] *hair*
pelota [f] *ball*
peluquero/a *hairdresser*
pena [f] *pity;* **what a shame!:** *¡qué pena!*
pendientes [m] *earrings*
pensar *to think*
pensión [f] *bed and breakfast, small hotel;* **pensión completa:** *full board;* **media pensión:** *half board*
peor *worse*
pepino [m] *cucumber*
pepita [f] *pip*
pequeño/a *small*
pera [f] *pear*
perder *to lose, to waste (time, chance)*
perderse *to get lost, to miss;* **¡vete a la porra/mierda!:** *get lost!*
pérdida [f] *loss;* **pérdida de tiempo [f]:** *waste of time*
perdido/a *lost*

perdón *sorry, excuse me;*
pedir perdón: *to apologize*
perdonar *to forgive*
perdone/a *excuse me*
perezoso/a *lazy*
perfecto/a *perfect*
perfume [m] *perfume*
periódico [m] *newspaper*
periodista *journalist*
permiso [m] (permiso de conducir) *driving licence*
permitir *to allow*
pero *but*
perro [m] *dog*
persona [f] *person*
personaje [m] *character (in play/cartoon/novel)*
pesadilla [f] *nightmare*
pesado/a *heavy, tedious, dull;* **ponerse pesado/a:** *to be a pest;* **¡qué pesado/a eres!:** *what a drag you are!*
pesca [f] *fishing*
pescado [m] *fish*
pesimista *pessimistic*
peso [m] *weight*
petanca [f] *boules, (game of balls)*
peto [m] *dungarees*
piano [m] *piano*
picadura [f] *sting*
picante *hot, spicy*
picar *to sting*
picnic [m] *picnic*
pie [m] *foot*
piedra [f] *stone*
piel [f] *skin*
pierna [f] *leg*
pieza [f] pieza de recambio [f]: *spare part*
pila [f] *battery*
píldora [f] *pill*
piloto [m] *pilot*

pimienta [f] *pepper*
pin [m] *badge*
piña [f] *pineapple*
pincel [m] *paintbrush (artist)*
pinchada *flat (tyre);* **tener un pinchazo:** *to have a flat tyre*
pincharse *to puncture*
pintar *to paint*
pinza [f] *tweezers, peg*
piscina [f] *swimming pool*
Piscis *Pisces*
piso [m] *flat, floor (level)*
pista [f] *track (sport), hint (clue);* **pista de hielo [f]:** *ice rink*
pistacho [m] *pistacchio*
pistola [f] *gun*
pito [m] *fag**
plano/a *flat (adj)*
planta [f] *floor (level), plant;* **planta baja [f]:** *ground floor* **plantar** *to plant;* **dejar plantado/a:** *to dump a girl/boyfriend*
plástico [m] *plastic*
plataforma [f] *platform*
plátano [m] *banana*
plato [m] *dish, plate*
playa [f] *beach*
plaza [f] *square*
plomo [m] *lead (metal), boring* (adj) e.g.* **ser un plomo:** *to be a drag/a bore*
pobre *pour*
poco/a *little, not much*
poder *to be able, can*
podrido/a *rotten*
poema [m] *poem*
policía [m/f] *police officer, cop, police*
política [f] *politics*
pollo [m] *chicken*
pomelo [m] *grapefruit*

poner *to put*
ponerse *to put on;*
ponerse + adj: *to turn, to become;* **ponerse a:** *to start;* **ponerse a llorar:** *to burst into tears;* **ponerse colorado/ a:** *to blush*
popular *popular*
por favor *please*
por fin *at last*
por qué *why*
por todos sitios *everywhere*
por *by, through*
porque *because*
portero [m] *goalkeeper, caretaker, goalie*
posible *possible*
positivo/a *positive*
posponer *to postpone*
postal [f] *postcard*
postre [m] *dessert*
potable *drinkable,* **no potable:** *non drinkable*
práctico/a *practical*
precio [m] *price;* **precio fijo [m]:** *set price*
preferido/a *favourite*
prefijo [m] *area code*
pregunta [f] *question*
preguntar *to ask*
preguntarse *to wonder*
premio [m] *prize*
preocupado/a *worried*
preocuparse *to worry*
preparado/a *ready*
presentar *to present, to introduce someone*
prestar *to lend*
pretencioso/a *pretentious*
primavera [f] *spring*
primero/a *first;* **primer plato [m]:** *first course /main course*
primeros auxilios [m] *first aid*

primo/a *cousin*
principal *main;* **los 40 principales:** *the top 40 charts*
principiante *beginner*
principio [m] *start, beginning*
prioridad [f] *right-of-way, priority*
prismáticos [m] *binoculars*
privado/a *private*
probable *probable, likely*
probadores [m] *changing rooms (in a shop)*
probar *to taste*
problema [m] *problem*
procesamiento de textos [m] *word processing*
profesor/a *teacher*
profundo/a *deep*
programa [m] *programme*
progreso [m] *progress*
prohibido *forbidden;* **prohibido fumar:** *no smoking;* **prohibida la entrada:** *no entry*
promedio [m] *average*
promesa [f] *promise*
prometer *to promise*
pronóstico del tiempo [m] *weather forecast*
pronto *soon*
propietario/a *owner*
propina [f] *tip (money)*
proponer *to suggest, to propose*
prórroga [f] *injury time*
prostituta [f] *prostitute*
protección [f] (protección del medio ambiente [f]) *environmental conservation*
proteger *to protect*
provocar *to provoke, to instigate*

próximo/a *next*
prudente *careful*
prueba [f] *proof*
publicidad [f] *advertising, publicity*
público [m] *audience, public*
pueblo [m] *village*
puente [m] *bridge*
puerro [m] *leek*
puerta [f] *door, airport gate*
puerto [m] *port, harbour*
puesta de sol [f] *sunset*
puesto de periódicos [m] *news stand*
pulcro/a *neat*
pulsera [f] *bracelet*
puñetazo [m] *punch*
puño [m] *cuff (sleeve)*
punta [f] *tip, end*
punto [m] *point, dot*
puré de patatas [m] *mashed potato*
puro/a *pure*

que *who, which than, that*
¡qué! *how! what!*
¿que? *what? which?*
¿que hora es? *what time is it?/what's the time*
quedarse *to stay;*
quedarse dormido/a: *to drop off (fall sleep)*
quejarse *to complain*
quemadura de sol [f] *sunburn*
quemar *to burn*
querer *to want;* **querer decir:** *to mean*
querido/a *dear*
queso [m] *cheese*
quien, quienes [pl] *who(m) which*
quincena [f] *fortnight*

quiosco [m] *news stand*
quitar *to take away*
quitarse *to take off*
quizás *perhaps*

racista *racist*
radiador [m] *radiator*
rádio [f] *radio*
rana [f] *frog*
rápidamente *quickly*
rápido/a *fast, quick*
raqueta [f] *tennis bat, racket*
raro/a *rare, unusual, weird*
rascar *to scratch*
rasgar/ desgarrar *to rip*
rastro [m] *second hand market, flea market*
ratón [m] *mouse*
raya [f] *stripe;* **de rayas:** *striped*
rayo [m] *lightning*
razón [f] *reason;* **tener razón:** *to be right*
razonable *sensible*
realmente *really*
rebajas [f] *sales*
rebeca [f] *cardigan*
recepción [f] *reception*
receta [f] *recipe*
rechoncho/a *plump*
recibir *to receive*
recoger *to pick up*
recomendar *to recommend*
reconciliarse *to make up (become friends again)*
reconocer *to recognize*
recordar *to remember, to remind*
recto/a *straight;* **todo recto:** *straight ahead*
recuerdo [m] *souvenir*

red [f] *net, trap*
redondo/a *round*
reducir *to reduce, to limit*
regalar *to give (as a present)*
regalo [m] *present*
regar *to water (the garden)*
regatear *to bargain*
régimen [m] *diet;* **estar a régimen:** *to be on a diet*
región [f] *region*
regla [f] *rule, ruler, period*
regular *regular*
reina [f] *queen*
reirse *to laugh;* **echarse a reir:** *to burst out laughing*
reja [f] *iron gate, grid*
relación [f] *relationship*
relajado/a *relaxed*
relajarse *to relax*
religión [f] *religion*
relleno/a *stuffed*
reloj [m] *watch, clock*
remar *to row*
remo [m] *oar*
remoto/a *remote/far away*
remover *to stir*
RENFE *(Spanish railways)*
reñir *to quarrel, to tell off*
reparar *to repair*
repente (de repente) *suddenly*
repetir *to repeat*
reponer *to replace, put back*
reportajr [m] *report, article*
representación [f] *performance*
repugnante [m/f] *disgusting*
resaca [f] *hangover*
reserva [f] *booking, reservation*

reservado/a *reserved*
reservar *to book, to reserve*
respuesta [f] *answer*
resfriado [m] *cold*
resfriarse *to cool, to catch a cold*
respirar *to breathe*
responder *to answer, to reply*
respuesta [f] *answer*
restaurante [m] *restaurant*
resto [m] *rest*
resultado [m] *result*
retén [m] *lock on steering wheel*
retirada [f] *withdrawal*
retraso [m] *delay;* **con retraso:** *late*
retrato *portrait*
retroceder *to move backwards*
reunión [f] *meeting*
reventar *to burst*
revés [m] *reverse side, wrong side, backhand (tennis);* **al revés:** *inside out, upside-down*
revisor [m] *ticket inspector*
revista *magazine*
rico/a *rich*
ridículo/a *ridiculous*
riendas [f] *reins (riding)*
riesgo [m] *risk*
rígido/a *stiff*
rimel [m] *mascara*
riñón [m] *kidney*
riñonera [f] *bum bag, money belt*
río [m] *river*
ritmo [m] *rhythm, beat*
rizado *curled (hair)*
rizo [m] *curl;* **rizado:** *curly*
robar *to steal/rob*

robo [m] *burglary, theft*
roca [f] *rock*
rock and roll [m] *rock'n roll*
rodilla [f] *knee*
rojo *red*
romántico/a *romantic*
romper *to break*
romperse *to get broken*
roncar *to snore*
ronda [f] *round of drinks*
ropa [f] *clothes*
ropa interior [f] *underwear*
rosa *pink*
rosa [f] *rose*
roto/a *broken*
rubio/a *blond;* **el rubio/la rubia:** *the blond one*
rueda [f] *tyre, wheel*
ruido [m] *noise*
ruinas [f] *ruins*
rumor [m] *rumour*
ruta [f] *route*

sábado *Saturday*
sábana [f] *sheet*
saber *to know*
sabor [m] *taste, flavour*
sacacorchos [m] *corkscrew*
sacar dinero *to withdraw money*
sacar fotos *to take photos*
saco de dormir [m] *sleeping bag*
Sagitario *Sagittarius*
sagrado/a *sacred*
sal [f] *salt*
sala de espera [f] *waiting room*
salado/a *salty; funny*, witty*, charming**

salami [m] *salami*
salario [m] *salary, wages*
salchicha [f] *sausage*
salida [f] *departure, way-out, exit;* **salida de emergencia [f]:** *emergency exit*
salir *to go out*
salmón [m] *salmon*
salón [m] *living room;* **salón de té [m]:** *tea room*
salsa [f] *sauce*
saltar *to jump*
salud [f] *health*
salvaje *wild*
salvar *to save*
sandía [f] *watermelon*
sandwich [m] *sandwich*
sangrar *to bleed*
sangre [f] *blood*
sano/a *healthy*
saque inicial [m] *kick-off*
sarcástico/a *sarcastic*
sartén [f] *frying pan*
saxofonista [m/f] *saxophonist*
saxófono [m] *saxophone*
se alquila *to let, for hire/rent*
secador [m] *hair-drier*
secadora [f] *tumble dryer*
secar *to dry*
seco/a *dry*
secretaria [f] *secretary*
secreto [m] *secret*
secundaria [f] (ESO) *secondary school*
sed [f] *thirst;* **tener sed:** *to be thirsty*
seducir *to seduce*
seguir *to follow*
según *according to*
segundo *second*
seguramente *probably*

seguridad [f] *safety;* **cinturón de seguridad [m]:** *safety belt*
seguro [m] *insurance*
seguro/a *sure*
self-service [m] *self-service*
sellar *to stamp*
sello [m] *stamp*
semáforo [m] *traffic lights*
semana [f] *week*
Semana Santa [f] *Easter*
señal [f] *sign*
señalar *to point, to underline*
sendero [m] *path*
señor [m] *Mr, Sir*
señora [f] *lady, madam, Mrs*
señorita [f] *Miss*
sentado/a *sitting down*
sentarse *to sit down*
sentido [m] *sense;* **no tiene sentido:** *it doesn't make sense;* **sentido común [m]:** *common sense;* **sentido único:** *one-way*
sentir *to feel;* **lo siento:** *sorry, desolate*
sentirse mal/bien *to feel well/ not well*
separar *to separate*
septiembre *September*
ser *to be*
serenarse *to calm down*
serio/a *serious*
seropositivo/a *HIV positive*
serpiente [f] *snake*
servicio [m] *toilet, sevice*
servilleta [f] *napkin*
servir *to serve, to be used for;* **servirse:** *to help yourself*

sesión [f] *session, showing (of film, movie)*
sexo [m] *sex*
shandy [f] *shandy*
si *if*
sí *yes*
si no *otherwise*
SIDA *AIDS*
sidra [f] *cider*
siempre *always*
siglo [m] *century*
silbar *to whistle*
silencio [m] *silence*
silla [f] *chair;* **silla de ruedas [f]:** *wheelchair;* **silla de montar [f]:** *saddle*
sillón [m] *armchair*
simpático/a *friendly*
simple *simple*
sin *without*
sin blanca (estar sin blanca*) *to be broke (without money)*
sincero/a *honest, sincere*
sino *if not*
sintetizador [m] *synthesizer*
sitio [m] *place*
sobre [m] *envelope*
sobre todo *above all*
sobrina (f) *niece*
sobrino (m) *nephew*
socio/a *partner*
socorrista [m/f] *lifeguard*
software [m] *software*
sol [m] *sun*
solamente *only*
solapa [f] *lapel*
soldado [m] *soldier*
soleado/a *sunny*
sólo *only*
solo/a *alone, lonely*
soltero/a *single (unmarried)*
sombra [f] *shade*
sombrero [m] *hat*

sombrilla [f] parasol
sonar to sound
soñar to dream
sonido [m] sound
sonrisa [f] smile
sopa [f] soup
soportar to bear; **no soporto:** I can't stand ...
sordo/a deaf
sorpresa [f] surprise
sótano [m] basement,
su her, his, their
suave soft
subir to go/walk up
submarino/a underwater
subterráneo/a underground
subtítulo [m] subtitle
sucio/a dirty
sudar to sweat
suegro/a father/mother-in-law
suerte [f] luck
sufrir to suffer
Suiza Switzerland
suizo/a Swiss
sujetador [m] bra
sujeto [m] subject
suma [f] sum
superficial superficial
supermercado [m] supermarket
supersticioso/a superstitious
suplemento [m] supplement
suponer to suppose
supositorio [m] suppository
sur [m] south
suspender to fail (exam)
susurrar to whisper

tabaco [m] tobacco
taberna [f] inn, pub
tabla [f] board; **tabla de**

windsurf [f]: windsurf
tacaño/a stingy
tal such
tal vez maybe, perhaps
talentoso/a talented
talla [f] size
taller [m] workshop
tallo [m] stalk
talonario [m] cheque-book
también also, too
tampón [m] tampon
tan ... como as ... as
tanteo [m] score
taquilla [f] ticket office
tarde [f] afternoon
tarde late
tarifa [f] fare; **tarifa completa [f]:** full fare; **tarifa reducida [f]:** reduced fare
tarjeta de crédito [f] credit card
tarta [f] cake; **tarta de cumpleaños [f]:** birthday cake
Tauro Taurus
taxi [m] taxi; **taxista [m/f]:** taxi driver
taza [f] cup
té [m] tea
teatro [m] theatre
techo [m] ceiling
tecla [f] key
técnico [m] mechanic, technician
tejado [m] roof
tela [f] fabric
teleférico [m] cable car
teléfono [m] phone; **teléfono de tarjeta [m]:** card phone; **teléfono de monedas [m]:** coin phone
telenovela [f] soap opera
telesilla [f] chair lift
telesquí [m] drag lift

televisión/tele [f] television
temblar to shiver
temperatura [f] temperature
templo [m] temple
temporada baja [f] off season
temporal temporary
temprano early
tenedor [m] fork
tener agujetas to feel stiff
tener cuidado to watch out
tener to have
tenis [m] tennis; **tenis de mesa [m]:** table tennis
tensión [f] tension, blood pressure
tenso/a tense, up-tight
tentador tempting
tercero/a third
terminar to finish
termo [m] flask
termómetro [m] thermometer
ternera [f] veal
terreno [m] plot of land
terrible dreadful
tez [f] complexion
tía [f] aunt
tiempo [m] weather, time; **¿qué tiempo hace?:** what's the weather like?; **tener tiempo:** to have time; **tiempo libre [m]:** spare time
tienda [f] shop; **tienda (de campaña):** tent; **tienda de discos [f]:** music store
tijeras [f] scissors
tímido/a shy
timo [m] (es un timo) it's a rip off
timón [m] rudder, helm

tío [m] *uncle, guy**
típico/a *typical*
tipo [m] *type*
tirar *to throw, to throw away, to pull, to shoot*
tisana [f] *herbal tea*
titular [m] *headline*
título [m] *title*
toalla [f] *towel*
tobillo [m] *ankle*
tobogán [m] *toboggan*
tocar *to touch;* **te toca:** *your turn*
todavía *still;* **todavía no:** *not yet*
todo *all, everything;* **todo el mundo:** *everybody;* **todo lo demás:** *everything else;* **todos los demás:** *everybody else;* **todos los días:** *everyday*
tomar el pelo *to tease, to have someone on*
tomar el sol *to sunbathe*
tomar *to take;* **tomar algo:** *to have a drink;* **ir a tomar** *algo: to go for a drink*
tomate [m] *tomato*
tontería [f] *nonsense;* **decir tonterías:** *to talk nonsense*
tonto/a *silly*
topless [m] *topless*
torcedura [f] *sprain*
torcer *to turn*
tormenta [f] *storm, thunderstorm*
tornillo [m] *screw*
torre [f] *tower*
tortilla [f] *omelette*
toser *to cough*
tostado/a *toasted*
trabajar *to work*
trabajo [m] *work, job*
tractor [m] *tractor*
tradicional *traditional*

traducción [f] *translation*
traducir *to translate*
traer *to bring*
tráfico [m] *traffic*
tragar *to swallow*
tragedia [f] *tragedy*
traje [m] *suit, costume,*
traje de buzo [m]: *wetsuit;* **traje de esquí** [m]: *ski suit*
trampolín [m] *diving board*
tranquilizarse *to calm down*
tranquilo/a *laid-back, peaceful*
trasero [m]/ **culo** [m]* *bottom*
trastos viejos [m] *junk*
trastornado/a *disturbed*
travesía [f] *crossing (by boat)*
tregua [f] *truce*
tren [m] *train*
trenza [f] *plait (hair), braid*
trimestre [m] *term*
triste *sad*
trompeta [f] *trumpet*
trozo [m] *piece*
trueno [m] *thunder*
tú *you*
tu *your*
tu/tus *your*
tubo de respiración [m] *snorkel*
tumbarse *to lie down*
tumbona [f] *deck-chair*
túnel [m] *tunnel*
Túnez *Tunisia*
turismo [m] *tourism;* **oficina de turismo** [f]: *tourist office*
turista [m/f] *tourist*
turístico/a *touristy*

UE *Unión Europea* [f]
EC *European Community*
un/una/uno *a,an,one*
único/a *unique;* **el/la único/a:** *the only one;* **hijo/a único/a:** *only son/daughter*
universidad [f] *university*
urgencia [f] *emergency*
urgente *urgent*
usar *to use*
usted *you (pol. sing.)*
ustedes *you (pol.pl)*
usual *usual*
útil *useful*
uvas [f] *grapes;* **racimo de uvas** [m]: *bunch of grapes*
V.O *(versión original) original version (film/movie)*

vaca [f] *cow*
vacaciones [f] *holidays*
vacío/a *empty*
vacuna [f] *vaccination*
vagabundo/a *tramp*
vagabundos [m] *the homeless*
vagón [m] *wagon;* **vagón-restaurante** [m]: *restaurant car;* **coche-cama** [m]: *sleeping car*
vainilla [f] *vanilla*
vale *OK, all right*
valiente [m/f] *brave*
valor [m] *value;* **objetos de valor** [m]: *valuables*
vaqueros [m] *jeans*
variado/a *varied*
vecino/a *neighbour*
vegetariano/a *vegetarian*

vejez [f] *old age*
vela [f] *candle, sail;* **vela mayor [f]:** *main sail*
velocidad [f] *speed*
venda *bandage*
vender *to sell;* **se vende:** *for sale (sign)*
vendimia [f] *grape harvest*
venenoso/a *poisonous*
vengarse *to get your revenge*
venir *to come*
ventaja [f] *advantage*
ventana [f] *window*
ventanilla [f] *bank counter*
ventilador [m] *fan*
ver *to see*
verano [m] *summer*
verdad [f] *truth*
verdadero/a *genuine, true*
verde *green*
verdulería [f] *greengrocer's*
verdura [f] *vegetable*
vereda [f] *pavement, path*
vergüenza [f] *shame,* **¡qué vergüenza!:** *how embarrassing!*
vespa [f] *moped*
vestido [m] *dress*
vestirse *to get dressed*
vestuario [m] *changing room*
vez [f] *time, occasion*
viajar *to travel*
viaje [m] *journey, trip;* **viaje de novios:** *honeymoon;* **¡buen viaje!:** *have a good trip!*
viajero/a *traveller*
vid [f] *vine*
vida [f] *life;* **en mi vida:** *never in my life;* **ganarse**

la vida: *to earn one's living;* **nivel de vida [m]:** *standard of living;*
darse/pegarse la gran vida: *to live it up*
vídeo [m] *video recorder, video tape*
viejo/a *old*
viento [m] *wind;* **hace viento:** *it's windy*
viernes *Friday*
vigilar *to keep an eye on*
vil *vile*
viña [f] *vineyard*
vinagre [m] *vinegar*
vinagreta [f] *french dressing*
vino [m] *wine;* **ir de vinos:** *to go on a drinking spree;* **vino blanco/ tinto/ rosado:** *white/red/rosé wine;* **vino de la casa:** *house wine;* **vino de mesa:** *table wine;* **vino peleón:** *plonk*
violación [f] *rape*
violín [m] *violin*
violoncelo [m] *cello*
Virgo *Virgo*
visera [f] *visor*
visitar *to visit*
vista [f] *view, sight*
vitrina [f] *shop window*
viudo/a *widow/ widower*
vivir *to live*
vivo/a *lively*
volante [m] *steering wheel*
volar *to fly*
voluntario/a *voluntary*
volver *to return, to go back;* **volver la espalda:** *to turn one's back*
volverse *to become*
vomitar *to vomit, to be sick*
vosotros/as *you*

votar *to vote*
voz [f] *voice*
vuelo [m] *flight*
vuelta [f] *return*
vuestro/a/os/as *your*

Walkman [m] *personal stereo*
windsurfista [m/f] *windsurfer*

y *and*
ya *already*
ya basta *it's/that's enough*
yate [m] *yacht*
yema [f] *egg yolk*
yerno [m] *son-in-law*
yo *I, me*
yoga *yoga*
yogur [m] *yogurt*

zalamero/a *flattering, suave*
zanahoria [f] *carrot*
zapatería [f] *shoe shop*
zapatilla [f] *slipper*
zapatillas de deporte [f] *trainers*
zapato [m] *shoe;* **botas de escalada [f]:** *climbing shoes*
zarzamora [f] *blackberry*
zodíaco [m] *zodiac*
zoo [m] *zoo*
zoom [m] *zoom*
zopenco/a* *daft, stupid*
zueco [m] *clog*
zumbado/a* *crazy, mad*
zumo [m] *juice*
zurdo/a *left-handed*